HELLHOLE

HELLHOLE

By GINA DAMICO

Houghton Mifflin Harcourt

Boston   New York

www.hmhco.com

Text set in Minion Pro

Library of Congress Cataloging-in-Publication Data
Damico, Gina.
Hellhole / by Gina Damico.
pages cm
Summary: "Max Kilgore has accidentally unleashed a
devil — and now the big, evil oaf is living in his basement.
If Max doesn't meet the devil's demands (which include
providing unlimited junk food and a hot tub), everyone
and everything he holds dear could go up in smoke."
— Provided by publisher.
ISBN 978-0-544-30710-0
[1. Devil — Fiction. 2. Conduct of life — Fiction.
3. Interpersonal relations — Fiction. 4. Sick — Fiction.
5. Mothers and sons — Fiction. 6. Single-parent
families — Fiction. 7. Humorous stories.] I. Title.
PZ7.D1838Hel 2014
[Fic] — dc23
2013042827

Manufactured in the United States of America
DOC 10 9 8 7 6 5 4 3 2 1
4500510276

For my godparents, Lolly and Uncle Dave,
who have always been and who continue to be
so enthusiastic about my existence

ACKNOWLEDGMENTS

Even though many crunchy and delicious snacks were devoured to keep the insanity at bay over the course of writing this book, I fear I still may have dragged several people down with me into the depths of hell during its creation. As always, I am indebted to them for their patience, support, emergency delivery of said snacks, and many reasons more.

In the first circle of hell, we've got the always-marvelous team at Houghton Mifflin Harcourt: Julia Richardson, Betsy Groban, Lisa DiSarro, Jennifer Groves, Joan Lee, Lisa Vega, and Maxine Bartow; plus Katie O'Connor at Audible and Roxane Edouard at Curtis Brown. Thank you for your hard work, and for continuing to champion and humor my weird, wacky writing.

Second, to the Apocalypsies, fellow writers, bloggers, librarians, and teachers I've met in person and via the interwebs — you guys have been great, still are great, and probably will continue to be great until the heat death of the universe.

Third, to Jessica Almasy, audiobook narrator extraordinaire, because up until now I have neglected to thank you, and that certainly has to be one of the deadliest sins of all. Thanks for bringing my books to life and making my jokes sound funnier than they are.

Fourth, to Dad, lover of crossword puzzles and instiller of my love for crossword puzzles. And to Puzzlemaster Will Shortz, thanks to you too! Remember when you met me and my dad backstage at that talk you gave and we took a photo with you? Of course you do; it's probably framed on your wall.

Fifth, to Mom, giver of pep talks and over-the-phone hugs, procurer of tasty treats for bookstore events, and guerrilla publicist. Thanks for telling me I'm awesome even when the state of my kitchen sink suggests I am the exact opposite.

Sixth, to Lisa: I just want to tell you both good luck, we're all counting on you.

Seventh, to my agent, Tina, for her advice on which characters need sex changes and which ones should just die altogether. Thank you for being the best, deadliest agent ever.

Eighth, to my editor, Julie Tibbott, who, when I begin an email with "Okay I know this is nutballs but HEAR ME OUT . . ." responds with an emphatic "I love it!" Thank you for your enthusiasm, guidance, and permission to be nutballs.

And in the ninth and undeniably hottest circle of hell, because you're the one stuck with living with me: Will, thank you for insisting, against all rhyme, reason, and logic, that I should continue this writing bonanza of mine, and for not kicking me out of the marriage when I do things like use the dining room table as my personal bulletin board. You're a saint.

And one final thank-you to all my readers and fans, for your heaps of emails, letters, art, and fandom. I hope you enjoy this book as much as I enjoyed writing it, in blood, atop an altar made of skulls.

To hell with you!

CHAPTERS/CLUES

Across

1. Stolen
4. Excavate
7. Malevolence
9. Demolish, variation
10. Start over
11. Frequently (two words)
12. Obsessive-compulsive type
14. Kind of party
15. Devised a plan
19. Center of the earth
20. Fairy-tale beginning
22. Kerfuffles
23. Hot spot
24. Surveillance
25. Accomplished

Down

1. That girl
2. Where things heat up
3. Torrent
4. Adventurer in Surrealism
5. Escapes injury (two words)
6. Snare
8. Can't stomach
9. Went berserk (two words)
13. Driving aid
15. Sort of jerk
16. Cut short
17. OK place
18. 666 – 15
19. Secret weapon
21. Epilogue

HELLHOLE

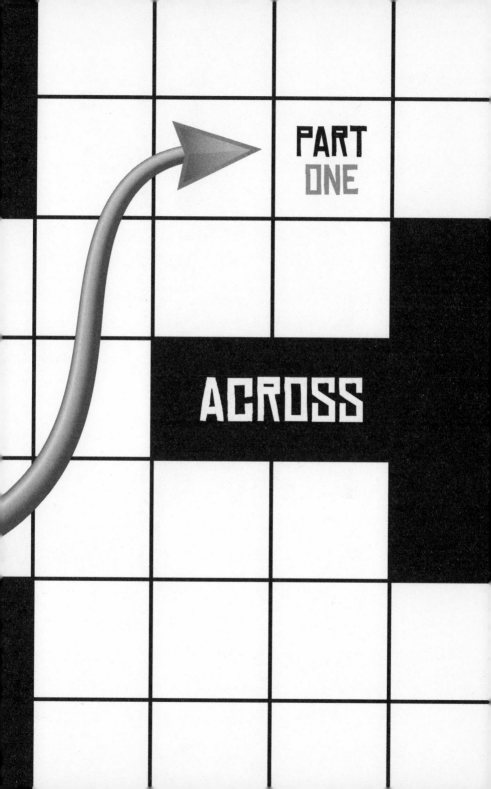

PART
ONE

ACROSS

STOLEN

MAX'S LIFE OF CRIME STARTED POORLY, with the theft of a glittery pink bobblehead in the shape of a cat.

His boss had burst out of the back room moments earlier. "Forest-green Honda Civic license BNR one seven five!" she yelled in a heavy Greek accent as she waddled out the door of the small convenience store, chest heaving and dyed-red bouffant hairdo bouncing. Stavroula Papadopoulos was neither young nor physically fit, but she hadn't let a gas-and-dasher go without a fight for well on thirty years, and she wasn't about to start.

Max's gaze followed her bobbing hair to the abandoned gas pump but got hijacked by the cat, sitting in all its glory next to the cash register. He could hardly believe his luck.

It's breathtaking, he thought.

In actuality, the thing was hideous — poorly made, terrible paint job, practically falling apart. Stavroula must have ordered it from one of those crappy gift store catalogs she was so fond of. Max normally would never have dreamed of taking it, no matter how much irresistible enchantment it exuded, but something strange had come over him. One minute it was sitting there on the counter, all smug and catlike and made in China, and the next it was in his hands, the glitter already beginning to coat his palms.

He wiped his hands on his stiff blue employee vest — then, realizing that this was only incriminating him further, he turned the vest inside out and put it back on. The cat he rammed into his backpack, its head nodding up and down as if to say *Yessiree, I'm contraband!*

Sweat started to seep through Max's T-shirt. His hands were shaking, his stomach queasy. He told himself to knock it off, to sack up already. This was not the sort of behavior befitting a felon.

He was a hardened criminal now, and it was time to start acting like one.

• • •

Seventeen-year-old Max Kilgore suffered from the unfortunate curse of having a name that was far cooler than the person it was attached to. *Max Kilgore* evoked images of Bruce Willis mowing down every law enforcement officer in Los Angeles with a single machine gun, then lassoing a helicopter, stealing the Hollywood sign, and blowing up an army of cyborgs, all in the name of Vengeance.

But the real Max Kilgore was not one to break the rules. He did his homework every night. He never talked in class. He obeyed every bicycle traffic rule in the bicycle traffic rule book — which he had requested from the library and read cover to cover, lest *God forbid* he ever be pulled over by a police officer, a thought that made him want to vomit up a kidney or two. Trouble was something that kids with piercings and sculpted calf muscles got into, and as he had neither, he toed the line like a perpetually paranoid parolee.

As far as Max could tell, this phobia didn't stem from any traumatic events in his childhood, which had been relatively happy. His father had exited the picture long ago, being a "rotten hippie" his mother had slept with "on a dare" and had soon after kicked out of the house owing to his "lack of deodorizing and parenting skills." His mother had picked up the slack just fine, raising him as if single parenthood were as natural to her as breathing clean, patchouli-free air.

Of course, Max had made it easy for her, well-behaved as he was. And until his sophomore year they'd been doing okay on their own, just the two of them. Now life was a bit harder. Now, instead of paying real American dollars for a plastic animal with eyes facing in two different directions and ears that looked as if they'd been designed by someone who had never seen a cat firsthand, he had to break the law and steal it.

And not even in the name of Vengeance.

• • •

The sound of jingling bells snapped Max to attention as Stavroula returned to the store, a flood of Greek words — probably of the swearing sort — gushing out of her mouth. "Second one this week," she spat. "I leave old country for this? Headaches and scoundrels?"

"Headaches and scoundrels" was Stavroula's favorite phrase — Max heard her utter it three or four times over the course of each of his shifts at the Gas Bag — and with it came a pang of guilt at the thought of stealing from her. Grouchy though she may be, Stavroula had given him a job when he'd needed it most, and he knew it wasn't easy for her to have taken over her husband's business when he'd died a few years earlier.

But it was only a small pang. One he could live with.

"Bah!" She threw her hands up in the air, still vexed. "Tomorrow I buy shotgun."

The fear of getting caught was interfering with Max's ability to speak properly. "You said that last week," he said, his voice cracking.

"Last week I buy pistol. This week I buy shotgun."

"What we really need is a trained velociraptor."

She made the same face she always made at his dinosaur references, then frowned, leaning in on the counter until he could see each and every whisker above her lip. "I hate thieves." She narrowed her eyes. "I *despise* thieves."

She knows, he thought with a rush of terror, cat-shaped spots flying across his vision. *She knows, and she's going to call the police, and I'm going to go to jail, and I'll need to figure out how to use cigarettes as currency or I'll become someone's bitch — Oh, who am I kidding, I'll become someone's bitch no matter what —*

Just when Max was sure the sweat accumulating on his forehead was about to cascade down his face in a majestic, disgusting waterfall, Stavroula pounded a fist on the counter. "Restock the meat sticks!"

Max exhaled, taking great pains not to emit a nervous honk as he did so. "The Slim Jims, you mean?"

"Is what I said. Thin Jims."

Perhaps cheerfulness would mask the foul stench of wrongdoing. "You got it!" he chirped.

As he crouched down to retrieve the last remaining box of Slim Jims from beneath the counter — Audie was going to be so pissed — he pushed the incriminating cat farther into his backpack, and only once it was out of sight did his pulse begin to settle back into a normal rate. *You're fine, you're fine,* he chanted to himself, to the beat of his heart. *You were out of the security camera's line of sight, and she wasn't even in her office watching anyway, and even if she was, she stopped watching those tapes once the Booze Hound retired. You're fine.*

Meanwhile, Stavroula took out her iPhone and dialed the police station. "Hello, Rhonda? Yes, we get another one. No, I no break windshield this time —"

She rattled off the numbers of the license plate all the way back to her office and slammed the door shut. Relieved, Max ran a hand over his drenched forehead and into his ridiculous hair, which was black and short except for the front, which stuck out over his forehead like an awning at a Parisian café. Old people liked to say that it was "hair you could set your watch to," whatever that meant. Max just took it to mean that his head was permanently shaped like a batting helmet and there wasn't anything he could do about it.

Although he was beginning to recover most of his faculties, he still felt on edge. As if he could be struck down at any moment by God, or whichever deity it was that handled knickknack robberies —

His cell phone vibrated.

Max's eyes bulged. *Is it the police? Did they somehow see what I did? Do police make courtesy calls before they arrest people?*

He watched it dance across the counter, a beige, bricklike plastic thing designed exclusively for the elderly, with gigantic glowing numbers and a frustrating lack of caller ID. There wasn't really room in his budget for a phone at all, but the situation with his mother required that he be reachable at all times.

His shaking hand knocked against the counter as he picked up the Beige Wonder, wishing yet again that he'd had enough money to afford a communication device that wasn't a glorified coconut radio. "Hello?" he said tentatively.

"You got the stuff?" a gruff voice answered.

It wasn't the police. Or a supreme being. Though maybe Audie did have a little bit of divinity in her — how else could she sense that Max was restocking the Slim Jims at that very moment? "Sorry, Aud, I can't spare any this week," Max said, ripping the cardboard open. "It's our last box. I'll have to reorder."

"So reorder, punk!" his best friend replied, punching every word with a blast of pure concentrated glee. If Audie were candy, she'd be a bag of Skittles: bright, shiny, and bursting with real fruit flavor.

Max, on the other hand, would be a bowl of stale licorice, bland and unwanted. "I don't like reordering," said Max, waving his large hands about. "The customer service guy is named Izzy, and he's really awkward, and every time we lapse into an uncomfortable silence, I end up saying, 'It isn't easy, is it, Izzy?' and it just devolves from there."

"Yeah," Audie said, deadpan. "Izzy sounds like a real freak."

"I know, right?"

Audie let out a sprightly sigh, no doubt twisting her fingers through her spiky dreads as she always did when her patience was being tested. People said she looked like a cross between Rihanna and a palm tree, but to Max she'd always be the girl next door who made him eat a worm when they were six, then a firefly when they were seven. He swore for weeks that it made his pee glow, until the day she demanded he prove it and the topic was mysteriously dropped.

"Anyway," she said, "you coming to the game?"

Max cleared his throat and looked down, pretending to count the pennies in the take-a-penny tray, even though Audie couldn't see him. "I can't."

"Come *on,* man," she whined, a twinge of hurt in her voice. "You haven't come to a single game this season! What are you so busy doing on Friday nights? And *don't* say you got a hot date —"

"I do have a hot date."

"With someone who hasn't been dead for seventy million years?"

"Hey, I'll have you know that with recent 3D imaging, *Ichthyosaurus communis* is more *alive* than ever!"

"Talk like the Discovery Channel all you want, but a book of fossils and a tub of plaster does not an orgy make."

"Gross, Aud." Max reddened as he glanced at the smutty magazine rack behind the counter, then switched to his reflection in the window. With his big brown eyes and thin, pointy nose, he could easily be mistaken for a barn owl. Audie liked to assure him that there were plenty of girls who would go for that sort of look—Gaunt British Standup Comedian, she called it—but always with the caveat that he wouldn't be encountering such girls until he got to college and joined the Science Society, or "whatever it is that lamewads congregate in."

"A gaggle of geeks?" Max often suggested.

"A warp of nerds?" Audie would counter.

"A woot of dweebs?"

"A bunch of virgins?"

And so forth.

He returned the Slim Jims to the shelf under the counter. Of course he'd save them for her; he always did.

"I'm just sayin'," Audie was just saying, "if you can't master the art of small talk with a jerky meat salesman, you're never going to be able to manage it with a lady."

"You make a variety of fine points."

Audie yelled at someone in the background, then came back to the phone. "Gotta run. Thanks for the laughs. Come to the game."

"Goodbye. You're welcome. Can't, but good luck."

Audie muttered a sarcastic "Can't" as she hung up.

"Sorry," Max said to the dead phone.

And he *was* sorry. But a date was a date.

He dug around in his backpack—ignoring, for the moment, the demonic glassy-eyed cat—until he found his crossword book and a pen. He readied his digital watch, a cheap glob of rubber and plastic emblazoned with the *Jurassic Park* logo. He never took it off, for two reasons: (1) it had been a semi-ironic eleventh birthday gift from his mother and his tweenage self had solemnly sworn to her that he'd never remove it; and (2) he had since repurposed it into his own personal crossword timing device. And okay, there was a third reason: he secretly really loved it.

His current crossword record stood at twelve puzzles in six hours. He triggered the countdown timer, narrowed his eyes, and set his voice to movie trailer voice-over mode.

"Let's DO this."

• • •

Six hours and eight crossword puzzles later, the watch alarm beeped. Max threw his pen to the counter and pounded his fist on the rumpled book. "Damn you, Thirty-Two Down! Roast ye in the fiery bowls of HELL!"

After composing himself, he packed everything into his backpack and picked it up gingerly, not wanting to ignite a glitter storm. He was *so* close to pulling off the cat heist.

He tried to keep the waver out of his voice as he yelled to the back room. "I'm heading out, Stavroula!"

The door opened. Stavroula emerged and approached the counter. "Sure you don't want to stay till close? I pay you overtime! You save up for car? Take nice girl out?"

"No thanks." He made a beeline for the exit lest she spontaneously develop x-ray vision and demand that he empty the contents of his bag. "Any other night I would, you know that."

"Psff," he heard her huff as he left. "You and your precious Fridays."

Once he rounded the corner and unlocked his bike, Max let out a final sigh of relief. He'd gotten away with it. "The purr-fect crime," he whispered, followed by a strong urge to punch himself.

The town of Eastville was known for four things: its renowned hospital, its renowned high school football team, its renowned granite quarry, and its stupid, stupid name. No one could say with authority what Eastville was supposed to be east *of*, as it was located in a fairly nondescript area far from the highway, in the wilds of western Massachusetts — west of Boston, west of Springfield, west of anything significant. The only thing it was east of was a big, ugly hill (known locally and affectionately as Ugly Hill) that was covered in a variety of shrubs and brambles that looked brown in the summer and browner in the winter. They didn't even glitter prettily in the snow, because snow didn't bother to stick to them. It recoiled from their thistles in disgust.

Max threw a glance at the hill as he pedaled through town, surprised at his ability to perceive its outline. Normally E'ville was anything but bright, but owing to the lights of the football stadium bouncing off the low clouds in the sky, it was as if a dome had encased the town in a glowing, reddish hue.

The crisp September air bit at his face. A loud cheer mushroomed up out of O'Connell Stadium as he rode past, and there was Audie's voice, booming out of the speakers. In the school's hundred-year history, there had never been a female football announcer at Eastville High — not until the day Audie marched up to the athletic director and flashed that irresistible smile of hers, informing him that she was going to be on ESPN one day, and if he ever hoped to score some tickets to the Super Bowl, he'd give her the job.

He gave her the job.

"And what will *you* be, young man?" Max muttered to himself in a spot-on imitation of Audie's mother.

A convict, he imagined the cat meowing from inside his bag. *It's death row for you, bub. You'll probably get the chair. I'm a very important cat. Back on my home planet, I was a queen, I tell you! A queen!*

Max was not adapting well to the criminal life.

He rounded into the parking lot of the Food Baron, stopped in front of the exit, and looked at his watch. It was 9:03 p.m., the T. rex skeleton informed him. He took exactly $4.81 out of his pocket and waited.

Two seconds later the automatic door swished open. Out poked a sweating bottle of sparkling apple cider. Max exchanged it for the money, then expertly slid it into his bag.

"Hey, Paul," he said to the person formerly attached to the cider, a short, pimple-faced kid wearing a Food Baron apron.

"Hey yourself" was the standard reply.

Paul had been the only other student to show up for Mr. Donnelly's after-school Paleontology Club last year, an endeavor that had clearly been doomed from the start. (Even Mr. Donnelly hadn't cared enough to show up.) The two of them had chatted and exchanged their favorite geologic periods — Jurassic for Max, Cretaceous for Paul — and from then on had sat at lunch together every day. Slowly, accidentally, Paul became Max's friend, or at least served as a decent pinch-hitter friend once Audie got too popular.

And it was a good thing, too, because Paul looked even more the part of a dweeb than Max did. A curly-haired ginger, he possessed glasses that wouldn't have been out of place at a nursing home, and a bucktoothed overbite fighting an epic battle against a complicated set of braces. But Paul was a nice kid, if a little dull, and his propensity to repeat the same word over and over sometimes got distracting.

"Busy night?" Max asked.

"I'll say. We got a big squash shipment, but the squash was really dirty, so I had to wash each squash."

"Oh my gosh."

"Do *you* want to buy a freshly washed squash?"

"No, thanks, I'm good with the cider. Have a good night!"

The errands continued. Max hung a left onto Main Street — the founders of Eastville had apparently expended every drop of their creative juices on the town name — and biked past the dark storefronts, most businesses having closed early because of the football game. Only a couple of them were still open — a quirky gift shop whose owners cared nothing for sports, and a pizzeria, in front of which Max came to a practiced stop.

"Hi, Mario," he said with a nod as he entered.

Mario the pizza guy smiled through his bushy mustache and opened the oven. Max hadn't even needed to place an order; that large cheese pizza was already waiting for him, just as it was every Friday night at 9:05 p.m.

He paid for the pie and then — because he was still coasting on the high of his successful theft and feeling really crazy — added an order of onion rings.

Mario's eyebrows went up. "Big night?"

Max stuffed the onion rings into his bag. "You have no idea."

• • •

The squat ranch-style house that awaited Max was its usual dark and foreboding self, the kind of unkempt pile of shingles and shutters that neighborhood kids sometimes likened to the abode of a witch. Its once-white aluminum siding had long ago turned a sickly shade of brown. The lawn was overgrown and scorched yellow in the late-summer heat; Audie's father often threatened to fine Max for not mowing it, but only in jest, as it made his own lawn look all the more pristine by comparison.

The backyard was another story altogether.

Max flipped open the mailbox to find two bills and a DVD. He scowled at the bills, but the DVD lit a tiny, happy spark inside him. He grinned, tossed all the mailbox's contents into his backpack, and walked up the driveway.

His cat — a real one named Ruckus, not the stolen plastic atrocity — greeted him at the door by way of hissing and swiping at every available inch of skin, as Ruckus's favorite hobby was climbing atop the refrigerator and dive-bombing hapless kitchen entrants until they were forced, bleeding and broken, to retreat. "Ow!" Max shouted, then immediately shushed himself. Red, puffy scratch marks were already popping up from his skin. "Out of my way, spawn of Satan," he whispered, swatting the orange furball away.

Two plastic champagne flutes, the bottle of cider, a stack of paper plates, and the onion rings all got piled on top of the pizza box as Max headed into the hallway. He stopped in front of the first door on the right, then, struck by an idea, put everything on the floor and pulled the bobblehead out of his bag instead.

He opened the door a crack and stuck the misshapen pink head in. "Mrow!" he squeaked.

"Ruckus, is that you?" the voice inside said. "My — my *God*, what have you done to yourself? You got a makeover! Let's see, I'm sensing exfoliation, sequin implants, corrective eyeball surgery, and is that . . . decapitation?"

"Mrow." Max made the cat nod, bouncing its spring-loaded head back and forth.

"Well, dahling, you look stunning. Only a matter of time before Bravo gives you your own show. You'll be the most intelligent thing on the network."

Max snickered, entered the room, and leaned over the rails of the hospital bed to give his mother a kiss. "You like it?"

"It's breeeeathtaking," she said in a perfect imitation of the ridiculous way the ladies on QVC said it, her eyes sparkling in jarring contrast to the rest of her. Bulging collarbone, pale skin, sunken cheeks — she looked even thinner than she had when Max kissed her goodbye before school that morning, he thought.

But he didn't let his face show it. "I thought you might," he said, handing her the cat.

"Look! No matter where I move it, still it stares," she said in awe, holding it at different angles. "Where on earth did you get this?"

He hoped to sound nonchalant when he said, "Work."

She frowned and placed the cat on her nightstand. It joined an old-school beeper, plus a troll doll, some sort of unicorn-as-angel figurine, and a one-eyed koala dressed as a princess, each kitschy monstrosity more *breeeathtaking* than the last. That Goodwill Store had been a treasure-trove until it closed a couple of months earlier, transforming into an upscale boutique where even the chintziest snow globes were out of Max's price range.

"I hope it didn't cost too much," she said. "Stavroula give you a discount?"

He nodded, for once thankful for the hair shelf that shielded his eyes. "Yep. Big one."

"Or maybe you stole it." Every one of Max's muscles seized, until he realized she was joking. "Maybe you're secretly the Booze Hound," she teased. "Robbing all those liquor stores, getting sloshed every night right under my nose."

"Ha!" Max laughed forcefully. "Yeah right, Mom."

That was too close. Quick, distract her with dairy.

He retrieved the pizza from the hall and placed it on the bed next to her blanketed legs. "Let the Petty Pizza Pity Party . . . commence," he said, opening the box.

His mom breathed in deeply, then moaned. "Crack. Pure crack. And—sakes alive, onion rings? I'm in heaven. Wait—have I died and gone to heaven and I don't even know it? Is this a *Sixth Sense* situation we've got going on here?"

Max snickered, poured the cider into the plastic flutes, and sank into the ratty armchair beside the bed. "How was your day?"

"Oh, thrill-a-minute," she said bitterly, helping herself to a slice and a ring, one in each hand. "What would you like to hear about, the newest Bowflex infomercial? Or the latest shipment of bimbos on *The Price Is Right*? Or—funny story—the time I got up to brush my teeth but all of a sudden felt so weak I dropped my toothbrush in the toilet?"

"You dropped your toothbrush in the toilet?"

"Yeah. Which reminds me—I need you to get my toothbrush out of the toilet."

"Will do."

She slurped up a wad of cheese and gave him a sad smile. "Oh, Maxter. What would I do without you?"

Chronic heart failure wasn't nearly as much fun as the name implied. Max's mom was young—she'd had him when she was only a few years older than he was now—so a viral infection was the only explanation the doctors had been able to come up with. She had survived the virus, but her heart just barely squeaked by, and she'd been in a state of decline ever since. As a nurse, she'd at least been able to handle her own medication, but she and Max both knew that she was past the point of getting any better.

Her former colleagues begged her to stay at the hospital, but she always refused. ("Yeah, like I want half my coworkers coming in to gawk at my emaciated body and trade small talk. 'Come on in, Phil, grab an IV pole and let's get this party started!'") Confident, stubborn, and fiercely independent, she'd spent the last two ailing years retreating from society, not wanting anyone but her son to see her in such a weakened and pathetic state. Her parents had thrown her out of the house when she'd gotten pregnant with him, and she hadn't been in contact with any members of her family for years, so she'd learned not to rely on anyone but herself.

And Max.

Max had not minded the added responsibility of caring for his mom; she'd done it for him by herself for so many years that he certainly owed her the same courtesy. But when he wasn't kept up all night by the idea of her going into sudden cardiac arrest, he was ceaselessly worrying about the financial strain. Every moment he wasn't in school he was at work at the gas station, forgoing any and all extracurricular activities and socializing, should he ever discover what that word meant. He was barely able to put food on the table and pay the bills every month, let alone cover his mom's medical expenses, to say nothing of the desperately needed heart transplant they'd never be able to afford.

He glanced at the beeper on her nightstand, the one that would send an alert from the hospital should a spare organ ever drop into their lives. It hadn't gone off yet, though, and Max had all but given up hope that it ever would.

"So, what's playing tonight?" his mom asked, going in for a second slice. She really wasn't supposed to be eating all that cheese, but when she'd threatened to set herself ablaze at the thought of a life devoid of mozzarella, her doctors had agreed to exactly two slices per week. Which translated, in her opinion, to four. "If John Cusack's involved, I'll have to brush my hair first." She combed her fingers through a flat, lifeless strand, then snorted. "Provided I can still hold a comb."

Max shook his head. "You're too good for John Cusack, Mom. The guy hasn't put out a decent movie in years."

"You bite your tongue, young man. *Say Anything . . .* ? Lloyd Dobler standing outside the bedroom window with the boom box? John Cusack is one of America's finest — what's that?"

When he'd pulled the DVD out of his bag, one of the overdue bills had come with it. He stuffed it back in. "Nothing."

It's only a second warning, he thought. *They don't cut the electricity until after the final one.*

"Hey, here's a question for you," he said brightly, holding up the DVD. "What happens when two hopelessly romantic business rivals hate each other in real life but fall in love over the Internet?"

Her eyes lit up. "*You've Got Mail!*"

She clapped as he popped it into the DVD player. "Oh, Max, you're the best. You have no idea how much I needed this."

Cheesy romantic comedies put the "petty" in their weekly Petty Pizza Pity Parties, for reasons that soon became obvious.

"Die, Meg Ryan!" Max's mom shouted at the screen as the actress flounced around her children's bookstore. "Get crushed underneath a bookcase of Harry Potters and DIE."

"Won't work," Max said. "Her perkiness will save her."

"And yet, inexplicably, Tom Hanks will only find her all the more charming." She narrowed her eyes. "What a loser. Living on a boat. Boat hobo."

"Mom, you're the only person on the planet who hates Tom Hanks."

"Good," she said, peeling blobs of cheese off the bottom of the pizza box. "Then I get to be the one who slays him."

They continued to rip the movie to shreds, with analyses both profound ("You know why he needs to make friends on the Internet? Because in person, women keep laughing at him when they see the size of his—" "Mom, stop."); vindictive ("She's faking that cold. No one looks that cute when they're gushing mucus."); and cruel ("'Daisies are the friendliest flower'? Who *talks* like that, other than people with brain damage?"). Max joined in on the barbs, even though he sometimes secretly liked those kinds of movies. They always had happy endings, a precious commodity that was not guaranteed in real life.

Plus, Tom Hanks gave him hope. The man's head looked like a loaded baked potato, yet he always got the girl in the end.

When at last "The End" was typed out on the screen and a cursor hovered over it and clicked it away ("Lame."), Max rubbed his eyes and stood up. His mom leaned back into her pillows with a contented sigh.

"Thanks, hon," she said, squeezing his hand. "You did good."

"I try." He picked up the pizza box and his backpack, then leaned over to kiss her on the forehead. "Night, Mom. Love you."

"Love you too, babe," she said, her eyes already fluttering. "Thanks again for the mutant cat."

Max snickered and closed the door behind him. He thought for a moment about heading into the basement to log some hours on the Xbox in the hopes that he might one day beat Audie at *Madden*, but the tendrils of a headache were beginning to spread through his skull, worming into the spaces behind his eyes. He told himself this was due to the stress of stealing the cat. Definitely not from the effort of holding in tears at the end of the movie.

Look, he couldn't help it. Tom and Meg were just too charming.

When he got to his bedroom, he dropped his backpack to the floor, the overdue bills along with it. He'd deal with them tomorrow. Or, rather, he'd check the family bank account balance, confirm that there wasn't enough money in it to pay said bills, and throw them into the garbage bin tomorrow.

He fell into bed but couldn't sleep. He stared out his window at the perfect view of Ugly Hill that it provided, but its blahness only depressed him more. The familiar refrain of *what am I gonna do, what am I gonna do* ran through his head like a stampede of collection agency wildebeests. One concern led to another, a chain reaction with no end in sight.

Well, there was one end—but he didn't want to think about that.

He tossed and turned, yet sleep refused to come. He watched the clock on his nightstand flip over, one minute at a time—2:59, 3:00, 3:01—until finally, unable to endure another minute of worry, he got dressed and grabbed his shovel.

EXCAVATE

MAX WAS OUTSIDE IN LESS THAN A MINUTE, wearing his crummiest pair of jeans and a jacket that was far too thin for how chilly it had gotten. Not that there was any danger of getting lost and dying of exposure out there; he knew the overgrown hiking trails of Ugly Hill by heart. Everyone in E'ville did, as it was the only halfway decent place to make out. Or do more than make out.

Or, in Max's case, dig holes.

Aside from being notably hideous, Ugly Hill had one additional claim to fame: about ten years prior, a paleontology team from Harvard University had discovered a rare fossil beneath its ugly dirt. It was so rare they hadn't been able to identify it, and as far as Max knew—since he had periodically emailed Dr. Cavendish, the professor and expedition leader, about it—they were still stumped a decade later.

The discovery garnered a lot of attention when it happened—Eastville even made the national news for a day or two. But once the excitement died away, any and all scientific interest went with it. The original discoverers had been a team of bored undergrads who thought Paleontology 101 would be an easy A and had already moved on with their lives, and the few honest-to-God paleontologists who showed up to properly search the area ended up finding nothing but more ugly dirt and a bunch of used condoms. So everyone gave up on it.

Except for Max.

The discovery had come at the height of his childhood obsession with dinosaurs, and it had lit such a fuse within him that he made it his goal in life to keep the investigation alive. So intent was he on finding The Next Big Fossil that he trudged up the hill every chance he got, shovel in hand, and dug until calluses formed on his fingers and his clothes were soaked with perspiration. He never found anything, but he liked digging, and the thrill of possibility was enough to keep him coming back. Of course, with his mother's health problems, he hadn't been able to return as much over the past couple of years, but every once in a while he still went up there for old times' sake.

Or to vent some pent-up frustration.

So it was from the top of Ugly Hill that Max planted his shovel, sank it deep into the ground, and dug. He went at it for a solid hour, muscles screaming, cones of dirt piling up around him as he tried out different spots. The wind stung at his sweaty face, but it felt amazing, and the aches in his arms were good aches — they took away his cares and worries, one knot at a time.

Max shone his keychain flashlight down into the hole he'd just made. Seeing nothing, he put the light back in his pocket, chose another spot, and started all over again. In, out, in, out, in —

In . . .

In . . . ?

The shovel kept right on going, swallowed by the earth. Max lost his balance and stumbled forward, catching himself at the last second — just before the ground started to collapse.

He let out a shout and wrenched his body backwards to keep from falling in. Landing flat on his butt, he scuttled back like a crab, hands and feet frantically scrambling away from the sinking dirt. The abyss grew and grew, all while a low rumble sounded through the air, as if the planet itself were growling.

Then: silence.

Max groped in his pocket for his flashlight, clicked it on, and pointed the beam into the darkness. The dirt had stopped falling, but the damage was done. Stretching out before him was a massive dark hole.

Shaking, Max got to his feet and started to make his way around the void, confusion growing with every step. It was a perfect circle, about six feet in diameter. Dust stung at his eyes; a sour stench choked his lungs. He could taste something awful on his tongue, like the gagfest that results from drinking orange juice right after brushing one's teeth. But other than an occasional, eerie clicking noise coming from deep within, he couldn't hear a thing.

Max took a cautious step up to the rim. He could see only blackness inside, the hole so deep his flashlight couldn't reach the bottom. A gentle pulse of warm air puffed up into his face, the smell of sulfur tickling his nostrils. And in that moment—he was sure he was imagining this, but that didn't make the sensation any less intense—an overwhelming *something* came over him, an emotion he'd never felt before that was sadness and terror and suffocation and grief all at the same time.

Max had been up on Ugly Hill hundreds of times, alone and in the dark, but this was the first time he'd ever been truly scared.

"What the hell?" his voice quivered.

Just then an air pulse sent up small fleck of ash—black, as light as air, a gothic snowflake. It floated out of the hole, then descended and landed on the back of Max's hand. He tried to wipe it off, but all that did was create a black smear across his skin.

And then, as abruptly as it had come, the strange fear began to fade. Sleep tugged at his body, and Max started to feel a little foolish. He hadn't been up this hill in months; maybe the gas company had done some faulty pipeline laying or someone had begun construction on a cell phone tower. Or something. He didn't know *why* a giant circular hole might have opened up out of nowhere, but Max was sure there was a reasonable, corporate, environmentally unfriendly explanation for all of this.

As an afterthought, he grabbed a nearby rock and tossed it into the hole, waiting for a thump to signify that it had hit the bottom.

A minute later he was still waiting.

But he was cold now, exhausted, and a sudden fear rose in his chest—what if his mother needed him? What if she was having an episode right now and was desperately calling out his name, dialing the number of a cell phone that he hadn't remembered to bring with him?

He sprinted home.

Only when he opened her door with fumbling hands and saw her lying there, safe and alive, did the panic stop ringing in his ears.

"You okay, Max?" she said blearily, through squinted eyes. "What's wrong?"

"Nothing," he said, his voice cracking. He cleared his throat. "Nothing. Thirsty. Just getting some water."

"You look sweaty, hon. Did you have a nightmare?"

He didn't know what to say to that.

Maybe?

MALEVOLENCE

THE NEXT MORNING, MAX SLEPT IN. Only by five minutes, but those five minutes translated into five minutes late showering, five minutes late getting dressed, and, ultimately, five minutes late for the verbal beatdown Stavroula was all too willing to deliver.

"We open five minutes ago," she scolded as he rushed in.

"I know, I know." He pulled his blue vest out from under the counter and put it on, praying that she wouldn't notice the glitter shower that ensued. "I'm sorry."

"*Five minutes ago.* And where is my cashier? Watching goats mate on the computer?"

"I — no! Why would you think that?"

"I don't know what you kids do on that box!" she said, throwing up her arms. "All I know is that you are late. Tell me why."

Max's mouth was devoid of saliva. Even if it wasn't for the cat, he still hated being in trouble. And truth be told, he was still a bit shaken by what he'd seen up on Ugly Hill. If not for the dirt caked on his shoes, he might have thought he dreamed it.

"Last night, I — um, couldn't sleep, and —"

"And, and? I no sleep in six years since my husband die, bless his soul."

Max joined her in making the sign of the cross. "It's just — I —"

He didn't want to do it. He hated trotting out this excuse, this despicable, manipulative excuse, but she was staring at him so hard he was willing to do anything to make her stop.

"It was my mom," he said in a low voice, taking care to inject double doses of Sorrowful Despair and Soldiering On in the Face of Adversity.

Stavroula's scowl diminished, replaced by a look of sympathy, or perhaps disappointment at not being able to keep yelling at him. "Ah. Yes. Is she all right?"

He nodded and spoke in clipped words. "Yeah. Fine."

"Good." She waggled her finger at him as she walked back toward her office, but any anger was long gone. "Just don't let it happen again."

The door slammed.

Max exhaled. After making sure that his resting heart rate had been restored, he reached for his book of crossword puzzles. Over the entirety of last Saturday's double shift, he'd solved twenty-one in fourteen hours, resulting in a rate of only 1.5 puzzles per hour, which simply would not do. Fatigue had set in. Fatigue was the enemy.

Determined to do better this time, and even more determined

to put the Ugly Hill incident out of his mind, he set his watch for fourteen hours — his shift lasted fifteen, but he had to allow a spare one for lunch, dinner, and those pesky interrupting customers. He uncapped his pen, got to work, and didn't stop until halfway through puzzle number five, when the door jangled and Audie walked in.

"Greetings, hermit!" she said.

Audie had exactly two moods: exuberant and slightly less exuberant. Nothing in between. Today: a rare appearance by the latter.

Max hit the Stop button on his watch and gave her a withering smile. "I can make it up to you."

"You damn well better." Audie attempted to look stern but failed immediately, as her face just didn't bend that way. "With meats. Chop-chop!"

Max retrieved the box of Slim Jims he'd stashed and plopped it on the counter. "Today I've prepared for you a selection of plastic-wrapped charcuterie, featuring a rustic gastrique of artisanal pig anuses and a decadent mélange of mechanically separated chicken," he said in the style of the chefs on all those cooking competition shows his mother complained about wasting her life watching, yet watched anyway. *"Bon appétit."*

"You're such a freak," Audie said with a giggle, tossing a wad of money at him and attacking the wrapper. "But thanks."

"How do you find the mouthfeel, ma'am?"

"Ew. Lifetime moratorium on that word."

"What, 'mouthfeel'?"

"Stop it!" she cried, giving him one of those fake smacks on the arm that she had perfected since the age of five.

Max dodged it with a smile. "What are you doing up and about so early on a Saturday?" he asked, taking a Slim Jim for himself.

Audie nodded toward the window. Her father was outside, pumping gas into the family car while her mother squeegeed the windshield. A third person was asleep in the back seat. "I'm giving Wall a ride to the airport. Which of course means we're *all* giving Wall a ride to the airport because Mom and Dad *insisted* on coming. Like they think I'm gonna be so heartbroken about him going away for the weekend that I'm gonna bang him right there atop the check-in kiosk."

"That's a fun visual."

"I agree. Little fantasy of mine."

"Then maybe their suspicions aren't unfounded."

"Hey, don't take their side." She took another bite. "He's not even conscious, anyway. Killer game last night, not that *you'd* know."

As they munched, Max toyed with the idea of telling her about what he'd seen up on Ugly Hill. Maybe she could —

— kindly inform me that I've lost my mind? his brain butted in. *She'll think I'm bonkers. And if God forbid her father catches wind of it, he'll go up there to investigate, and then I'll lose my private digging spot, and if he God forbid decides to question me any further, I'll totally cave and confess the theft of Frankencat, and then I'll be arrested and go to jail and will almost certainly need to learn how to sharpen a toothbrush into a shiv to defend myself, which is a skill I should probably start honing now . . . I wonder if you can whittle a Slim Jim —*

The door bells rattled as a human refrigerator walked into the store. It leaned on the counter and smiled at Audie with a mouth full of straight, achingly white teeth.

"Hey, girl."

Audie's mood ramped right up into high gear. *Click!* Full steam exuberant. "You're awake!" Her face glowed as he grabbed her hand, twirled her around, then dipped her almost down to the floor, planting a big wet kiss on her laughing mouth.

The giant pulled her back up, then turned to Max. "Hey, hoss."

"Hi, Wall," Max replied in a voice as microscopic as he felt.

The real name of E'ville's star linebacker and Audie's boyfriend of three years was Emmanuel, but on the football field he basically turned into a concrete parking garage with a little helmet on top, so Wall was the nickname that stuck. He was a nice guy, yet Max still felt like the *Microceratus gobiensis* to Wall's *Brachiosaurus altithorax*. Max just didn't know how, as an athletically challenged and thoroughly unimpressive human being by comparison, he could ever find anything in common with the guy. Max didn't know a thing about football. He didn't know how to bridge the popularity gap. And he didn't know what a hoss was, either.

The office door pounded open. "No!" Stavroula yelled upon seeing Wall snap into a Slim Jim. "No more! You football brutes eat up all my meats!"

"Roula, Roula, Roula," Wall said, propping a massive arm over her shoulder as she approached the counter. "You know I need my meats. I'm a growing boy."

She made a *psff* noise. "You grow anymore, you hit head on

ceiling, break sprinklers, flood store. Bah." And she was off again, shuffling to the back room with a dismissive wave.

Max stuffed more Slim Jim into his mouth. Now that Wall was here, he didn't dare bring up Ugly Hill. "So, did you win the game?" he asked.

"Did we win the game?" Wall answered, his mouth full of nitrates. "He's asking if we *won the game!*" he shouted in disbelief to an invisible crowd, then let out a hearty laugh, followed instantly by a death glare, a combination that could be pulled off to perfection only by himself and a Mr. Denzel Washington.

Max genuinely feared for his life for a second there, but Wall had already started laughing and ruffling Max's hair. It went askew for a moment, then settled right back into its default golf visor position.

The door chimed yet again. Max stood a little taller, preparing for the double whammy of Audie's increasingly intimidating parents. There hadn't been anything too scary about growing up next door to a teacher and a policeman, but subsequent promotions in their respective fields had put them in a much more imposing light. It was that whole authority figure thing again. Something about them made him want to constantly smooth his shirt and glitter-precipitating vest in their presence.

"Max!" Audie's dad said. "Haven't seen much of you lately! How are you doing?"

"Fine, Chief Gregory."

Audie's mom joined him at the counter, her smile frozen in place. "And how's your mom?"

"Fine, Principal Gregory. I mean, she's the same," he added when she made a doubtful face. "Sleeps a lot."

Audie's mom leaned in and spoke in a whisper that was dripping with compassion. "You know, Max, you can call us. Whenever you need something. I just feel so bad thinking of her cooped up in there, all alone all day."

"Yeah, but you know how she is," Max said, squirming. "She doesn't like people to see her when she's . . ."

He trailed off. Back in the day, his mom and Mrs. Gregory had been good friends. Now he couldn't remember the last time they spoke.

She frowned. "I know, but —"

"Mom, give it a rest," Audie said. "He knows the drill."

Principal Gregory threw up her hands. "Sorry! Can't turn off the mom in me!"

Max was willing to do anything to get out of this conversation, up to and including talking to Wall. "Where are you headed, Wall?"

"College visit for the weekend," Wall said. " 'Bama."

"Oh." Max tried to nod knowingly. "Sure. Go Gators."

They all looked at him as if he'd kicked the Pope in the junk.

"Max," Audie said, aghast, "it's *Roll Tide*."

"Roll Tide!" the other three echoed in unison, pumping their fists.

Max tried to punch the air in a similar enthusiastic fashion, but he looked ridiculous and everyone knew it, so he switched to swatting at an imaginary fly instead.

"The coaches there are *very* interested in him," Audie said, gazing adoringly into Wall's eyes. He took Audie's chin in his massive hand, moving in to kiss her.

"Emmanuel!" Chief Gregory interrupted, clapping his hands on Wall's back. "Come out and help me check the tire pressure."

Wall gave Audie a wretched look and slumped out the door.

Principal Gregory paid Max for the gas. "Here," she said, handing the change to her daughter, "buy yourself a drink." She turned back to Max. "And you—remember what I said. Whatever you need, hon."

"*Mom.*"

"Thank you," Max said. "I'll remember."

After she left, Audie let out a long, exasperated breath. She grabbed a bottle of water out of the refrigerator, then rounded on Max like a feral dog. "So. Why'd you skip my game last night?"

Max decided to feign choking on his Slim Jim to escape this line of questioning, but the jangle of door bells saved him from having to resort to such theatrics. Three girls walked in, two of them talking loudly. The third girl headed straight for the snack food section. Max watched as the top of her straight brown ponytail bobbed down the aisle, then stopped, hovering above the Cheetos. Giggling, the other two followed.

"You know what?" said Audie, a wicked grin spreading across her face as she watched the girls. "I don't even want to hear your feeble excuses." She pointed the remains of her Slim Jim into his face. "You know there's only one way to make this up to me."

Max waved his hand, dismissive. "I'm not doing this today, Aud. I'm very close to beating the crossword record."

"Oh, screw the crossword record."

Max narrowed his eyes. "How *dare* you."

"Come *onnn*," Audie said in that whining voice she used when she knew full well she'd already won. She nodded toward the girls. "Try. For me."

Max grumbled. Ever since that fateful night their thirteen-year-old selves decided to finally French it up — a kiss that garnered such rave reviews as "slimy" and "like kissing my brother" — any potential sparks between them got permanently switched to Off, unplugged from the wall, and buried in the backyard, never to be spoken of again.

This was totally fine with Max; he'd felt the same way about that gross kiss as she had. But once she started dating Wall, he got relegated to permanent third-wheel status, and now Audie was constantly getting on his case about nabbing a girlfriend. "We could go on double dates!" she'd insist, a prospect Max found especially nauseating. To get a date, one generally needed to be able to string words together in a coherent manner around the opposite sex, or at the very least be able to smile charmingly. Both Audie and Wall did these things quite well, whereas Max had all the flirting ability of a packing peanut.

The venerably popular Krissy Swanson approached the counter with an armful of snacks and sodas. Audie stood behind her and made a go-ahead gesture at Max, followed by something much more vulgar. "Fine," Max mouthed at her as Krissy dug through her purse.

When she looked up, Max smiled. "Find everything okay?" he asked.

"What?" she said in a distracted voice, as if surprised to learn that the counter kid spoke Human. "Uh, yeah."

Wiggling his eyebrows, Max held up the bag of Cheetos. "Processed cheese snacks," he said with a knowing nod. "I like that in a woman."

Audie had to excuse herself.

Krissy gave Max a look. "They're not for *me*. *I'm* getting the soy chips and diet protein water."

"Oh, yeah, you gotta have protein," he said, scanning the rest of her items and placing them in a plastic bag. "Amino acids are, like, the shit. You like veal?"

"I— What?"

"Me neither. It's baby cows, did you know that?" Max could already feel this thing going south, yet he pressed on, as always. "I don't think I could eat a baby anything. Except baby corn. Those things are so weird. It's like, are you real corn, or were you shrunk by a shrinking ray, or what's going on here?"

Krissy's eyes darted to the security camera. "Am I on a reality show right now?"

"No," Max said. "Why?"

"Okay. Um, here," she said, tossing him a twenty-dollar bill and grabbing the plastic bag.

"But it's only twelve—"

"Keep the change!" She grabbed the elbows of the other two girls and plowed out the door, barely able to keep her giggles in as she relayed the tale of her encounter with the troglodyte cashier. Brown Ponytail threw a languid glance back at him as they left.

Audie emerged from her hiding place behind the motor oil, holding her stomach. "You should be studied by scientists," she said between laughs. "Veal? *Veal?*"

Max shrugged. This was nothing new. Humiliation in the face of the opposite gender was an unfortunate plague he'd simply had to get used to, like high milk prices or the continued existence of the Kardashians.

"So what are you doing after you get back from the airport?" he asked Audie just as the door opened. He nodded hello at the new customer, a guy sporting heavy black eyeliner, several piercings, and a visible hangover. The man nodded back, making a beeline for the coffee machine.

"I don't know," Audie replied with a shrug. "Maybe go see the new Michael Bay explodathon."

"Spoiler alert: Everyone dies."

Audie rolled her eyes, having grown sick of Max's standard spoiler-alert joke long ago. "We'll see. I was gonna devote the day to *Madden*" — here she cracked her knuckles as she always did at the mention of the game, like a Pavlovian response — "but my Xbox is busted."

Max gasped.

His voice dropped to a horrified whisper. "The red ring of death?"

"'Fraid so."

Max's main fear in life was, *of course*, that his mother could drop dead at any given second . . . but if he was being completely honest, the prospect of the same thing happening to his Xbox struck him with an almost equal amount of terror. "Well, you can go play on mine if you want."

"Really?" She did her Audie-is-super-excited-about-something hop, bouncing from one foot to the other. "Key still under the mat?"

"Yep. I'll call my mom and tell her not to bash the intruder's head in."

"Thanks, man!" She lunged across the counter and gathered Max into a headlock. "All is forgiven. As long as you come to my game next week."

"I'll . . . see what I can do."

"Just once before the season is over! That's all I ask!"

"Okay, okay."

"Or at the very least, come to the pep rally this Wednesday. You don't have any secret dates with fictional people on Wednesdays, do you?"

"I do not."

"Then come." She tossed the empty Slim Jim wrapper at him. "And thanks for the meats."

"Any time."

Audie laughed as she exited the store.

Guyliner brought his coffee up to the counter, his eyes bleared and tired. "And a pack of smokes. Whatever's cheapest."

"Sure." Max rang up the purchase and placed the cigarettes on the counter.

The guy let out a small laugh. "You were there too?"

"Huh?"

He showed Max the back of his hand, which featured the faded slash of a black Sharpie. "At the concert," he said, nodding at the similar mark smeared across the back of Max's hand.

From the ash that floated up out of the hole. Max hadn't noticed until just then that it was still there. *But I took a shower . . . ?*

"Killer show, right?" the guy said, handing Max some money. He took a long gulp of coffee. "Lucky I didn't black out in a gutter somewhere. Anyway, cheers." He held up his cup in thanks and exited the store.

Max examined his hand. He licked his thumb and rubbed it against his skin, but no matter how hard he tried to wipe off the mark, it wouldn't go away.

• • •

When his watch alarm went off at the end of his shift, Max slammed his pen and crossword book onto the counter and pumped his fists into the air.

"I win at LIFE!" he shouted, enjoying for a moment the delusion that completing twenty-five crossword puzzles in fourteen hours meant he'd won at anything at all.

Stavroula's grumpy face poked out from behind the Funyuns. "Why you yell?"

"Oh, sorry," Max said, lowering his arms. "I just —" But talking about his victory would make it sound even sadder. "Nothing."

She looked at her watch. "Okay, ten o'clock. You go home now."

He took off his vest, threw out the wrapper from his Hot Pocket dinner, and stuffed his crossword book into his bag. "Thanks, Stav."

"And tell your mom I say feel better."

The sting of the earlier lie prickled in his stomach. He nodded gravely. "I will."

He biked home under a moonlit sky. Bracing for the worst as he opened the mailbox, he was relieved to find nothing more than a Home Depot catalog. That, he could handle. They made good shovels.

On his way to the back kitchen door, he assessed the house. Dark, except for the flicker of television visible through his mother's bedroom window and the rectangle of light coming from the basement. The leaves of his mom's beloved ficus tree inside blocked the view of the small den down there, but judging by the guttural noises and whistle blows coming from within, Audie was well into her *Madden* conquest.

After dumping his stuff onto the kitchen table and wondering why Ruckus hadn't greeted him with a friendly claw to the face, neck, and torso, Max grabbed a granola bar and headed to the basement. Sporty football music hit his ears as he descended the stairs. "This was my plan all along," he sang down to Audie. "You wear your thumbs down with hours of playing and then I swoop in to kick your ass." He unzipped his hoodie as he neared the bottom of the steps. "Jesus, Aud, it's like a hundred degrees down here—"

He stopped.

The granola bar fell to the floor.

Perched on the edge of the plaid 1970s-era couch, where Max had fully expected to find Audie, was a man in a teal-blue velour tracksuit. His beard was rust colored and shaggy, as was his hair, out of which poked two white, jagged horns. And though he was currently dumping the remains of a bag of Flamin' Hot Cheetos into his mouth with a cheese-dusted hand, the coloring didn't end at the edges of his fingertips.

Every visible inch of his skin was red.

He shook the controller at the television with his other hand and flashed Max a garish grin, food globs flying out of his mouth as he spoke.

"This shit is awesome."

DEMOLISH, VARIATION

"AAAAAAAH!" MAX SCREAMED, then added another "Aaaaaa-
AAAAAaaaaah!" for good measure.

He spun around and bolted up to his mother's bedroom, pounding the door open so forcefully she nearly fell out of bed in surprise.

"Max!" she shouted, fumbling with her covers. "Jesus Christ,
what's wrong?"

He blinked several times, terrified that he'd just ruptured her
aorta. "Are you okay?"

"Yes! Why are you so freaked out?"

Max swallowed. He wanted to tell her, but shocking her into
cardiac arrest was not optimal. "I'm . . . not," he said slowly, trying
to force blood back into his cheeks. "I just — I heard ambulance
sirens on my way home, and I worried."

The tension washed out of her face, giving way to a smile.
"Well, sorry to disappoint there, pal. I'm still here, healthy as a glue-
factory-bound horse."

He hated when she brought up the glue factory. "Okay. Uh, I'm just going back downstairs to . . . play some video games with Audie. Yeah. So if you hear anything weird, that's . . . what we're up to."

She raised an eyebrow. "You're not doing drugs, are you?"

"What? No!"

"Sorry. I'm contractually bound to ask." She picked up the TV remote as some screaming reality show contestants began to throw mud at each other. "Have fun. Tell Audie I said hi."

Audie. Max sprinted back down the hallway and headed for the front door. When he opened it, a piece of paper taped to the door fluttered in his face.

"Sorry to refuse your most generous Xbox offer," it said in Audie's handwriting. "But Mom made me go clothes shopping instead. Pray for my poor, doomed soul."

He flipped up the doormat — the key was still there. *Okay. So she was never here. Good.*

He grabbed the key, then a fireplace poker on his way through the living room. Pausing at the top of the basement stairs, he took his cell phone out of his pocket.

"I'm calling 911!" he shouted down.

"No, you're not!" the man yelled back.

Instantly, the Beige Wonder went dead. Max stared at it, his eyes doubling in size. He ran back into the living room to click on the cordless but found only dead air, no dial tone.

He planted himself at the doorway again. "How are you doing this?"

"Stop yelling and get down here. We'll have a nice, reasonable chat."

Squeezing the poker, Max slowly made his way down the stairs. The man hadn't moved — he was still on the couch, still playing *Madden*.

Somehow, with his eyes glued to the screen, he sensed Max's intent to harm. "Go ahead," he scoffed. "Do your worst."

Max's worst wasn't very terrible at all, but years of shoveling had at least given him some decent upper-body strength, despite a poor showing in other areas. And there were laws about self-defense and protecting one's own home, right? So he gave it a shot, hurling the poker straight at the man's torso, where, amazingly, it hit its target.

It even stuck. The poker sank several inches into the man's beer gut, and yet . . . he didn't flinch. He didn't *bleed*. A second later he took one hand off the controller to casually pull the rod out, but in doing so, he gave up a touchdown and lost the game.

"Damn it!" he shouted, hurling the controller to the floor. "See what you made me do?"

Max watched, aghast, as the yawning stomach wound got smaller and smaller until it disappeared. "Sorry . . . ?" Max stuttered, unsure whether apologizing to the man who'd broken into his house was sound etiquette.

Unfazed, the man began licking the Cheetos dust off his fingers one at a time. "No worries. I get that a lot."

Now unarmed, Max settled into what he thought, based on countless movies and television shows, was a fighting stance. "Listen —"

"Relax, kid, will ya? I'm not going to hurt you." He reached for the Cheetos bag, then, remembering that it was empty, frowned. "You got anything else? Combos?"

"No."

"Cheez-Its?"

"No."

"Meth?"

"What?" Max shouted, horrified. "No!"

"Ugh," the man groaned. "No one *ever* has meth."

Max shook his head. Maybe *he* was on meth. Had Stavroula slipped some into his Hot Pocket?

The man was now picking his teeth with the fireplace poker. Max backed up against the wall, hoping to be camouflaged by the horrid wood paneling. "Who *are* you?"

"Hmm?" The man paused in his dental work to shoot Max a disinterested glance. "Oh. I'm Satan."

Max blinked. "You're . . . Satan."

"Well, I'm *a* Satan. There are six hundred and sixty-six of us, not that anyone's counting. But you people always seem to want to lump us together into one all-powerful, malevolent being, so I like to give my audience what it wants." He started to sink into a deep bow, but he burped in the middle of it and the moment was ruined. "The name is Burgundy Cluttermuck, devil-at-large. I do bachelorette parties and retirement galas, but *no more* children's birthdays." He sucked in some air through his teeth. "Too much screaming."

Max could no longer feel his extremities. "Burgundy Cluttermuck?"

"Please, call me Burg," he said with a smile, his beard widening. It wasn't a well-trimmed beard, but rather the feral, unkempt kind that resulted from a weeklong bender, with Cheetos debris sprinkled throughout. His forehead was tall, his brow cavemanlike. His hair probably had things living in it. And his horns, while white and polished and slightly iridescent, ended in ragged, cracked tips.

In short, he didn't look like the devil. He looked like the kind of early-forties, thrice-divorced alcoholic who owned a grungy car wash and had to become a sperm donor to pay rent.

Max swallowed. "I'm not —"

" — sure you need a devil in your life? Well, can't help you out there, kid. You brought this on yourself."

Max racked his brain. There *had* to be people on this terrible earth who were far, far more evil than he was. Unless it was because he'd stolen that cat — but it was just a stupid plastic *cat,* for chrissakes!

"This has to be a mistake," he said.

"No mistake. You must have done something to deserve me. What'd you do, kill a guy?"

"I stole a bobblehead!"

"Huh. Well, we can't all be Mansons."

Max shook his head, then shook harder. "No. It *must* have been someone else."

"Pretty sure it's you. You're the one with the shovel, right?"

Max froze. *Ugly Hill.* "Yeah, but —"

"You even kind of look like a shovel. All skinny in the middle, big head, wide feet. May I call you Shovel?"

"My name is Max."

"Revolutionary new tactic, Shovel, if I may brag so myself. Can't wait to share it with the guys below." Burg polished his horns. "See, any act of evil can bring up a devil, but the big ones exert the strongest pull; murders are very popular, because they require the least amount of effort on our part. But the smaller ones can work too, with a little advance planning. So I got myself into position close to the surface — loaded myself into the gun, so to speak, which you then fired by stealing. Since you so graciously dug a hole for me, popping out was a cinch."

"But I didn't *mean* to!"

"Too damn bad. What's done is done. I'm on an extended vacation now, homeslice, and you're my brand-new pool boy."

Max started to feel dizzy. He put his hand on the wall to steady himself.

Burg pointed to the streak of ash on Max's hand. "See, there's your proof right there, Shovel. I'm *allll* yours. It's like you went down to the pound and picked me out and — oh!" He clapped with glee. "I'm a rescue!"

"You are not a rescue," Max said, trying to keep his voice even. "You are not *mine*. I'm sorry I opened up your . . . hole . . . but I swear it was an accident, and what I really need right now is for you to go back to wherever it is you came from!"

"Hell."

"Well, go back to hell, then. Please."

"Too late for that." Burg lifted his sweatshirt to scratch his belly. "You've been marked. That means that until you find me some shelter of my own, you're responsible for sharing yours."

"I never agreed to that!"

Burg shrugged. "Your hand begs to differ. Now!" He rubbed his palms together and started to stroll around the room. "I'll require a hot tub — obviously — and a walk-in closet, three spiral staircases, a full-size meat locker, a bumper car racetrack, a sex dungeon, and a llama. Those last two are unrelated."

"I can't get you a house with all that stuff," Max sputtered. "I can't get you a house at all!"

Burg flung himself back onto the sofa. "Well, I'm not leaving this couch until you do, so you'd better find me some pillows and sheets while you're at it. Egyptian cotton. Twelve hundred thread count."

Max was pacing now, frantically trying to come up with a solution. "Look, there has to be some way around this. I can't keep a devil in my basement."

Burg burped again and picked up the remote, switching the television from Xbox to cable. "Tough titties, Shovel. You know the saying, 'You can't fight city hall'? Well, hell is a lot worse. Lot less forgiving. OH MY STARS AND GARTERS!"

Max had another heart attack. "What?"

"I LOVE THIS SHOW." Burg scooted up to the edge of the sofa and eagerly leaned forward. "Oh bitch, you did *not* just squeeze that other bitch's husband's ass. Shove a martini glass down her throat!"

The rich housewife flipped a table and wobbled away, only to trip over a teacup poodle and face-plant onto the floor. Burg hooted with laughter. "That's what you get! Time for a new nose!"

"You know this show?" Max asked. "You get cable in hell?"

Burg looked at him as if he were the dumbest kid in the world. "Uh, yeah. It's *hell*."

Max decided that if there were ever a time for him to grow a spine, now would be good. "As I was saying," he said, his squeaky voice already undermining his attempts at bravado, "you can't stay here."

"Can and will. Stab her with your stiletto! Go for the jugular!"

"And what if I say no?" Max shouted over him, puffing out his chest. "What if I refuse?"

As the show went to commercial, Burg finally looked at him. "Oh, I'll kill your family," he said in a casual voice. "Destroy everything you hold dear. Deliver hellfire and brimstone, etcetera and miscellany, so on and so forth."

Max tried to emit a skeptical scoff, but a tightness was creeping into his stomach. "Kill my family? Yeah, right."

Burg's eyes sparkled, as if he'd been waiting for Max to challenge him. He put his thumb and forefinger into the shape of a gun and fired it at the big ficus plant. "Bang."

Max watched, mouth agape, as the tree flopped to the floor. Within a second its leaves withered and turned brown, like one that had been dead for months.

The tightness in Max's stomach got worse, forming into a hard ball. "Shit," he whispered under his breath, nausea rolling over him in waves. "Shit, shit, shit."

"Now," said Burg, sitting back and hurling his legs up onto the coffee table, "it pained me to do that, as it was one of the lovelier ficuses I've seen in some time. But you wanted proof, so there you have it. Now find me a house."

Max pondered. He thought he'd read a book about this once. Or seen a movie. Possibly a musical.

"Am I allowed to bargain?" he asked.

Burg slowly tore his gaze away from the television. "Huh," he said, his apathy replaced by a look of intrigue. "Didn't think you had it in you, little Faust."

"Well? Am I?"

"Some people would consider the whole 'you find me a house and I refrain from slaughtering your loved ones' thing a pretty good deal as it is, you know. I wouldn't get too greedy, if I were you." He balled up the empty Cheetos bag and hurled it at him.

Max caught it, frowning. "Hey, where did you get all these snacks? We didn't have any in the house." He picked up one of the empty boxes on the table. "Devil Dogs?"

Burg snickered. "Couldn't resist. Been a while since I got my plunder on."

Max squeezed the box. "You stole these?"

"Yes. Fun fact: Your local grocery store doesn't have any security cameras."

"You just sauntered right in and took them?"

"Well, I could have burst through the wall like the Kool-Aid Man, but I wouldn't want to cause a scene, would I? Seems like word travels fast in this shithole town of yours."

"What is the matter with you? You can't just go around stealing whatever you want!" Max shouted in a spectacular display of hypocrisy. "I suppose you expect my gift of a house to be stolen too?"

"Yep," Burg said with no trace of sarcasm. He turned back to the television. "I can only utilize things obtained through ill-gotten means. Like this cable you're pirating, for instance."

Max bristled. That had been his mom's doing, and he'd always been uncomfortable with it. But the cable company hadn't caught on for years — how could this guy tell after an hour? "But the TV and Xbox aren't stolen!" Max countered. "I paid good money on Craigslist for those!"

"Well, whoever you bought them from didn't."

"So? That shouldn't count!"

Burgundy held up his hand and tilted it back and forth. "We devils love dealing in gray areas. It's kind of our thing."

Max clenched his fists to his sides and stormed out of the den into the unfinished area of the basement, the part used by his mom for storage and by him as a workshop for his dinosaur-related geekery. He needed to think.

"There has to be a way out of this," he quietly said to himself. "How many *Law and Order* reruns have you watched with Mom? You just need to get him on a technicality, find a crack in his —"

He stopped as his eyes fell on a dusty green lump in the corner.

"*Yes,*" he whispered, doing that making-a-fist-and-pulling-the-elbow-downward move that is supposed to symbolize victory but only made him look like an eight-year-old.

When he returned to the den, Burg was talking to the television again. "You used *frozen* scallops?" he shouted at the hapless chef on the screen. "Are you *trying* to lose?"

"Ahem," Max said.

Burg turned to look at him. "What do you want?"

Max tossed the green nylon bag to the floor, where it landed with a metallic clang. "I found you a home."

Burg's lip curled. "What is that?"

"It's a Coleman Elite Sundome, complete with hinged-door system and rainfly."

"A what?"

Max smirked. "A tent."

The smirk might have been too much, because Burg's face

abruptly changed into that of a full-fledged, terrifying demon. He stood up, the frame of his body stretching as he did. His chest got broader. The tips of his horns punctured the ceiling tiles, sending bits of crackled plaster to the floor.

"A tent," Burg growled, displaying a mouth full of sharp, shark-like teeth, "is not a house."

Max felt that he would very soon need to change his pants, but for the moment he stayed strong and maintained eye contact. "Well," he said, his voice quivering, "you didn't say 'house.' Not at first. You said, and I quote, 'Until you find me some shelter of my own, you're responsible for sharing yours.' *Shelter.* Which, according to Webster's crossword dictionary, can mean habitat, abode, digs, or, um, tent."

Burg exhaled smoke.

"*And* it's stolen," Max rushed to add.

"Is it now."

"Sort of. Gray area." Max omitted the rest of the story, of that fateful Boy Scouts camping trip when he'd fallen naked into a bush of poison ivy and was confined to the good ole Coleman Elite for the rest of the weekend, wallowing in a severe rash that managed to worm its way into some very unpleasant places. Martin Schultz had not, for some reason, wanted his tent back after that. "You can set it up wherever you want. Maybe go back to Ugly Hill and live near your hole. But you wanted shelter, and here it is. So, you know. Boo-yah."

Max braced for the plume of fire that was surely about to envelop him in a shrieking mass of flame, but Burg shrank in size as he rubbed his chin, thoughtful. "Interesting. You're not as dumb as you look, sound, and act." He glanced with disdain at the tent, then sneered back at Max, tapping his fingers together. "Very well. A bargain it is."

Max stood firm. "Except, um, we no longer *need* to bargain. I got you shelter, so you have to leave."

"Or," Burg said slyly, "you can take what's behind door number two."

"Huh?"

"Technically, yes, you have given me shelter. But if you'd be so kind as to give me an upgrade, I might be so kind as to grant you a favor in return. Which, by the way, I *never* do. You're getting a real steal here, Shove, so I'd take it if I were you."

Max couldn't shake the feeling that he was being manipulated, but he was also starting to realize that he didn't have much choice in the matter. "I'm listening."

"If you find me a house — a real house, with a roof and plumbing *and* a hot tub, that's nonnegotiable — then I'll do something" — he winced, as if the word itself caused him pain — "*nice.* For you."

"Like what?"

Burg groaned. "Oh, come on, kid, just think of something. Want a new laptop? A car? A nice piece of tail to aid you in losing your virginity?"

"How do you know I'm a —"

Burg made a skeptical face.

"Hmph," said Max.

"So, what'll it be?" Burg said. "Gift card to the Outback Steakhouse? Money? Fame?"

Max perked up. "Money?" *I could pay off those overdue bills. Get Mom a visiting nurse and better meds. Maybe even save up for college.*

"Sure," said Burg. "Name your price. Uh, within reason. Whatever I can nab from the local bank."

The ideas kept churning. How much did a pacemaker cost? They'd never been able to afford one before, but —

Wait a minute.

Max licked his lips. "Can you . . . heal?"

"Pardon?" Burg said, eyes narrowing.

"Can you make people better? People who are sick?"

"Kid, I don't know if you fully understand the concept of 'evil incarnate,' but —"

"Yes or no?"

Burg held his gaze. "Yeah," he said, gesturing offhand to the ficus. "I can heal."

Max whipped around. The plant was back to normal. Even greener than before, it seemed.

"Okay," Max said, feeling as if he were going to burst. "Okay. So. My mom has a bad heart. You fix her, and I'll find you a house. I promise. You can even stay here in the basement until I do."

"You find me a house *first*," Burg said slowly, "and *then* I'll fix your mom."

"Come on, I'm not going to fall for that," said Max. "Those are my terms. You want a hot tub or not?"

The room took on a reddish hue as Burg ballooned back to his full size, snarling.

"House first, then heart," he said in a quiet, sinister voice that scared Max more than if he'd yelled it. "Or I'll run upstairs and gnaw the diseased thing right out of her chest."

A vision not of Max's own creation screamed its way into his head, that of his mother's bedroom smeared with blood, her lifeless eyes staring at him —

"Okay! Okay," Max whispered meekly. "Deal."

Burg shrank back to his frumpy form. "Great!" He held out his hand. "Hold that thought in your head while we shake on it."

Max did as instructed and shook Burg's hand, then recoiled as if he'd touched a hot stove. "Ow!"

"There's your contract," Burg said, pointing at Max's burned hand. "You'll want to put a little ice on it before bed."

• • •

Petrified, Max grabbed a package of frozen peas out of the freezer and eased it through his blistering fingers.

He tried to relax. He tried to stop freaking out over the fact that there was a DEVIL. In his BASEMENT.

He tried instead to focus on the tangible, positive aspects of this development.

This COMPLETELY BATSHIT DEVELOPMENT.

No, no, he argued with himself. *Constructive progress has been made. A deal has been brokered.*

Yeah, with a devil. Quit skipping over the devil part.

But I could save my mom's life! he countered. *Maybe this is a good thing!*

This is literally the WORST thing! Remember what the road to hell is paved with? You can barely keep your own home together — how are you supposed to procure an entire house, complete with hot tub? And through nefarious means, at that?

The how doesn't matter, he told himself with finality. He just had to figure out a way; it was that simple. *For Mom.*

He checked in on his snoring mother, then went back to his room and endured yet another sleepless night. This time, though, he sat straight up on the edge of his bed and stared wide-eyed at the door, the frozen peas in one hand and a makeshift T. rex femur weapon in the other.

START OVER

MAX WOKE UP TO THE MOUTHWATERING SMELL OF BACON.

"Mmmmm," he moaned, still half asleep. He loved bacon. His mom used to make it every Sunday morning as part of their prehistoric brunch — bacon-strip dinosaurs, sausage-toothed tigers, pancakes in the shapes of woolly mammoths, and sunny-side-up eggs guest starring as meteors plummeting toward earth to destroy them all in a fiery, yolky wave of destruction —

Wait a minute, Max thought with a start, poking himself in the eye with the femur he'd fallen asleep clutching. They hadn't had a prehistoric brunch in years. His mom hadn't made bacon in years. They didn't even have any in the house.

Oh no.

He leaped out of bed. Halfway down the hall, he spun around and checked on his mom, who was gamely drooling on her pillow, still asleep. He shut her door tight, then stuffed a towel in the crack underneath, lest the almighty scented power of bacon awaken her, too.

Max's fears were realized as he rounded the corner into the kitchen, though admittedly not in the way he'd imagined.

"Morning!" Burg chirped. Standing in front of the stove, he was wearing the same teal tracksuit top, an apron that said KISS THE COOK, and a gigantic smile. And no pants. "Want some bacon?"

With his bare hand, he plucked a sizzling slice of bacon from the pan and tossed it at Max, who managed to bat it to the floor before it could sear third-degree burns into his eyeballs. "Ow! What is the matter with you?"

"What is the matter with *you?* Don't tell me you don't like bacon."

"Not when it's a million degrees and flying directly at my head!"

"Puny little humans. So weak. So soft." Burg picked up another slice and popped it into his mouth, the fat dripping down his chin and into his beard. "Mmm," he said with a satisfied quiver. "If there's anything on earth more delicious than a hot, dead pig, I don't want to know about it."

Cautiously, Max took a seat at the kitchen table and held his hands up in a way that made it clear he did not want to be pelted with any more searing grease. "Listen —"

"You got any stolen lard?" Burg crossed to the cupboard and began to noisily open and slam shut its many wooden doors.

"No, we don't. Stop that!" Max jumped up and held the doors shut. "Keep it down!"

Burg put his hands on his hips. "How can you not have lard?"

"I don't know, because it's not 1965?"

"Fine. FINE." Burg approached the refrigerator. "Butter will have to do."

Max watched, dumbfounded, as he removed several more items from the fridge. "What did you do, embezzle the whole breakfast section?"

"Pretty much," Burg said, dropping a couple of eggs onto the floor. Yolk splattered up onto Max's bare shins. "Good thing I did, too. This kitchen was tragically understocked. What do you people eat, dirt?"

Max cupped his hands around his eyes to form blinders, as Burg's tighty whities had startled to jostle in a way that Max did not care to behold. "No. Peanut butter sandwiches and granola bars, mostly."

"Unacceptable." Burg opened the box of butter and removed a fresh stick, which he unwrapped by peeling down the sides of one end like a banana. He wiggled his eyebrows at Max.

"Ew," said Max, catching on. "No."

"Yes."

"Don't."

"I'm gonna."

He chomped away half the stick of butter, leaving a perfectly formed bite mark. "Glaaaaaghmmmuuugh!" was approximately the noise he made, slurping it around his mouth. "Want a bite?"

"No!"

Burg narrowed his eyes, the centers of which started to glow red. "Eat the butter, Shovel."

Max thought carefully before he spoke, something that he

realized he would have to start doing much more often from now on. "But if you give some to me," he said slowly, "there will be less for you."

Burg continued to glare at him, then abruptly laughed and slapped a greasy hand on Max's back. "Smooth move, kid. There may be hope for you yet." He placed the bacon plate on the table.

Max took a slice and shoved it into his mouth, chewing and thinking. Ruckus slunk into the room and rubbed up against Max's legs, then began licking the egg that had splattered there.

"Listen," Max said finally, turning back to Burg. "We need to —"

But instead of looking into Burg's face, Max found himself staring at empty air.

He looked down.

Burg had dropped to the floor. He was kneeling with his body folded, head down and arms straight out in front of him, as if bowing to a supreme being.

Max blinked. "What . . . are you doing?"

"I didn't realize you had a cat!" Burg said into the linoleum.

Max looked at Ruckus. Ruckus licked his chops. "Is that a good thing or a bad thing?"

Burg glanced up but quickly bowed his head several more times, his hands clasped in supplication. Ruckus scratched behind his ears and left, unimpressed.

"It's a thing I should have been made aware of," Burg said testily, getting back to his feet once Ruckus had left the room. "Cats are to be feared. And *loved,* of course, and *respected!*" he shouted, for Ruckus's benefit. He lowered his voice and eyebrows. "But also feared."

"I don't get it. You're scared of cats?"

"I'm not scared of anything. But cats . . ." He blew out a puff of air and shook his head. "Those soulless eyes. That depraved indifference. Cats are *evil,* dude."

Max thought of the claw scars decorating his own skin. He couldn't disagree. "Well, I'll keep him out of your way. He seems to be avoiding you anyhow."

"Not that he wouldn't be welcome!" Burg shouted after Ruckus with a defensive, nervous chuckle.

"Shh!" Max scolded. "Listen, we need to establish some ground rules. You can't make so much noise up here. In fact, you can't even *be* up here, okay? That's rule number one. You have to stay in the basement."

"But there's no embezzled bacon in the basement."

"I will *bring* embezzled bacon to the basement," Max said through clenched teeth. "And butter, and whatever other artery cloggers you want. Okay?"

"Yeah, whatever," Burg said, whisking a bowl of pancake batter into a mug and taking a large swig. "As long as it's all stolen."

"Stolen. Right." Max's breath skipped away as he remembered that little detail. "Why can't you steal your own snacks? And your own house?"

"I'm on vacation, remember? We devils have a terrible benefits package, only get time off once a century or so. I ain't lifting a finger while I'm up here."

Max wrung his hands. If only the Max of two days ago could see him now, so worried about stealing a plastic cat. Now he had to steal three square meals a day for this dickhead?

Burg was squeezing a long string of syrup into his mug and talking to his concoction. "Oh, Mrs. Butterworth, you saucy little minx, you —"

"Hey, I'm not done," Max said.

But Burg wasn't listening. He was now holding a second bottle of syrup, making it walk like a puppet. "Aunt Jemima, I didn't hear you come in! Why no, I'd *never* be opposed to a ménage-à-trois, *especially* not when syrup is involved —"

"Stop talking to the condiments and listen to me!"

Burg dropped the syrups and leaned back against the counter, folding his hands in front of him in a laudable impression of Mrs. Butterworth. "Proceed."

"Rule number two," Max said, "is that you can't make any noise. My mom is just down the hall. If she hears you, she'll freak out and have a heart attack and die."

Burg was nodding. "Before I get the chance to kill her myself," he said thoughtfully, stroking his chin. "Yes, I can see why that would be undesirable."

Max let this slide, if for no other reason than the mere possibility made him too lightheaded to form a response. "Third, you can't mess up any of our stuff. I don't want to come home from school and find a smoking crater where my Xbox used to be. You can use it, just don't break it. And don't poke any more holes in the ceiling with your horns."

"Hey, these bad boys go where they want to go," Burg said, polishing his horns with his buttery hands. "I can't be held responsible for their natural urges."

"Speaking of which — where are your pants?"

"I'm not a fan of pants."

"Yeah, well, fourth rule: Pants. Pants at all times."

Burg pushed himself away from the counter and towered over Max. "What exactly makes you think you're in a position to tell me what to do? Need I remind you again of my insatiable bloodlust?"

"I'm good, actually, on the reminders of the insatiable bloodlust," Max said, averting his eyes, which were frantically darting across the linoleum as he had a panicked internal conversation with himself.

This is never going to work. You can't treat a being of the underworld like a disobedient toddler. You can't give him a time-out if he breaks the rules. He'll burn your friggin' house down.

But I can't get rid of him, either. Not yet.

You're never going to be able to find a house, let alone steal one.

Then what am I going to do? The longer I take, the more pissed he'll get, and then he's gonna kill us!

So stall. STALL.

"Here's what I'm thinking," Max blurted. "You work hard in your daily life, down there in hell, doing . . . whatever it is you do. Probably a lot of paperwork. So why cut short your once-in-a-century getaway to earth? Sure, you *could* kill me and my mom and engulf the town in a blaze of hellfire, but there's no point in doing all that right off the bat if you could instead luxuriate in all the junk food and video games you want. Pretty good gig, right? And all you have to do is follow my puny little human rules. Which, you know, are just so lame and so puny, right?"

Burg let out a snort. "*So* puny."

"Exactly. What do you think?"

Burg stared at him for a moment. "I think that seems fair," he said, taking off the apron and flopping it into Max's hand. "As long as you really do make it feel like a vacation. And bring me all that stuff you just promised. And do the dishes," he said, nodding at the pile of dirty pans he'd piled up on the stove.

"Got it," said Max, relieved. "I mean, I will."

"Good." Burg grabbed his mug of pancake batter and started to make his way toward the basement door, then turned back to speak into Max's ear. "Oh, and if that flowery little speech of yours was the best your negotiating skills can offer, you may want to read up on my kind. This ain't my first barbecue, Shovel."

Max paled.

"And don't even *think* of locking that basement door," Burg continued. "I laugh in the face of your locks. Hahaha! Ha!"

He got halfway to the basement door before running back into the kitchen and sweeping the two syrup mavens into his arms. "I'm taking these ladies with me. I won't elaborate on why."

• • •

For the first time in his life, Max was riffling through a phone book.

"I can't believe people used to live like this," he said, smearing ink on his sweaty fingers. Whatever electronic temper tantrum Burg had triggered the night before had not only knocked out all the phone lines in Max's house — cell and land — but had extinguished the Internet connection on his crappy computer as well. And the library was closed on Sundays. So here Max was, back in the Stone Age, using the yellow pages at an old pay phone down the street to look up Satan Worshippers.

Except that such a category did not exist. Nor did Devil

Exterminators. Or Demonologists. The closest thing he could find to a paranormal solution was an ad for "Mythica's Discount Clairvoyant Readings: Where P-S-Y-C-H-I-C spells S-A-V-I-N-G-S!"

It was bad enough that he'd had to call Stavroula to say he wouldn't be at work; she had not been pleased, for the first time muttering a "headaches and scoundrels" in which Max surmised that he was both the source of the headache and the scoundrel in question. With a frustrated grunt he tried to hurl the phone book to the ground, but since it was attached to the booth with a heavy cable, it happily swung back around and smacked him in the groin.

Max limped down the sidewalk. He looked up at the sky and pleaded with the clouds, as if the answer might come from above.

To his surprise, a heavenly chorus sounded.

Grinning with bliss, he staggered forth, angelic voices calling him toward salvation.

• • •

Sneaking in through the back door of a church in the middle of services was probably not going to be earning him any brownie points with the guy upstairs, but Max was desperate. Besides, he wasn't there to see Him anyway.

"Audie!" Max whisper-yelled, ducking down behind the bleachers of the gospel choir. Luckily, she was in the back row, and luckily, the singers were belting and clapping too loudly for anyone to notice him. He pulled on the hem of her robe. "Audie!"

She sank to her knees, the soprano section forming a satiny cocoon of noise around them. "Max? What are you doing here?"

He ducked out of the way as a dancing foot swung perilously close to his head. "I need your help."

"I'm kind of in the middle of something."

"I know, but this is important! I have a big problem!"

"This song ends in about two minutes, so unless your problem can be solved in that amount of time, or unless you spontaneously develop the ability to hit a high C, you best be scramming."

"Tell me everything you know about Satan!" he shouted, unfortunately doing so just as the chorus cut out to allow for a solo. A very large woman looked down at him with confusion and a fierce desire to kick his scrawny ass.

"Satan?" Audie repeated, incredulous. "Like, the devil?"

"No, Steve Satan, hairstylist to the stars. Yes, the devil!"

Audie looked adorably lost. "What makes you think I'd know anything about the devil?"

"I don't know." Max's mom had never been religious, so his views on what happened at church were somewhat spotty. He knew that some places gave out free wine, while others made you play with snakes. He was unclear on pretty much everything else. "Isn't it part of the package deal that comes with all of this?" He gestured at the altar, inadvertently getting his hand caught in the hem of another woman's robe and feeling a little more leg than necessary.

Audie looked scandalized. "Max, are you okay? Did something happen to you? You smell like bacon."

"I'm fine," Max said. "Come on, anything at all. I need it for a . . . school project. I just remembered it's due tomorrow and I'm desperate."

"For school? What class?"

Max didn't always think well under pressure, which is why he was so impressed with himself for being able to remember that neither Audie nor any of her friends were in his section of — "Calculus."

The self-congratulations faded rapidly.

She stared at him. "Calculus. You need to know about Satan for math class."

"Yeah," he said, swallowing. "I'm trying to, uh, disprove him. Using . . . derivatives."

Audie rubbed her temples. She'd officially become only minorly exuberant. "Max," she said, "you're giving me a headache."

"Are you sure it's not the singing? It's really loud —"

"You need to go." She began to shove him away from the bleachers. "I don't know what's gotten into you, or why on earth you need to know about Satan at ten o'clock on a Sunday morning, but it's called Wikipedia. Look it up."

"I *can't* —" He fell to the floor with a thud. "Aud, please. Anything you can tell me will help," he said, pulling himself back up and talking to the back of her legs. "Anything at all."

She squatted back down with a huff. "Lore Nedry," she said. "That's the best I can do."

"Who?"

"Remember her from elementary school? She switched to Westbury Prep after sixth grade, then last year transferred back to Eastville High. There were rumors that she's a Satan worshipper, or used to be. She wore all black, and Chuck Bryant told me she kept a dead rat tacked up in her locker. Give her a ring, I'm sure she'll be overjoyed to chat with you. Now *get. Out.*"

The voices of the chorus rose to a deafening pitch, and even

Max could tell that they'd reached the final notes of the song. He stumbled toward the back door that he'd slunk in through and exited into the unseasonably humid morning air.

Max knew he had no right to be upset with Audie, seeing as how he'd burst into her house of worship and demanded some really strange information from her and all, but he was generally quite frustrated with the world at the moment and didn't know who else to take it out on. "Gee, thanks, Aud," he said out loud, kicking a rock as he shuffled back down the street. "What am I supposed to do, just call her up and be all like, hey girl, wanna talk about Satan?"

• • •

"Um, hi," Max breathed into the phone. "Wanna talk about Satan?"

"What?" said the voice on the other end.

"Or — sorry, the Prince of Darkness. Or, um, His Evil Lordship. Whatever you call him. I don't want to be disrespectful."

"Who is this?"

Max nervously drummed his fingers on the fiberglass of the small pay phone enclosure, feeling a sudden swell of affinity for the antiquated thing. Its phone book had given him the right number, after all — only one listing under the name Nedry — and she'd picked up after the first ring. He didn't want to think about how he would have reacted if a parent had answered instead.

He took a deep breath to calm himself. "This is Max Kilgore."

A pause.

"Isn't that the new Michael Bay movie?"

"I can see why you might think that, but no," he said. "I go to your school. I don't think we're in any of the same classes — actually, I don't even know what you look like —"

"Then it must be hard for you to picture the face I'm making right now," she answered dryly. "I'll give you a hint: it's the one that precedes me hanging up the phone."

"Wait, don't hang up!" Max wiped a drop of sweat from his eye. "I was hoping you might be able to help me. I've heard that you dabble in the satanic arts, and —"

A long, guttural noise rumbled out of the earpiece.

Once it was complete, she grumbled, "I don't do that stuff anymore."

"Oh."

Max did not have a Plan B, so he had to resort to Plan C: awkwardly breathing into the phone until she elaborated.

Which she did not.

"Um," he said after a time, "why not?"

Another pause, as if she was being careful to think before she spoke. "It was just a phase. Not that I need to explain myself to you, whoever you are."

Max's palms were so sweaty they could barely grip the receiver. Confrontations always did this to him. He was practically hyperventilating, fighting a strong urge to sink to the ground and start rocking back and forth in a fetal position. "Look, I'm sorry to have bothered you," he heaved. "I heard that you were into satanic worship, and due to some unforeseen circumstances that have recently cropped up in my life, I am now very desperate for more information on the matter. But obviously that rumor was untrue, and obviously it's kind of a sore subject for you, and obviously I'll just be hanging up now and dying of embarrassment, so have a nice life, bye-bye then —"

"Wait."

Max paused, then coughed because his throat was so dry. "Hmm?"

"Why do you need to know more about Satan?"

He blew out a puff of air. "You wouldn't believe me if I told you."

More silence.

"Meet me later tonight at the craft store on Main Street," she said.

Max nearly dropped the phone. "Huh?"

"Just Glue It. Around six thirty, back door, near the dumpsters."

"Uh, okay. Sure. Thanks!"

Max hung up, so thrilled at this positive turn of events that he forgot about the vengeful swinging phone book, still hell-bent on destroying his crotch.

FREQUENTLY

MAX SPENT THE REST OF THE DAY sitting in his living room, looking at his dinosaur watch, and listening to Burg play *Call of Duty*. It wasn't the game Max would have chosen; the near-constant firing of machine guns didn't exactly soothe his troubled soul. But as long as virtual soldiers were being killed downstairs, no real people were being killed upstairs. Hopefully his mom would think he was the one playing, and not abandon her Sunday reruns to come out and investigate.

At one point — and then another point, and another — Audie rang the doorbell and demanded to be let in, but Max had turned off all the lights and locked all the doors. He knew that she knew that he wasn't really out, but there was no way he was letting anyone inside the house, for their sake and his.

He made a peanut butter sandwich. He ate it.

He did a crossword puzzle. Then another.

He killed a fly, taking note of the way the gunshots stopped for a brief moment as the yellow goo oozed out onto the table, as if Burg could sense the death. As if he were enjoying it.

Max shuddered a little.

He shuddered some more.

When six o'clock finally rolled around, he stood up, opened the basement door, and crept halfway down the stairs.

Burg was sitting on the couch in his underwear, shouting at the TV screen, and bending an old tennis racket in half, violating rules four, two, and three, respectively. The presence of his mom's old tennis racket meant that Burg had ventured into the storage/workshop area of the basement, which would probably lead to some troublesome developments in the future, but for now, all Max wanted to do was get out of the house, and fast.

"I'm going out," he announced in a voice that was more high-pitched than he wanted it to be. "To, uh, steal you some dinner."

"Great!" Burg said. "I'll have twin lobsters, a filet of elk loin, a vat of truffle oil, and a package of Twinkies."

Max sighed. "I can obtain exactly one of those items."

"Ugh, *fine*. Make the elk rare, with a side of mint jelly."

Max stood there a moment longer. Once he was satisfied that Burg was well into what he called his "Gutsplosion Campaign," he snuck back upstairs to peek into his mom's room. She appeared to be sleeping, but then she stirred and waved him in.

"Hey," he said softly. "I was just gonna run out for some food. How are you feeling?"

"Exhausted," she muttered, still half asleep. "Must be that marathon I ran yesterday. Rocketed right past the Kenyans. ESPN'll be here later for an interview. Put out some quiche."

"Got it. Quiche. Anything else?"

He was answered with a snore.

•　•　•

Sweat was becoming a big problem in Max's life. The amount of time he spent in the throes of nervous panic had gone up exponentially, and with it, the amount of perspiration. Not only had Burg somehow settled the basement into a permanent setting of a hundred-plus degrees, but now that Max had been forced to interact with a strange girl about a subject he had no earthly idea how to broach in a tactful, non–police-alerting manner, his hands were the clammiest they'd ever been. They became so wet on the way to the craft store that they kept slipping around the handlebars of his bike, at one point causing him to veer into traffic and almost be run over by a Little Debbie delivery truck, because getting flattened by a giant supply of devil's food cake mix would have been just the most darling, ironic cherry on top of the shit sundae his life had become.

Just Glue It sat between a seafood restaurant and a laundromat in a small block of storefronts along Main Street. Max hopped off his bike and walked it down the narrow alley behind the building, scrunching up his nose as he passed several trash cans and a river of malodorous, fishy slime snaking its way out the back door of the restaurant.

At last he reached what he assumed to be the craft store's dumpster, judging by the amount of sparkly debris surrounding it. He propped his bike against the wall, took out a granola bar, and waited, chewing and wondering how it had come to pass that every major traumatic event in his life these days seemed to involve a splash of glitter.

The back door abruptly slammed open.

Startled, Max began to choke on a cashew. Really choke — airway blocked, face turning blue, fingers clawing at the wall, as if tunneling through to the store and grabbing a handful of pipe cleaners was the best way to resolve the situation. Without missing a beat, the door opener smacked him hard on the back.

Out came the nut. It ricocheted off the dumpster and sped off into the trees, where — Max fleetingly thought in what had to be a flash of near-death psychosis — it was found by a lucky squirrel, taken home to its squirrel family, and enjoyed as a jubilant part of Squirrel Thanksgiving, which, as everyone knows, traditionally takes place not in November, but in September, when half-swallowed flying nuts are more plentiful.

At some point Max realized that he was saying all of this out loud to the girl, who was standing there and listening and not, astonishingly, emptying a can of pepper spray into his face.

"What are you babbling on about?" she asked.

Max blinked and cleared his throat a few more times, his mind settling back down to a level of low-to-moderate insanity. Only then did he feel ready to make eye contact, and when he did, he thought he might start choking again.

It was Brown Ponytail. The one who came into the Gas Bag the day before. She wore a blue and green plaid skirt — the kind worn as part of a Catholic school uniform — plus sneakers, no socks, and a white polo shirt with rhinestones arranged in the shape of dancing teapots.

A year earlier, some of the douchier boys at school had compiled a ranking of the girls in their class, from hottest to ugliest, and if Max recalled correctly, Lore had ended up somewhere near the bottom. (It had stuck in his mind because she shared a last name with Dennis Nedry, the traitorous computer programmer in *Jurassic Park,* which was infinitely cool, though at that point he hadn't been able to put a face to the name.) He thought it was a mean thing to do anyway, especially since he was sure that if there had been a list for the boys, he'd have ended up so far down at the bottom he'd have fallen off, like a grungy barnacle clinging to the underside of a boat.

But Max didn't think she was ugly at all. Dark birthmarks peppered her pale face, as if she'd been splattered by a paintbrush. Big brown eyes that looked perpetually sad blinked back at him. She was taller than he was, and a shade on the curvier side — wide hips, chipmunkish cheeks — but her shoulders were broad and her arms looked strong. Strong enough to dislodge a cashew, at least.

"I'm fine now," said Max. "Airway cleared. Thanks. For that."

She stared at him quizzically, then reached behind the dumpster and pulled out a bike of her own. Max's insides gave a happy leap. What had Audie always told him? *Find something in common to bond over. Establish a connection.*

"You have a bike," he said unnecessarily.

She stared at him. "Yep."

"I also have a bike."

"I can see that."

"We are connected, then," he said. "Through the bikes."

She raised an eyebrow. "I'm sorry, did you say we went to the same school? Are you sure you don't go to a . . . special school?"

"No, same school." Max pointed at her ponytail. "And I saw you the other day. At the Gas Bag. You came in with your friends."

She studied him. "Oh yeah, that *was* you," she said, nodding slowly. "You look different without your vest."

"Do I?"

"Yes. Less concave."

Max wasn't sure whether this was a compliment or an insult, though he suspected the latter. "Are you the one who picked out the Cheetos?"

"I'm sure not the one who wanted all that soy nonsense."

She spoke in the most deadpan voice Max had ever heard. It made him think of a seismometer, the kind of device that measures earthquakes, and how her inflections wouldn't even register as a tremor.

"Anyway, they're not my friends," Lore added. "We got grouped together for an ethics debate project and were heading over to Krissy's house to work on it."

"Oh," said Max. "How did it go?"

"They thought 'euthanasia' referred to 'children in Asia' and supported it wholeheartedly. How do you think it went?"

Max responded by continuing to gawk at her, zeroing in on her hair. Messy bangs in irregular lengths swept in front of her eyes, and now that he got a good look at it, the brown ponytail in question didn't really resemble the tail of a pony or any other member of the equine family. It was more like a volcano. Situated high on the top of her head, it steadily gushed hair out on all sides, so that it fell around her head like one of those circular curtains in a hospital room.

Thus far in life, Max had had limited experience with the

opposite gender, but he was almost positive that *your hair looks like either a volcano or one of those circular curtains in a hospital room* was not one of the things girls liked to hear. He'd certainly never heard Tom Hanks say it to Meg Ryan.

"I like your shirt," he said instead.

She looked down at the sparkly teapots. "I don't. My boss made it. She said a bedazzled shirt would project an 'air of craftiness' to the customers. I think it projects an air of 'I'm a fifty-three-year-old hoarder who lives chest-deep in alternating layers of fast-food wrappers and dead cats,' but what can you do?"

Max gave a commiserating shrug, as if he encountered this problem all the time. "Nothing," he agreed. "Once I had a shirt that —"

"Okay," she said, crossing her arms, "as much as I love the smell of rotting fish heads and the stirring conversation topic of 'shirts,' could you get to the part where you tell me why you need to know about Satan? Because I spent a large portion of my day explaining to a blind old lady the difference between sequins and spangles, and I'd really like to go home."

"*Is* there a difference?"

She gave him a death glare. "I'm leaving."

"Wait, wait!" He moved to block her path. "Okay. Satan."

He stopped there because he didn't know how to start. This would be hard enough to explain to anyone, but this girl was a lot more direct and confident than he'd expected her to be, and he was starting to get a little scared of her.

He took a deep breath and the word-bile spewed forth. "I was digging over on Ugly Hill the other day and I opened up a hole and something came out of it and his name is Burg and I think he's the devil and he ate a stick of butter and I have to find a house for him to move into and I'm really up shit creek without a paddle and I need your help or he's gonna kill my mom or at the very least kill all our houseplants."

Lore held up a finger. "Fun fact: I didn't understand a word you just said."

Perhaps that was for the best. Max gushed out the rest of the air in his lungs, composed himself, and started over again with a less alarming approach. He didn't want to frighten her away. "I would like to know more about devils."

"Why?"

"I'm . . . dabbling in recreational Satanism?"

This turned out to be the wrong tactic. Her eyes narrowed. "I do *not* have time for this," she spat. Her tone was angry, but Max thought it sounded as if her voice had gone up an octave. And she was speaking a lot faster than she had before. "What happened — you got a little crazy with a Ouija board and now you're looking for tips on the best way to draw a pentagram, best brand of black eyeliner?"

"No," Max insisted. "You don't understand."

She put on her bike helmet and snapped the strap shut. "Listen, if sitting around in your bedroom and reciting terrible gothic poetry is what gets you through high school without jumping in front of traffic, fine. But there are *actual* evil things in this world, and I'm not wasting my time with any of this wannabe satanic bullshit."

Max was getting desperate. He didn't know what else to do, short of throwing her over his shoulder and lugging her back to his house, caveman-style. Girls weren't usually on board with that, though.

She started to walk her bike down the alley at a rapid clip. Max followed, trying not to slip in the dumpster juice. "But I'm not a wannabe!" He reached out to grasp her handlebars —

And she stopped. Her eyes fixed on his hand. The mark on his hand.

For a split second her eyebrows went up.

Then she gave her bike a yank, causing the wheel to buck up and hit her in the shin. A blob of blood appeared, but she took no notice, resuming her escape and muttering something that sounded like "I can't get involved in this."

"What was that?"

"I said leave me alone!"

She increased her speed, putting more distance between them. She was almost at the end of the alley when Max, desperate, yelled, "COME OVER TO MY HOUSE AND I'LL SHOW YOU AND WE CAN EAT QUICHE."

Lore stopped once again, turned around once again, and stared at him, taking in the full extent of his pitifulness. Her teeth bit at her lip as she considered his proposal.

"Did you say quiche?"

• • •

For the first time in years, Max had a bike buddy.

He and Audie used to ride down to the lake together when they were younger, but ever since she'd started dating Wall, their bike outings had gone the same way as their firefly hunts. He kept sneaking glances at Lore as they rode. He hadn't realized how much he missed someone pedaling next to him, sharing that rush of air, hearts pumping at the same velocity —

"Pole," she said.

"Huh?" Max snapped his head forward and swerved just in time to avoid hitting a signpost.

He pedaled back up to match her speed, wobbling uncontrollably. "Hah!" he barked, masking his embarrassment with volume. "What was that doing there?"

"Probably as a warning not to hit that pothole."

"What pot —"

The ground finished that thought for him. Max got up and dusted off his pants. "Just a flesh wound!" he announced, pointing at the scrape on his elbow.

Lore impatiently tapped her fingers on her handlebars. "I've known you for about ten minutes and you've almost died twice. Think you can get to your house without contracting smallpox?"

"Actually —" he started, noticing their surroundings. "I need to stop at the grocery store for a minute."

She looked at her watch. "Look, this isn't going to turn into a whole thing, is it? I've still got some homework I need to finish before tomorrow —"

"I know, I know. I'll be quick. You watch the bikes and I'll be out in five minutes, promise." Before she could answer, he propped his bike against the wall of the Food Baron and ran inside.

He grabbed a cart and loaded it with some lemonade mix,

antiseptic spray for the scrape on his arm that in truth hurt like a bitch, a quiche, and some Cheetos for Lore, since she liked them so much . . .

Max paused in the middle of the snack aisle. He'd been so pleased by his success in getting Lore to come back to the house with him that he'd forgotten the horror that awaited them there. And how hungry it would be.

He looked to his left, then to his right. There was nobody else in the aisle. He looked up at the ceiling. Burg was right — no cameras.

Before he'd really even decided to go through with it, his arm shot out, grabbed a package of pizza-flavored Combos, and shoved it into the pocket of his shorts. Without a second's hesitation he walked a few paces farther and nabbed some Chex Mix, tucking them into his other pocket.

Oh my God oh my God oh my God, his brain screamed at him, terror gripping his gut. *This is even worse than the cat!*

On autopilot now, he whisked around the end of the aisle and into the next one over — the cakey snacks section.

There they were. The Twinkies. But the box was too big and bulky — he'd never be able to smuggle it out of there unnoticed.

I can't believe I'm doing this, he thought as he tore into the box and removed the individually wrapped contents, dropping them one by one down his shirt. *I'm going to end up on one of those America's Dumbest Criminal shows, with the laugh track and goofy sound effects — they're going to call me the Twinkie Bandit — oh my God oh my God —*

He hurriedly tucked his shirt in so the stolen confections wouldn't fall out, hoping that he was already too much of a fashion disaster for anyone to notice. Huddling up against a paper towel display for a moment to calm himself, Max took a couple of deep, cleansing breaths. He couldn't look too suspicious or he'd never get away with it —

"Max?"

"I'm innocent!" he shouted, spinning around.

A pair of bugged-out eyes stared back at him. "Innocent of what?"

Max let out a hysterical giggle. It was only Paul!

"It's only Paul!" he shouted, to confirm. "Hey, Paul!"

"Hey yourself. Did you see our sale on beets? We're having a sale on beets. Two cans of beets for the price of one can of beets. It's a beets bonanza."

"Oh. Okay."

"I had to say that, it's store policy. So what are you innocent of?"

Max giggled again. The crazies had definitely set in. "Er — nothing," he said, pushing past Paul. "It's a line from, uh, *Monty Python*."

Paul's brow furrowed. He probably would have frowned, too, if his massive teeth hadn't rendered him permanently slack-jawed. "No, it's not."

"Ha, good one!" Max said, hustling to the front of the store. "See you later!"

He scuttled into the express lane, barely holding on to consciousness as he transferred the non-stolen goods from his cart to the conveyer belt.

"Hi," he said to the checkout lady.

"Hi." She scanned his items and gave him a tired look. "Anything else?"

"No!" Max said too loudly and too quickly and too guiltily. "Shipshape! Locked and loaded!"

He bit his tongue before it could keep shouting more ridiculous combinations of words. The lady raised an eyebrow but finished bagging his items and gave him the total.

Max practically threw her the money — the change Krissy Swanson had given him, in fact — and snatched the bag off the counter. Only when the sun hit his face outside did he start breathing again, and only in short, panting rasps.

"Let me guess," Lore said as he loaded the plastic bag into his bike's basket. "Asthma attack."

"I'm fine," Max said, still manic as he mounted his bike. "I'm just excited about, uh . . . the savings! Hot, hot deals at everyday low prices!"

Lore looked at her watch again.

They were only a couple of blocks away from Max's house when she spoke. "Hey —" She looked behind them, then back at Max. "What's going on?"

"With . . . what?"

"With the Twinkies your shirt is pooping out."

Max braked, almost vaulting himself over the handlebars. Dropping his bike to the ground, he ran back and collected the discarded Twinkies, one of which had exploded and left a splotch of creamy carnage across the road.

Lore walked up next to him to stare at the mess. "I think that one's a goner."

"Yeah."

"Shame. Only two days from retirement."

He made a desperate face. "There's a perfectly good explanation for this. I swear."

Lore looked at the bulges in his shirt, the Twinkies poking against the fabric like alien babies waiting to erupt.

Wordlessly, she went back to her bike, hopped up on the seat, and waited for him to join her.

• • •

"Store-bought quiche?" Lore asked, watching Max empty the groceries onto his kitchen table. "You sure went all out."

Max cut the pie into slices.

"Sorry," said Max. "But look, it's quiche Lorraine!"

He held it up at an angle, presenting it like a piece of fine jewelry. Lore stared.

"*Lore*-aine," he clarified. "Like your name. Get it?"

"I get it."

"I'm not sure you do."

Lore took a seat at the table. "Look, I enjoy puns as much as the next loser, but can we cut to the chase here?"

Max did not feel like cutting to the chase. He wanted to stall until roughly the end of time. The craziness he was about to unleash on her was like an escaped grizzly bear — once it was out of the zoo, it couldn't be put back without a considerable amount of unpleasantness.

"Sure. But first, quiche," he said, delaying the inevitable.

The inevitable, however, had no intention of being delayed. Max heard him before he saw him, as a belch erupted from the doorway.

A pantless Burg stood there, lifting his shirt to scratch his rotund belly. "Who's the broad?" he bellowed.

What followed was odd. To Max, it seemed as if the room had exploded into a million pieces of screaming and chaos, but after a second or so, he realized that that was all in his head. In reality, Burg had continued to stand there and scratch, Lore hadn't moved a muscle, and Max was still posing with the slice of quiche like Martha Friggin' Stewart.

Oh no. No, no, no.

Max sprang into action. He dropped the quiche, rushed at Burg, and pushed him with all his scrawny might toward the basement. "Rules broken: one, two, and four!"

"I also shattered a lamp."

"One, two, three, *and* four!"

They had just reached the top of the basement stairs when Burg said, "Who's the dame? I don't even get an introduction?"

Lore. If she hadn't bolted out the back door already, she had to be a nanosecond away from it.

"Go back downstairs," Max tried to tell Burg as nicely as he could. "I'll be right down, and I'll introduce you. Just let me give her a heads-up."

"Fine."

"And please put on some pants."

"Never."

Once Burg descended the staircase, Max sprinted back to the kitchen. Lore was still sitting where she had been a moment before, her jaw hanging open slightly, her eyes round and alert.

She got up and stood in front of him, her face coming to rest a couple of inches above his.

"Who . . . was . . . that?" she asked.

"I told you," Max whispered, cowering beneath her gaze. "There's a devil in my basement."

Lore worked her tongue around her mouth. Then she abruptly turned and walked out of the kitchen, grabbing the bag of Chex Mix on the way.

"Where are you going?" Max called after her.

"To talk to him," she answered. "Isn't that why you brought me here?"

"Yeah, but —"

"Alone," she said, her hand on the basement doorknob.

"Wait!" Max ran up to her, grabbed her elbow, and snatched the Chex Mix out of her hands. "I can't let you do that. He's dangerous. And unpredictable."

Lore cocked her head. And just for a moment Max thought he saw a spark in her eye where there hadn't been one before.

She snatched the Chex Mix back. "Well, would you look at that? So am I."

With that, she walked through the door and closed it behind her.

Max didn't know what to do next. He shakily sat down at the kitchen table and waited — for a piercing shriek of terror, for the scent of burning sulfur to waft through the house, for a plume of fire to knock the door off its hinges.

But none of those things came to pass.

Five minutes elapsed.

Halfway through the fifth minute the door clicked open. Lore walked into the kitchen and sat across from Max.

"What happened?" he asked, afraid of the answer.

She crossed her arms. "He made some ungentlemanly remarks about my chest."

"That sounds about right."

She fell quiet again.

"Anything else?" Max asked. "Did he hurt you?"

Lore briefly looked touched that he had asked that, but she shook her head. "No. He didn't even get up from the couch. Just sat there and housed that Chex Mix like a — a —"

"Like a cheetah devouring the entrails of a zebra?"

She put her elbow on the table, propped her chin in her hand, and bore a glare directly through to his soul. "Start at the beginning."

OBSESSIVE-COMPULSIVE TYPE

RECOUNTING THE WHOLE SORDID TALE took the better part of an hour. By the time it was over, Max's voice had gone hoarse, Lore's face had gone slack, and the quiche had been all but demolished.

"And that's why I stole the Twinkies and shoved them down my shirt," Max finished, noting that this was maybe the oddest way he'd ever ended a story.

"I see," said Lore. She wiped her mouth with a napkin, then folded her hands in front of her.

Max leaned forward, the better to hear the valuable knowledge she was surely about to dispense. "So?" he prompted.

Lore looked around, as if expecting someone else in the room to answer. "So what?"

"So what do I do about all this?"

"How should I know?"

Max blinked. "You're the expert!"

"I never claimed to be an expert." She was back to talking

swiftly, as she had at the dumpster. *"You're* the one who called *me,* all because of a rumor suggesting a persona and lifestyle I have long since shed and was never all that committed to in the first place. That'll teach you to listen to gossip, huh?"

"But you have to help me!" Max was getting that panicky, nauseated feeling again. He'd brought this complete stranger over to his house, exposed her to a demonic being, threatened her safety, jeopardized the secrecy of the situation, and for what?

"Why?" she shot back. "I don't even know you."

The anxious feeling swiftly morphed into the fluttering one that accompanied confrontation. "I'm sorry," he said, waving his hands. "You're right. I am so sorry I brought you into this. Now he knows who you are and what you look like and—oh, crap." He reached for the nearly empty tin of quiche. "I forgot to save some for Mom."

"You think she slept through all this?" Lore asked.

"She sleeps through everything." He transferred the microscopic sliver of quiche onto a plate, cut it up into even smaller pieces, poured a glass of water, folded a napkin, and arranged everything on a tray, all in the space of about fifteen seconds.

Lore watched him dart around the room. "Done this before?"

"Yeah. My mom is— she's sick. I take care of her."

Lore looked stung. She eyed the floor, while Max's ears reddened. He never understood why he got so weird about his mom. There was no reason for it, nothing to be ashamed of. But it crept in anyway, against his will, like a stubborn rash.

"I'm sorry," Lore said.

Max didn't know how to reply to this, so he turned and headed for the hallway. "I'll be back in a few minutes."

"Okay. I'm gonna go."

"Wait, what?" Max spun around, sloshing some water onto the quiche, further ruining what was already a pretty lousy dinner. He came back into the kitchen and put the tray down. "You're leaving?"

"Sorry. Need my beauty sleep."

"Aw, no you don't," Max said automatically, before realizing the implied flirtation and subsequently panicking. "I mean, I guess we can all be a little *more* attractive, relatively speaking, but it's not like you're any *less* attractive than anyone else. Like, you're not *ugly*. Your face has all the requisite features, and none of them are any larger or smaller than they should be, everything is in proportion, and you don't have any irregular moles or growths, so —"

You're doing it again, he thought. *Have we learned nothing from the veal incident?*

"I like your last name," he finished weakly.

Lore blinked at him. "Beg pardon?"

"Nedry. Like Dennis Nedry, in *Jurassic Park*? Sorry, I'm sure you get that all the time."

"No. This is a first."

He shook his head, trying to hit the Restart button. "You can't leave. What am I supposed to do about . . . him?"

"Look, I think things could be a lot worse," she said in a breezy tone that, to Max, sounded just a little too breezy, as if she were forcing it. "I mean, he's just some dude. An asshole, to be sure, but just a dude. He likes snacks. So give him snacks." Her voice turned bitter. "You got off pretty easy, if you ask me."

Max felt that the best response to this was some massive sputtering. "But I'm also supposed to find him a house!"

She was definitely agitated now. She got up and walked toward him. "I don't know what to do about that. You're absolutely right, you shouldn't have gotten me involved. You made your own mess, *you* clean it up."

It wasn't until Max's tailbone hit the kitchen counter that he realized he'd been backing up as she spoke. He brought a hand up to his face, and it felt hot, flushed. Lore's face was red too — he could see this because it was only about a foot away from his.

Her mouth was trying to form too many different words at once, twitching, trying to escape from her face. Finally, instead of saying anything more, she whipped her head around — brushing Max's face with her ponytail in the process — and stormed out the kitchen door.

Max stood there, stunned.

"What just happened?" he asked the empty room.

As if arriving specifically to taunt him, Ruckus sashayed into the room, rubbed his cheek against the cabinet, and let out a meow that sounded suspiciously like *Ha, ha!*

"Shut up, you," Max said. He looked out the window and saw Lore struggling to pick up her bike and put on her helmet all at the same time. Finally clicking the helmet strap shut with an angry *snap,* she pushed off and disappeared down the street. Max opted not to chase after her.

As if you could catch her, noodle legs! Ruckus implied with a disdainful arch of his back.

Max gave his head a hard shake. *I really need to stop imagining cat dialogue.* He picked up the tray, vowing to salvage the only good deed he could accomplish on this awful, accursed day. He stood outside his mother's door for a moment and attempted to compose himself. The trembling in his hands started to go away, but the ill feeling in his stomach remained.

At least his mother had been watching *Adultery Cove* at full volume, which meant she probably hadn't heard any of the escapades in the kitchen. "Quiiiiiche!" she cried, hitting the Mute button and clapping, though she stopped once she saw how little of it there was. "Geez, Max. You bulking up for the winter?"

"I . . . guess I got a little carried away," he said, trying not to let her see his face.

But mothers always know. "Why are you all red? Hon, look at me."

He turned his head. "It's nothing. I was moving around some stuff in the basement and it was really hot down there."

Even Max was surprised by how easily the lie came out. As if that small, bad part of him that had stolen the Twinkies and the cat had now been given free rein to shoot up to the surface and slither out of his mouth whenever it wanted.

He stared at the transplant pager on her nightstand, that useless chunk of plastic that so steadfastly refused to help them. "Anyway—"

A loud roar sounded from downstairs. Max caught the

words "son of a bitch," followed by something worse, followed by something *much* worse.

His mother struggled to sit up. "What was that? And what are you doing?"

Max was surprised to find that his mouth was open, and a strange, sustained "lalalalala" was coming out of it.

"Singing," he explained.

She frowned. "What's going on down there?"

"Um"—he looked up at the ceiling—"it's this new game Audie brought over. It's called . . . *Swearstorm*."

There's no way in hell she's going to buy that, he thought, but she'd finally taken a bite out of the quiche and was set adrift in cheesy, hammy, eggy heaven. "Mmmm. Audie's here? Tell her I said hi."

"Oh, she already left. Had homework to finish." He began to make his way toward the door. "And I do too. So I'm just gonna go"—he stuck his head out the door, yelled "TURN OFF THE *SWEARSTORM*," looked back at his mother, and smiled sweetly— "and study."

She looked back at him with a confused expression, fork posed over the last bites of her meal. "Maybe go a little easy on the quiche next time, Maxter. Too much egg can addle the brain."

He kissed her good night and flew back down to the basement, only to discover to his horror that the door to the storage area was open and Burg was inside, standing at Max's workshop — a.k.a. the old Ping-Pong table Max had commandeered to work on his secret dinosaur projects.

Not so secret anymore, he thought upon seeing Burg, who was holding Secret Project #17 in his hand.

"What are you doing in here?" Max asked.

"Those rotten video games of yours keep telling me I lost, so I was looking for something to smash the TV with." He held up the item. "This'll do."

"No! Put that down," Max said. "Gingerly."

Burg dropped it to the table with a crash. "What is it anyway?"

Max picked up the pieces of the project he'd been painstakingly sculpting out of wire mesh, papier-mâché, and plaster. "It's supposed to be a T. rex skull."

"Looks pretty real."

"A true scientist always strives for accuracy," Max said.

"A *truuue* scientist always strives for *aaaccuracy*," Burg said, mimicking him in a high-pitched little-girl voice. "You're such a nerd." He walked farther down the Ping-Pong table and grabbed a rough curved object that somewhat resembled a talon. "What about this one?"

Secret Project #11. "That's a replica of a fossil found up on Ugly Hill about ten years ago," Max said, taking it from him and turning it over in his hands. "Last year I emailed the professor who found it, and he sent me a couple of high-definition photos, and I've been working off of those. No one knows what it is — Dr. Cavendish was beginning to theorize that it came from some bird-dinosaur missing link. But he died a few months ago, and everyone was starting to think he was a crackpot anyway. Now nobody cares but me."

Burg squinted at the talon. "That's not from a bird."

"A *prehistoric* bird. They were different. Bigger."

Burg shrugged. "Is that why you were digging up on the hill?"

"Yeah. I've always thought I could find more by myself, but . . ."

It sounded so idiotic when he said it out loud. Why was he saying it out loud anyway? And to Burg, of all people?

"Never mind," he muttered.

"What happened?" asked Burg. "Daddy wouldn't build models with you anymore?"

"No."

"Why? Because you're so lame?"

"No, because I don't have a dad."

"Oh? Were you conceived via asexual reproduction?"

"Okay, I *technically* have a dad, but I've never met him. He could be dead, for all I know. Maybe even in hell. Ever come across a guy down there with persistent body odor and hair shaped like a baseball cap?"

Burg held up his hands. "No way. Not my department. I've got nothing to do with the stiffs, their eternal judgment, any of that."

"Why not? You're a devil, aren't you?"

Burg put his hands on his hips, puffing out his voluminous belly. "Think of hell as one big corporation. You got your Satans, in charge of damnation and dead folk and all that heavy important stuff — the CEOs, if you will. Then there's middle management, the ones who oversee the dispersal of evil into the world. And then there's me and the rest of the operational staff, doing all the grunt work."

Max rolled the model through his fingers. "What sort of grunt work?"

"Well, for example, I'm in the Vice Department," Burg said. "We're the ones who cause humans to lust after all the dumb shit their reptilian brains can't help but become addicted to. Drugs, alcohol, caffeine, sugar, money, television, bacon. I'm an Associate Imp in charge of Salty Snacks."

Max blinked. "So . . . you're not really *evil*, then, are you?" he asked, for the first time feeling some of his panic dissipate.

"Oh, I'm evil. It's just that some devils are more evil than others. I don't know what goes on in the upper management offices, but I do know that those are the vilest bastards we've got. Not that there aren't some pretty serious assholes in my division. Take the Moneygrubbers, for example — the committee in charge of stimulating human greed. These are fourteen of the douchiest, slimiest guys you can imagine. Anytime you hear about a particularly nasty white-collar crime or bank robbery, that's all their doing. Then there's the Donut Team — I don't need to tell you how wicked those guys are. Oh, and then there's Rusty, that entry-level kid we got a few years ago. He handles those addictive cell phone puzzle games. Real ass-goblin, that one."

"Wow."

"We have fun," Burg said cheerfully. "But I needed some air. Needed to get away for a while. It's really hot down there, you know?"

"Guess I better go fill that hole in, then," Max muttered. "Before more of you sprout up."

"Yeah, probably should."

Max fumbled the talon. "Wait, really? I was just joking. That's a possibility?"

Burg gave an innocent shrug. "Maybe, maybe not."

Irritated at his vagueness, Max studied him. "What happened when Lore came down here?" he asked. "Why didn't you scare her or attack her or something? Not that I wanted you to," he rushed to add, "but our previous interactions led me to believe that you might rip the head off of anyone who invades your space."

"Nah." Burg walked back into the den, sank into the sofa, and took a long swig of Mountain Dew. "No challenge there."

"What do you mean?"

Burg took another sip. "She's too miserable."

"Lore? She's not—" Max stopped himself. "She's not *that* miserable."

Burg reached a hand down to the floor and fished around until he found a crumpled-up Mountain Dew can. He held it up to illustrate.

"This is your miserable friend," he said. "Already crushed. I can squeeze it into a tighter ball if I want, but it's hardly satisfying."

Max nodded, his face pale. He didn't like where this was going.

Burg tossed the balled-up can to the floor, then finished his current soda and held up the empty can. "This," he said, his left eyebrow arching up to form a point, "is that next-door neighbor of yours. Happy. Full of life. Bright, shiny future."

With a metallic *crunch*, the can imploded in his grip until there was hardly anything left, an aluminum apple core.

Fear sliced through Max's stomach, but he tried not to show it. "I don't know who you're talking about."

"Liar. I watched her through the window. Saw her skipping off to church this morning, giddy as a flag on Flag Day." With an unsettling leer he glanced out the window that faced Audie's house, then grinned back at Max. "I love a good challenge."

Max wanted to scream. It was hard enough to protect his

mother from this monster, and then he'd gone and roped Lore into it — now he had to worry about Audie, too? How many innocent lives could he endanger within a twenty-four-hour period?

There was a knock at the kitchen door.

Burg started to get up, that predatory look still in his eye, but Max cut him off. "Stay here," he ordered.

The leer was replaced by a petulant frown. "But I'm hungry."

Max ignored this and went back up into the kitchen. He couldn't blow Audie off forever. And he'd much rather cause a scene in his kitchen than in the middle of a crowded school hallway.

"Hey, Audie," he said, pulling the door open.

"That," said the visitor, "is not my name."

Lore stood on the stoop, her face red and sweaty from biking, her ponytail windblown.

"Oh," said Max. "Hi. Again."

Lore shifted her weight to one foot, then the other. "I'm sorry I yelled at you."

Max noticed a pair of dark circles under her eyes. Had those been there before? "That's okay."

"I'm just going through some stuff — *still* going through some stuff . . ." She looked frustrated with herself, then shook her head. "Whatever. It's no excuse. Sorry."

"Ain't no thang," Max replied, inexplicably.

"Because actually —" She brought her eyes up to his. "I changed my mind. I want to help you."

That he did not expect. "Really? Why?"

"I have my reasons."

"Uh, okay. But —" Max at least had the presence of mind to

know he shouldn't look a gift horse in its scowling, deadpan mouth, but he had to be up-front. About this, at least. "But it could be really dangerous. You know that, right?"

"I know," she said, examining her chewed-up, unpolished nails. "All the more reason to dispose of him, for your sake and your mom's sake. So here I am. Just a girl standing in front of a boy, asking him to accept her devil-expelling assistance."

"Okay. I mean — God. Thank you."

Lore walked past him into the kitchen, tossed her bike helmet onto the table, and turned around.

"Well?" she said impatiently. "We can't love it when a plan comes together if the plan doesn't come together, right?"

• • •

Max kicked off their brainstorming session that evening in the only way he knew how: with school supplies.

"Wow," Lore said, sitting on the living room sofa and taking in the two-by-three-foot posterboard easel in all its nerdly glory. "That is a thing that you own."

"Oh, this is just left over from the Paleontology Club," Max said. "I'd had high hopes for getting an *Ankylosaurus* swap meet going and — you know what, forget it."

"I'm already trying."

He uncapped a marker and wrote "IDEAS" at the top of the poster. "Now —"

"Hey!" Burg bellowed from the basement. "Where's my after-dinner snack?"

Max gave Lore a tight smile. "Excuse me for just a moment."

He went into the kitchen, grabbed the bag of Combos, and chucked it down the stairs like a missile.

"These come in *pizza flavor?*" Burg cried.

Max returned to the easel and readied the marker. "Okay. Go."

Lore had evidently done some brainstorming of her own during her bike ride epiphany; she immediately started ticking off items on her fingers. "Okay. Ways to procure a house out of thin air: We buy one, we build one, we dupe a real estate agent into selling us one for no money, we find an abandoned one and take it for ourselves, we break into one and kill its owners —"

"Whoa, whoa, whoa!" Max was aghast. "We can't do that!"

"Why not? I have a crowbar."

Max was getting all sweaty again. "Let's just start with a list. Say them again, slowly."

She did so, and he copied them down in rickety lettering. "I can't believe you just came up with these off the top of your head," Max said, jokingly adding, "Have you done this before?"

Lore clenched a pillow between her fists.

"Just trying to lighten the — okay, let's start with the first one," he said, hastily tapping the word "buy." "I, for one, am dirt-poor. You?"

"Oh, I'm loaded. I only wear the same skirt every day to throw kids off the scent of my many walk-in closets."

"So buying is out." He drew a thick line across the word. "What about building?"

"Sure. What with your architecture degree and my easy access to large quantities of airplane glue, the sky's the limit."

"Hardy-har," he said in a doofus voice, something his mom always did when he told a bad joke. "I don't suppose any of your immediate family members are contractors who do pro bono work on the side?"

"Nope."

Max tapped the marker against his head. "How can we convince someone to build a house for us for free?"

"How about Habitat for Humanity?"

Max was about to bust out the ole hardy-har again when he realized she was being serious. "We can't defraud a charity!"

"Why not? They build houses for people who are in need. *We* are in need. Probably more so than any of the other people who get free digs. None of *them* are plagued by evil demons threatening to kill *their* loved ones."

As a sign of just how far he had fallen down the ladder of righteousness, Max actually considered this for a second. Just for a second, though. "No," he said firmly, crossing out "building." "We can't get charities mixed up in all of this. That's just wrong."

She rolled her eyes. "We're stealing a house here, Max. There's going to be a staggering amount of 'wrong' involved no matter how you do it."

He didn't know what to say to this, so he went back to the board. "Real estate. You know any agents?"

"Nope. You know anything about real estate law?"

"No. Wait—I did play a lot of Monopoly when I was younger." He bit his lip. "Could we buy a deed? Or a . . . mortgage?"

"You don't even know what you're saying, do you."

Max crossed out "real estate."

A car pulled into the driveway next door, its tires swishing through the rain that had started to fall. Max hurriedly adjusted the curtains, making sure they covered the window completely.

Lore snorted. "Afraid your popularity stock will go down if you're seen with me?"

Max made a flabbergasted noise. It sounded a lot like the word "flabbergasted." "Me? I'm not popular."

Then came one of those rare instances in which Lore looked unsure of herself. "Aren't you friends with that guy on the football team?"

"Sort of. I mean, I'm really more friends with his girlfriend, Audie. She lives next door. We've known each other since we were two, and we kinda grew up together, and one time we touched tongues, but that was *only* part of an experiment to see if cooties were contagious—"

"Okay," Lore said, holding up her hands. "That's all the information I require."

"But *I'm* not popular. They are. I'm just the sad third wheel."

"Have you told them about your new roommate yet?"

"No." Max was about to explain why he couldn't—how Audie was bursting with happiness and puppies and rainbows, so he needed to protect her, while Lore was an abyss of misery and despair from which no joy could enter nor escape—but at the last second he decided that that might not be the sort of thing people like to hear about themselves.

Luckily, Lore cut him off. "Good," she said, fiddling with the seam of the pillow. "You should protect them. Don't bring them into this."

There was that clouded-over look in her eyes again, the one Max desperately wanted to ask about, but she'd already started speaking again. "Any other friends?" she asked. "Who we should be protecting?"

Max shrugged. "I mean, there's Paul, I guess. But he's mostly just the guy I sit with —"

"At lunch," Lore said, nodding. "Yeah. I know how that goes."

Max raised his eyebrows. "Yeah?"

Lore had relieved the pillow of some of its stuffing. She rolled it between her fingers. "You know what happens when you transfer into a school in your junior year? You're well and truly screwed. All cliques and friendships are solidified by then, and no vacancies are left. So I was this weird interloper who glommed on to the only group that would have me. They're nice, but . . . yeah. I wouldn't call them friends either."

Max felt an overwhelming urge to give her a hug, but he knew that acting on it would probably lead to more bodily harm. "You transferred from Westbury Prep, right?"

"Yeah."

"Why'd you come back?"

"There was an incident that happened while I was there."

"Oh. What kind of incident?"

She glared at him. "I killed a kid because he asked too many questions about my personal life."

Max coughed. "Gotcha." He looked back at the easel, as if

expecting it to burst into song to diffuse the tension. It did no such thing. "So . . . breaking in?"

"Yeah." Lore sank deeper into the couch and propped her legs up on the coffee table. "We find an abandoned house, we break in, make sure no one is living there, then squat."

Max stared at her. "Squat?"

"Yeah."

"You mean, like . . . go to the bathroom?"

Lore stared at him. "See, this is why you can't rely on board games to teach you all you need to know about life." She leaned forward, speaking slowly and brightly, as if hosting a bizarrely delinquent segment of *Sesame Street*. "Squatting is the term for when you live in a building that you don't legally own or rent."

"Oh."

Max added "squat" to the board, wondering how he'd never heard of it before. It was a good crossword word. "Well, that's out. We can't break into a house."

"Why not?"

"Because we'll get in trouble! We'll get caught!"

She rolled her eyes. "Not if you do it right."

"We're *not* breaking into a—"

"Hey!" Burg again shouted from downstairs. "I'm still hungry!"

Max plodded across the room and stuck his head in the door. "How can you still be hungry?"

"I'm watching *Iron Chef*. Battle Scallop is making me salivate."

"Well, I'm all out of snacks."

"But there's still a half-hour left! I'm *dying!*"

Max wholeheartedly wished this were true, but he checked his anger and spoke in an even voice. "What do you want?"

"Something with shellfish would be nice. Bobby Flay is making ceviche!"

Max stormed into the kitchen, found a months-old box of fish sticks in the freezer, and tossed it down the stairs.

This must have pleased Burg, because he began to sing the old commercial jingle. "Jeff, the Gooorton's Fishermaaan!"

"I think it's '*Trust* the Gorton's fisherman,'" Max shouted down.

"You're dead wrong there, pal!"

Max didn't think he was, but arguing further seemed pointless. "Hey," he called out to Lore as he made his way back into the living room. "Do you know if it's 'Trust the Gorton's Fisherman' or 'Jeff, the Gorton's' — ahhh!"

Lore had disappeared. Or rather, Lore had deftly ducked into the hallway closet, as evidenced by the small fingertips poking out to pull the door shut. *Why* she had ducked into the front hall closet Max couldn't understand until he saw his mother squinting at the thermostat, looking washed-out and frail and highly annoyed for having to get out of bed.

Mrs. Kilgore turned to her son. "I'm pretty sure it's 'trust,'" she said. "Not 'Jeff.'" Her brow furrowed. "Who are you talking to? And what's with the easel?"

Max's expression had frozen into an expression not unlike that of the fish Jeff had caught for his sticks, open-mouthed and frozen. "It's a school project," Max blabbed, then couldn't stop himself from adding, "for calculus."

For the love of all that is holy, he thought. *It's like a sickness.*

His mother looked at the list of words on the board — *buy, build, real estate, squat*—and opened her mouth to ask a question, but Max butted in before she could. "Can I get you anything, Mom?"

"I just came out to check on the thermostat," she said. "It's getting kind of hot in here —"

"Hey," a voice bellowed from the downstairs. "You got any tartar sauce up in this piece?"

Max twisted around, but it was too late. Standing there in the basement doorway, crumbs in his beard, pants AWOL, and in full view of Max's mother, was Burg.

KIND OF PARTY

MAX EXPECTED HIS BRAIN TO REACT the way it had the last time Burg scared him into another plane of existence — with that high-pitched, screaming sound buzzing through his head. But this time he just stiffened and squeezed his eyes shut. His mom was going to be killed right in front of him, and there wasn't anything he could do about it. He'd tried to protect her, and he'd failed.

Then his mom spoke.

"Hey, Audie," she said, a tight smile in her voice. "Long time no see."

Max opened his eyes, thinking that dementia had finally begun to settle in his mother's poor brain, but he was way off. For standing in the same spot Burg had been, holding the box of fish sticks, was unmistakably Audie. A perfect replica.

Lore, poking her head out of the closet, shot a look at Max that silently but clearly stated, *WHAT IN THE EVER-LOVING CRAP IS GOING ON?*

I DON'T KNOW, Max eye-yelled back, then glanced at his mom.

She, in turn, was giving Max a look that said, *I am SO mad at you but will maintain this pleasant charade in the presence of guests.*

Burg-Audie just smiled politely, twisting a finger through his newly acquired dreads.

"I didn't realize you had company, Max," his mom said tersely. And then Max watched in horror as she crossed the room to lovingly embrace the unholy evil that had become the bane of his existence.

After the hug, during which Max had to fight to keep his quiche down, his mother held Burg-Audie at an arm's length. "You sure have sprouted up, girl," she said in a tone that was at once cheerful, forced, apologetic, and embarrassed. "You taller than your dad yet?"

Burg laughed in a way that was so identical to the way Audie laughed that Max couldn't help but gag. *How did he get it just right?*

"Not yet," Burg replied with a shy smile. "And I'd better get home before he sends out a search party."

Max's mom leaned against the wall to support herself. "Fair enough," she said. "Hey, tell your parents I'm sorry that I haven't —" She paused, a pained look pinching at her mouth. "Tell them I said hi."

"Yes, yes, she'll tell them," Max said, grabbing Burg by the elbow and dragging him toward the front door. "But for now I really have to concentrate on this project. *Thanks for the video game you let me borrow, Audie,*" he said, delivering the exposition as loudly and obviously as he could while simultaneously grabbing a video game off the shelf and handing it to him. He opened the front door. "I'll see you tomorrow at school!"

"Sure, Max," Burg-as-Audie sang, giving Mrs. Kilgore a wink. "I guess the lovebirds want to be left alone, huh?"

Max's mom's eyebrows shot up. "The what now?"

An odd, forced laugh came out of Max's throat. "Ha! BYE, AUDIE." He shoved her outside and slammed the door.

His mom gave him a horrible look. "What has gotten into you, Max?"

"Nothing. I mean, I don't know. I mean —" His brain began shuffling through the litany of plausible excuses: *I'm overtired. I'm cranky because I haven't eaten. I'm a dumb, self-conscious teenager who does dumb, self-conscious teenagery things — that's the one!*

"Uh, the thing is," he said, arranging his face in an abashed expression. "There's a girl coming over soon. To work on the calc project with me. That's what Audie meant by lovebirds, but ha-ha, it's not like that! It's just for school. She'll be here any minute."

His mom frowned. "Isn't it kind of late?"

Max shook his head. "Nope."

He left it at that.

"Okay." She smiled uncomfortably. "Well then, work hard. Have fun. Other momly advice."

"Thanks! We'll try to keep it down."

She went back to her room and closed the door. Max watched her go, then, remembering that he'd just casually deposited a being of the underworld on his front stoop, dragged the fake Audie back inside the house. As he did, the air around her blurred, as if she were being censored for television. Max stared, trying to figure out how this was happening, but found that his eyes couldn't quite focus. But it was all over within a couple of seconds anyway; when the fuzziness cleared, Burg was back to his regular oafish self.

"Dude," he said. "Your mom is hot."

Max let go of him.

"At least I *think* she's hot," Burg continued. "It all happened so fast. Further observation is required."

"No, it is absolutely not. And what—how did you—why did you turn into Audie?"

"Would you rather I appeared to your mother in my natural form? Give her that heart attack you seem so intent on *not* delivering?"

"No. I just . . ." Max looked to Lore, but she was no help at all, emerging from the closet and watching Burg with wide eyes. "I just didn't know you could do that."

"Well, I can. And I did. Because the sooner I got rid of her, the sooner I could get back to Battle Scallop—though the judging is probably *over* by now, thank you very *much*—and the sooner my fish sticks could . . . wait a minute." He leaned in to Max and whispered. "Those fish sticks weren't for the cat, were they?"

"No," said Max. "Cat food is for the cat."

"Really? You don't prepare fresh-caught fillets for him for every meal? Served in a goblet? With a festive garnish?"

"Uh, no."

Burg looked at him in disbelief. "Whatever, Shove. When the

feline uprising begins, it's *your* head on a spike." He crossed to the basement door. "Now, then. As I was saying, I will require some tasty condiments to go with my tasty fish sticks. Tartar sauce, chop-chop!"

"We don't have any," said Max.

Burg sauntered over to the fireplace poker, which Max had put back in its rightful place after his failed spearing attempt. Without a second's hesitation Burg picked up the poker and hurled it at Max. It stuck in the wall behind him, ripping a couple of hairs out of his scalp as it landed mere millimeters above his head.

Before Max knew it, Burg was in his face. "How are we coming on that house of mine?" he growled, instantly furious.

Max could only squeak out a whisper. "Working on it."

"Better be."

With a snort that expelled a cloud of black smoke, Burg pivoted and headed down the stairs, humming a sinister version of the Gorton fisherman song as he closed the door behind him.

Shaken, Max crossed to the posterboard and drew a wobbly circle around the last words he'd written.

"Breaking in it is."

• • •

Audie banged on Max's front door eighteen times the next morning. He counted them off as he hid in the hallway, just out of view. Next, she moved on to the window; he heard a couple of taps on the glass, then a pause, as if she were peering in. He cowered further, not emerging even when the microwave dinged.

Finally, after making absolutely sure that Audie was gone, he slunk into the kitchen, grabbed the (by now cold) oatmeal he'd microwaved, and carried it to his mother's doorway.

"Mom?" he whispered into the dark room. "You awake?"

No response.

Max thought nothing of this; sometimes she slept until noon. He crept inside and, expertly navigating through the room using only the scant amount of light the heavy curtains allowed, set the bowl down on a stand.

But as he straightened up, he paused. The shadows on the walls were falling just a little bit differently than they normally did. Something felt weird.

He switched on the light —

And clapped his hand over his mouth to keep from shouting.

Burg sat in the armchair, staring at Max's mother. His face mere inches from hers, he took almost no notice of Max, glancing up only when Max started to make a choking sound.

"What are you DOING?" Max silently mouthed.

"Watching her sleep," Burg whispered casually, as if this were a totally normal, not horrendously creepy thing to say. "Further observation confirmed: she *is* hot."

Fueled by adrenaline, Max wordlessly grabbed Burg and dragged him out of the room. "That's it!" he half shouted once they were at the top of the basement stairs. "You are *grounded,* mister!"

"Wait!" Burg looked at Max imploringly and asked, "Can you put in a good word with her for me?"

With that, Max shoved Burg over the threshold and down the flight of stairs, taking a distinct pleasure in each bump and squeal that came from the darkness. "Stay down there! Forever!"

He slammed the door and, not caring whether this would get his throat slit in the middle of the night, locked it.

• • •

> Triple-checked the kitchen door: locked, locked, locked.
>
> Triple-checked the windows: locked, locked, locked.
>
> Ruckus: stationed at the top of the stairs, bribed with an extra-heaping bowl of cat food, with festive garnish. Might keep Burg from breaking down the door and coming upstairs. Last-ditch effort, but can't hurt.
>
> Mom: unharmed. Still sleeping peacefully. Did her cheekbones always protrude that much, though? And were her fingers that bony yesterday?
>
> Audie: gone. Saw her get into Wall's car and drive off.
>
> Officially safe to leave. Go.

His mental checklist complete, Max ducked out the back door, hopped on his bike, and rocketed out of the driveway, oblivious to the police cruiser whose windshield he instantly found himself sprawled across.

"Christ, Max, watch where you're going!" Audie's dad yelled, getting out of the car. "You okay?"

Max nodded and brushed himself off, nearly cackling at the cruel irony of it all. "I'm fine. Totally fine. Sorry, Chief Gregory."

Chief Gregory let out a relieved sigh. "You need a ride? Audie said she tried to find you before she left with Wall, but I guess you were in the shower or something —"

"No, that's okay," Max said. "I like to bike."

"All right." Max could see that the chief had raised an eyebrow behind his sunglasses. "Sure you're okay, Max? Audie said you were acting funny yesterday. And you're acting funny right now."

"Funny?"

Chief Gregory pointed to Max's armpits. "It's not even eight o'clock, and you're sweating through your shirt."

"I ran out of deodorant!" Max said gaily. "And yesterday — I was just tired. That double shift on Saturday kinda zonked me out."

The chief nodded slowly. "All right. And your mom —"

"She's fine too. We're all fine. Really, incredibly fine."

Max got the distinct impression, as he watched the cruiser disappear around the corner, that Chief Gregory did not believe him.

• • •

Max had been staring at the inside of his locker for so long he was no longer aware that he was doing it. His mind was elsewhere, everywhere, a million places at once.

Slowly he became aware of another presence, someone peering into the locker alongside him. "Anything good on in there?" Audie asked.

Max snapped himself out of his stupor, slammed the locker door, and gave her a toothy smile — the only kind of fake smile he could manage. "Just finishing up a movie. Spoiler alert: Everyone dies."

"Do they." Max had expected her to be in her secondary mood, but a smile was tugging at the corner of her lips, leading him to conclude that she was fairly jubilant. He suspected that this had something to do with Wall's return from his weekend college visit; he'd seen them making out in front of the water fountain.

Actually, he'd wanted a drink from said water fountain, as he could no longer count on his salivary glands to provide the amount of moisture his mouth required. His temples were pulsing, his nerves frayed. The effort he'd expended to convince the world that everything was fine in the Land of Max had paradoxically turned him into a paranoid speed freak. He felt as if he'd sprinted to the other side of the world and climbed up Mount Everest, then gotten the shit kicked out of him by an angry mountain goat.

"Are you all right?" Audie said, scrutinizing his bloodshot eyes. "You don't look so good. And what's that on your hand?"

He shoved his ash-stained hand into his pocket. "I'm fine. Just like I told your dad this morning. Why's your family so nosy, huh? Why did you have to tell him I was acting weird?"

"Because you *are* acting weird!"

"I am not," he said, backing away from her. "I'll talk to you later, okay? I gotta get to calc."

She put her hands on her hips. "For your Satan presentation?"

Dammit! Why did he keep bringing up the least believable class in his arsenal? "Yes. That is the one." He turned around and attempted to scoot away, but Audie grabbed the loop of his backpack and yanked him back.

"OH no you don't," she said. "Not until you tell me what that church interruption was all about. And why you lied to my face —"

"I didn't."

" — and why you're *currently* lying to my face."

The annoyed mood was about to make an appearance; Max could see it happening in real time, like a cloud drifting in front of the sun. He tried to breathe evenly, buy himself time to come up with something that wasn't *quite* a lie but was enough of one to throw her off the scent, even though . . .

Even though he wanted to tell her. He wanted to tell her everything. And he would have, if not for what Burg had told him with the visual aid of that crushed Mountain Dew can.

"I think I, uh — I think I lapsed into a fugue state," Max blurted. He'd seen a special on TV about this once, how people could fall into these special kinds of amnesia trances and forget large portions of their lives.

Audie pursed her lips. "A fugue state? You mean the condition that shady characters on TV shows claim they have when they want to cover up something they don't want other people to know about?"

Max nodded eagerly. "Yes, that's the one! I don't know where it came from — maybe I was overtired from work or something —"

"*Max.* In case you can't tell, which you can't because you are *spazzing out*, I'm not buying a word of this."

"Really?" Max scratched his hair, which had started to itch. "Well, that's one of the side effects, I've heard: that no one ever believes you."

She cocked her head. "Is this about a girl?"

He scratched deeper, way into his scalp. "Huh?"

"Because I saw one inside your house last night before you pulled the curtains shut. Do you secretly have a girlfriend and you're not telling me?"

"I do not have a girlfriend," he said, breathless. "That was just Lore Nedry, who I invited over on your advice to help me with my project —"

"You *actually* called Lore Nedry?"

"You told me to!"

"I was just trying to get you out of my church! Jesus, Max, you swindled that poor girl over to — what? Make fun of her Satan thing?"

"*No*, that's not what happened. She just came over to help me with my project, and in fact she *was* quite helpful, so there's no reason to — can I *help you?*" he shouted at the hapless freshman who had just tapped him on the shoulder. She handed him a yellow slip of paper, then darted back into the rushing current of students like a terrified tadpole.

"Sorry!" Max shouted after her.

Audie shook her head in disapproval. "Fine," she said, starting to leave. "You don't want to talk to me—be that way. Good luck pulling the same shit with my mom, though."

Max looked down at the slip from the principal's office as she left, then groaned.

• • •

Click. Clack. Click. Clack.

The clicky-ball contraption merrily clacked away on Principal Gregory's desk while Max sneered at it with unbridled hatred. It went back and forth, back and forth, like a pendulum, each click of the metallic spheres scraping against his spine like a rake across a chalkboard.

If he wasn't already on track to develop a nervous eye twitch by the end of the day, he would be after this.

Left. Right. Left. Right. *Oh. My. Friggin'. God.*

"Can you please stop that thing?" he asked.

Principal Gregory raised an eyebrow and, cupping her hands around the apparatus, put a stop to the torture. "Sorry. I find it helps me relax. You don't feel the same?"

"No. No, I don't." Relaxation was a foreign concept at this point. "Am, uh," Max started, but his throat was so dry his sentence petered out. He started again. "Am I in trouble?"

"Of course not." She gave him a warm smile. "It's just that Audie told me you've been acting strangely lately, and my husband said the same. So I thought I'd check in."

God! Max thought. *Doesn't this family have anything better to do than psychoanalyze my abundance of problems?*

"So talk to me, Max," she went on. "Let's get a dialogue going."

I'm going to puke all over your desk, he thought. *Does that count as dialogue?*

"It's nothing, really," he managed to say. "Just a bunch of things went wrong this weekend — our phones went out, and I didn't get much sleep —"

Principal Gregory was nodding thoughtfully, ever so thoughtfully. "And your mom's health?"

"She's okay," Max said, arranging his face into what he approximated to be an expression of human happiness. "Still waiting on the transplant, but she's stable. Feeling good." To stop himself from saying more, he held his tongue between his teeth.

"That's wonderful news, Max. And Audie also tells me you had a girl over last night?"

"No. No no no." He let out a nervous laugh. "I mean, yes, but we were just doing a project together." He swallowed. "For calculus."

"Oh. I see." She gave one of those insidious wink-wink conde-scending smiles that adults think make them look cool and in the know. "Calculus."

Max sucked on his bleeding tongue. "Can I go now?"

"Well . . . okay." She looked unconvinced. "But Max, please, let me know if you need to talk. About anything."

"Right. Will do. Thanks, Principal Gregory."

He sprang up from his chair and was almost out of the office when she called after him. "Max, is something the matter with your eye?"

"My eye?"

"It's twitching a lot. Is it bothering you?"

"Uh, no. I didn't even notice."

She frowned. "Well, if it gets worse, stop by the nurse to get it checked out. Maybe it's one of those nervous tics that are caused by stress."

Max held a finger to his spastic eye, all the while praying that he could just keep it together for a few more hours, that his mom was safe at home, that Burg wasn't at that very moment setting fire to an orphanage —

He swallowed. "I think stress is a distinct possibility."

· · ·

Staring at nothing was officially Max's new hobby. At lunch, he unwrapped his peanut butter sandwich and proceeded to gape at it for a full ten minutes. He would probably have continued this foray into insanity until the end of the period if a cobalt-blue lunch box hadn't slid across the table, blocking his view.

"Sorry!" The lunch box was retrieved and placed at the seat across from him. A tuft of orange hair followed.

"Oh. Hey, Paul."

"Hey yourself. Aw, crap!"

Paul jumped up and bobbled back to the counter to grab a straw. Max winced as he watched him go. The other thing about Paul was that his head had grown to adultlike proportions, but the rest of his body hadn't caught up yet, giving him the appearance of a walking, talking lollipop. Add to that the way he walked on the balls of his feet — bounced, really — and it made for a somewhat unsettling encounter.

Even more disturbing was the way he was currently huffing and puffing, small flecks of spittle gathering on his strained-to-the-max braces. "Er," said Max, eyeing him as he returned to the table, "something wrong, Paul?"

"I got fired from the Food Baron!" Paul said with righteous indignation, slamming his thermos on the table. "They thought I was stealing!"

Max's heart took a flying leap. His hands went clammy, and an anxious ringing filled his ears. "Really?" he said, taking care not to let his voice rise.

"Yeah." Paul pulled out a wad of aluminum foil and proceeded to unwrap it. Inside, Max knew, were exactly twenty-one boiled cocktail wieners. Paul didn't care for sandwiches.

"Why would they think that?" Max asked, choosing his words carefully.

"Because they're imbeciles!" Paul blared, waving a stubby little hot dog. "Like there's any way I could fit a Twinkie box in my apron, stuffing Twinkies into that tiny little pouch in front. And it's not like I could stash Twinkies anywhere else — pants pockets aren't big enough to fit Twinkies! Right?"

"Right." Max was starting to feel itchy again. He scratched at his neck, then his chest. "Maybe the Booze Hound came out of retirement."

"That's what I said! But they wouldn't believe me!"

Max scratched harder. Paul came from a big family. His dad drove a truck, and his mom stayed home with the four kids. Unlike Max's mom, none of them had hearts that disintegrated if you looked at them wrong, but Max knew that money was tight. Paul needed a job just as badly as he did.

"Hey, you think your boss is hiring?" Paul asked, eyebrows lifting.

Max was finding it difficult to get words out around all the guilt building up in his throat. "I don't know. I'll ask her."

"Thanks!"

Max tried to respond, but no noise came out. Only a dry wheeze.

He scratched himself again — the itch had traveled around to his back, where he couldn't reach it. He peeked down his shirt to find big pink splotches haphazardly splashed across his stomach. Were those hives? Hives were what you broke into when you were stressed, right?

It's not your fault Paul got fired, he thought to himself, as if that would make the splotches go away. But they remained, stubborn, growing even hotter and pinker as he stared at them.

There's nothing you could have done, he reworded, switching up his thinking. *You needed those snacks for you. To keep yourself and your mother alive. Survival of the fittest.*

Because two high school boys jockeying over grocery store jobs are on equal footing with the process of evolution now? the hives retorted.

Yes! Natural selection! his brain yelled. *And so forth!*

Impassioned pleading did nothing. The splotches got splotchier.

Just then, a crumpled-up piece of paper skittered across the table. Neither Max nor Paul batted an eye, as they had grown fairly accustomed to trash and other debris sailing across the cafeteria and landing in their vicinity. But after a glance at the brown ponytail bobbing out the door, Max reached for the paper and unfolded it.

Blow off the rest of your classes. Meet me at the small patch of woods behind the soccer field. Be stealthy.

The house hunt is on.

DEVISED A PLAN

"WHAT," LORE SAID AS MAX TRUDGED through the bushes toward her, "is on your head?"

Max tugged at the black ski mask covering his face. "We're robbers, right? Isn't this what they wear?"

"You look like the Hamburglar."

Max took the mask off. "Sorry. You said to be stealthy."

"I meant behaviorally."

"Well, I was an upright citizen before all of this started. I don't know the dress code for thievery."

"There is none." Case in point: Lore was wearing the same Catholic school uniform skirt and the same sort of bedazzled white polo shirt, though this one featured rhinestone flowers instead of teapots. "And besides, we're not stealing anything."

"We're stealing a house!"

"Keep it down." She turned and began to hike deeper into the woods. "This is where some kids come to smoke, so try not to be so overtly delinquent."

"Me? You're holding a crowbar!"

"I sure am." She gave it a tender pat. "This is Russell. Russell Crowebar."

"You named your crowbar?"

"Sure, why not?"

Max could not think of a good reason why not. "The googly eyes are a nice touch."

Lore wiggled the crowbar so that its plastic eyes went all spastic. "Thanks. I once had a spare five minutes and a preheated glue gun. Couldn't help myself."

Max followed her into the woods, brambles snagging on his jeans. The weather was just as sickly warm as it had been over the weekend, with baffled meteorologists saying that the unusual September heat wave was showing no signs of letting up. He was drenched within minutes; blood pounded in his temples with each step, and an odd, tinny ringing filled his ears. "So where are we going?"

"There's a trailer park just on the other side of this hill," Lore called back to him. "Their overgrown lawns would suggest that some of them have been abandoned."

"Trailers?"

She whirled around to face him. "Is there a problem with trailers?"

Max felt bad about getting whiny; at least Lore was coming up with ideas, while all he was coming up with were new cadences in which to whine. "Well, no. I just don't think Burg will go for something as dumpy as a trailer. He wants, like, a mansion."

She crossed her arms. "You want that guy out of your basement, right?"

"Yes."

"Then has it occurred to you that a trailer might be the perfect place for him to crash, removing him from the vicinity of your mother and your girlfriend —"

"Audie's not my girlfriend."

" — while we sort through all the nearby abandoned mansions and pick out just the absolute perfect one for His Highness?"

Max blinked at her. It sounded like a really flimsy idea. But what he said was, "That's a really good idea."

She turned and kept walking. "Of course it is," she muttered.

He ran to catch up to her. "You think he'll go for it?"

"I don't know. Maybe if you get him drunk."

"Oh, sure. Like stealing Twinkies isn't bad enough, now you expect me to steal alcohol?"

"You've never stolen alcohol before? Not even from your parents?"

"Parent," Max corrected. "And no, I haven't."

"Man, you really are squeaky clean."

Max blushed, as if being a good kid were a bad thing. "The last thing I want to do is get Burg drunk. He's uncontrollable enough when he's sober."

"Then how about a different tactic? Why not drug him?"

Max frowned. "I never thought of that," he said. "You mean like slipping him a Mickey? How would I do that?"

"Well, simply travel back in time to the twenties when that phrase was last used —"

"You know what I mean. Sleeping pills, or whatever? Alcohol's one thing, but stealing drugs? That's getting into some dicey territory," said Max, who had once seen a movie that did not paint drug dealers in the most flattering light. "I'd probably get got."

"Huh?"

"That's what they say," Max said, watching as his attempt to sound cool blew up in his face, yet powerless to stop it. "The drug lords. When someone steals their stash, they have to get got. Or wait — no, the person who does the stealing gets got. Either way, there is some got that is get. Gotten."

She squinted at him. "Are you having a seizure?"

"Stealing drugs is a bad idea," he proclaimed loudly and clearly. "Is my point."

"Even if you stole them from your mom?"

Max slowed his steps. "My mom?"

"I mean, she's bound to have some stuff lying around, right?"

"I can't take drugs that my mom *needs to live!*"

Lore rolled her eyes. "Not the ones that she needs to live, you moron," she said. "I mean like expired ones, stuff that's been forgotten inside the medicine cabinet."

Max started walking again. "Maybe," he muttered. "I'll look when I get home."

Lore pulled aside a branch and stepped out into a field. "Here we are," she said. "Paradise Fields."

Max thought she was being sarcastic, but as he squinted across the clearing, he saw a tilted, broken sign that said just that. Well, what it really said was PAR DI E FI L, since several of the letters had rusted off. Below that, chipped paint spelled out in a flowery cursive, HOME IS WHERE THE BLISS IS!

"Try not to be overwhelmed by the bliss," Lore said as she walked across the field, carefully sidestepping the shards of broken glass that littered the dry brown grass. "It's unbearable in some places."

"Like that backed-up sewer drain?" Max said, pointing.

"Yes. Feel the magic."

A bitter scent of diesel fuel lingered in the air. A creepy old stone well sat on the outskirts of the park, its opening sealed off by a large rock. The late September sun, blazing with the last gasp of summer, made Max feel as if he were swimming in his own juices. The buzz of the cicadas rose and fell, the sort of noise that always makes everything feel twenty degrees hotter.

Max wiped his forehead with the bottom of his shirt. He counted eight trailers, plus several rectangular imprints where absent trailers once stood, the ground flattened. Yet despite the overarching bleakness, the homes themselves appeared lived-in and well loved. One, painted a happy yellow, featured a string of colorful patio lights. Another had a garden of fresh herbs planted along its front wall. The largest was decorated with every lawn ornament ever crapped out of a Christmas Tree Shop, up to and including the ever-classy wooden cutout of a woman bending over and exposing her plump bottom.

"Now what?" Max said. "We can't break into these places. People live here."

"Not in that one." Lore nodded at a shuttered trailer close to the woods, its aluminum siding stained the same bright, distinctive shade of seafoam green as the Statue of Liberty. The blinds were pulled down, the door handle rusted. No knickknacks or anything graced the lawn, which was unmowed and wild.

Lore gripped Russell Crowebar, sending its eyes a-google, and marched onward without waiting for Max.

"You know what?" he said, once again having to run to catch up with her. "I changed my mind. I don't think we need the trailer–halfway house strategy. I'm okay with Burg in the basement. I mean, not totally okay, but more okay than I would be if we broke into that trailer and there was a chain-saw-wielding maniac in there who cuts people up and then sews them back together into scarecrows. *That,* I really wouldn't be okay with."

But Lore was already jimmying the door open. "You need to relax."

Her words had the opposite effect. "Lore, stop. Stop! *Stop!*"

With a crack, the door popped open. Picturing all sorts of terrible things happening, like a hail of bullets spewing out the door or the trailer exploding into a flesh-melting fireball, Max hurled himself to the ground and covered his head.

A second later he felt a tap on his shoulder. Lore was standing over him.

"You landed in the sewage puddle," she said.

Max stood up. His shirt was covered in something he didn't want to think about, and smelled like something he didn't want to sniff about. After a mini internal debate over whether he should take it off (*It smells like crap! But my pasty white torso is a travesty! But wearing a feces shirt is even worse!*), he peeled the foul thing off and dropped it to the ground.

"This plan is not going how I envisioned," he muttered quietly enough that he thought Lore couldn't hear him, but of course she did.

"Oh, really?" she said, her mouth playfully tugging up a millimeter. "This wasn't all an elaborate scheme to 'accidentally' grace me with a striptease?"

Max carefully thought this through. He detected a hint — a tiny, *tiny* hint — of something that might be construed as possibly being identified as flirting. Normally, in emergency situations such as these, he'd say something bumbling and off topic (probably about veal, as was his recent trend) and the whole thing would blow up in his face. Bad things happened when he attempted to flirt. He was basically required to stay fifty feet away from flirting at all times.

But for the moment he ignored all that. Maybe he could play this one right.

"Careful," he said to Lore, trying to shield the glare from his skin. *Don't say anything about veal, don't say anything about veal. Play it cool, play it off as a joke.* "If you look directly at it, you'll go blind. It's like an eclipse."

Lore kept looking anyway. That was a good sign.

"That," she said, "is pretty damned pale."

"It's several shades paler than pale, I think."

"I'd call it ecru."

"Really? I always thought of it more as a beluga whale in a snowstorm."

She frowned. "Not a polar bear in a snowstorm?"

"Oh. Yeah, that would make more sense."

She snickered. *She laughed!* Max thought. *Does that mean I did it right? Did I flirt good?*

As Audie was not around to inform him that he had or had not flirted good, Max was left to his own devices, which included staring wordlessly at Lore and expecting her to perhaps draft up a flirting report card. But all she did next was point at the empty doorway, and it was only then that Max remembered that he should be cowering in fear from the homicidal maniac.

Except there was no homicidal maniac. Just a mostly empty trailer, with a few odds and ends left behind — a sofa, some pillows, a lamp. The floor was littered with Schwill beer cans, but other than that, the place seemed altogether livable.

"This actually isn't bad," Max said, ducking his head in.

"Told you so," said Lore.

But something was nagging at him. Something about the ease with which Lore moved through the space, the air of familiarity she seemed to have with the trailer park. "Have you been here before?" he asked with what he hoped was an acceptable amount of tact. "I mean, what are the odds that the first trailer we look at —"

CLUNK.

The sound of rattling aluminum cans made them jump. Frozen in place, they whisked their gazes to the bedroom door, which was slowly swinging open.

Out darted a stray cat. Its tail sent a few more cans flying as it sped past their feet and out the door.

"Okay," said Max, clutching his chest. "You go ahead and check the rest of the place out while I sit right here on this ottoman and have a massive coronary."

"You are such a wimp," Lore said. So much for any flirty ground gained by the exposed chest. "We should be thankful for that little guy; he probably keeps the nasty-ass rats away."

"Maybe Burg would like an army of rats," Max said. "They could be his minions, do his evil bidding."

"All the more reason not to provide him with the option."

Max squinted at her. "Wait, you don't like rats? I heard you —"

Lore's face went hard.

"What," she said. "Did you hear."

"That you kept a dead one hung up in your locker."

Lore held his gaze, then looked at the dirty floor. "Not true."

"Oh. Sorry."

He started to speak a couple of times, desperately trying to come up with a joke to ease the tension, but Playful Flirting Fun Time had clearly come to an end. It was Full-On Stammering Awkward Time now.

Thankfully, Lore was back to focusing on the task at hand. "I can check out the rest of it if you want to wait outside, get some air."

Max opted to get some air. But the great outdoors wasn't much better than the cramped trailer. A drop of sweat fell from his forehead and onto his sneaker as he hopped down the stairs, the brown grass rustling as a hot wind blew through the park. The noise of the cicadas throbbed, filling the air.

Anxious, he began to wander around the trailer, hoping to find some shade. His muscles were pounding, and the ringing in his ears was getting louder. Was this what heat stroke felt like?

But he stopped at its back wall when something caught his

eye. Underneath the window, a few inches above the ground — he stretched out his fingers to touch it, to try to smudge it away, but it remained the same —

A week earlier, he wouldn't have looked twice at such a seemingly insignificant mark. Now he'd recognize that black streak of ash anywhere.

"Max?" Lore called from the door.

Max hastened around to the front. He didn't want Lore to know what he'd seen; he needed time to think about it.

"It's all clear in there," she said, though her eyes weren't meeting his. "In my highly unprofessional opinion, I think it's the perfect place for a denizen of hell to call home."

Max bit his lip. Could it really be this easy? It wasn't exactly what Burg was looking for — there was no hot tub — but maybe he'd take it anyway. At the very least, it wasn't all that different from the basement.

But Max was distracted by what he'd seen on the wall, and his voice sounded hollow when he said, "Great." He tried to nod enthusiastically. "Let's go tell Burg."

They were silent as they returned to the woods, neither of them commenting on the fact that something weird had definitely developed between them, that Russell Crowebar had barely gotten to fulfill his trespassing destiny, or that Max had a ton of questions for Lore. The cicada clicks again rose to a crescendo as they walked, a distinct oppressiveness worming through the air, a haze of unease that settled between them like a cloud of cigarette smoke.

Just before they reached the trees, Max broke the silence. "How did you know about this place anyway?" he asked.

Lore glanced back at the park, her eyes pausing on the sea-foam-green trailer for a split second before returning to the woods before them.

"Phone book," she said.

CENTER OF THE EARTH

THEY BIKED TO HIS HOUSE IN SILENCE, Lore without a smile and Max without a shirt, certain that the glare from his alabaster skin would cause several traffic accidents along the way.

But they pedaled without incident, giving Max the freedom to mull over the multiple-choice quiz he'd created for himself. Would he (a) casually mention what he'd found at the trailer park and discuss it with Lore like a levelheaded, rational human being, (b) wildly accuse her of colluding with the devil and lying to him from the very start, (c) b followed by a, (d) a followed by b, or (e) hide out in the bathroom until she left?

These options disappeared, however, the minute they stepped into the house. Ruckus was screaming — *screaming* — his little cat heart out, probably because something had gone dreadfully wrong with the thermostat. It felt as though they'd entered a sauna.

"Holy . . ." Max stuck his tongue out of his mouth like a panting dog and headed straight for the thermostat. "Why is the heat on full blast?"

The answer came via a burst of terrible falsetto singing from the basement. *"Hot-blooded! I'm hot-blooded!"*

"Oh, for the love." Max switched off the heat, then reached up to turn on the ceiling fan. "Stay here," he told Lore. "I gotta check on my mom and make sure she hasn't spontaneously combusted."

Lore nodded, took a seat on the living room sofa, and began to fan herself.

Max knocked on his mom's door. "Sorry about the heat, Mom, I—"

"Where have you *been?*"

Max stared at his mom, his mouth open. She was glaring back at him, fuming, her face red and sweaty and her hair wild. "Uh, I was—"

"I have been *roasting* here. Stick a meat thermometer in me, Max. I am *well done.*"

"I'm so sorry, Mom—the thermostat was broken—"

"You think?" Her voice was shrill, mean. Max couldn't remember the last time she'd yelled at him like this. "I couldn't even stand up, thought I was going to pass out! And here you come breezing right in, even had time to take off your shirt—"

Max looked down at his bare chest. "That wasn't—"

"I tried calling you, but the phones are out! Why are the phones out?"

"There was a problem with the phone company, I'm working on it—"

She rolled her eyes. "Full of excuses. Surprise, surprise."

Max wanted to figure out what on earth was making her act like this, but his first priority was to calm her down before her heart exploded. "Hang on a second, Mom, okay?" He darted a few feet into the room, grabbed the hot-water bottle at the foot of her bed, then ducked back out, as if she might bite if he got too close.

He ran into the bathroom across the hall and turned on the cold water full blast. He let it run for a full minute, getting it as cold as it could go. His worried, sweaty face stared back at him in the mirror.

What is going on?

When his unhelpful reflection couldn't provide an answer, he splashed some water on his forehead, filled up the bottle, and walked back across the hall.

"Mom?" he said softly, peeking his head in. "I got a cold compress."

She beckoned him closer with an impatient wave of her hand. Snatching the bottle from him, she held it to her forehead, closed her eyes, and took a deep breath. When she opened them again a few seconds later, the fury was gone.

"Thanks, Max," she said wearily. "That feels great."

He sat down on the bed and rubbed her hand. "I'm sorry the phones are broken. I'm sorry I let it get so hot."

"It's okay, hon."

"It's not okay! What if it had gotten so bad you'd —"

"Well, it didn't, and I'm fine." She gave him a weak smile. *She looks so old,* Max thought. "What's this on your hand?" She feebly held up his wrist and, in doing so, caught a glance at his watch. "And it's only two o'clock — why aren't you in school?"

Max felt it would be rude to point out that if the phones had been working, she would have pulled him out of school anyway. "I had free period at the end of the day," Max lied, hoping she'd drop the thing about his hand. "Got out early."

"Ah." For a moment she looked as though she were trying to remember her first question, but then let it go. "I'm sorry I yelled at you, hon. I got pretty damn cranky there for a minute, didn't I?" She shook her head, bemused. "Don't know what came over me."

Max tensed as something occurred to him. *This is Burg's doing. And if he came up from the basement to crank up the heat, maybe he even came into her room again . . .*

"What's wrong, Max?" she asked when his hand tightened around hers.

"Nothing. I'm . . . just trying to figure out what happened with the thermostat. No one, like, broke into the house or anything, right? You didn't hear anything weird?"

He tried to say it with a bit of laughter, which she miraculously echoed. "No one broke into the house, you little paranoid. And I didn't hear anything weird, but then again I was asleep for a large portion of the day. Missed the Showcase Showdown and everything."

"Hmm."

She gave his hand a squeeze. "Guess it's just a mystery, huh?"

"Mmm-hmm."

Max could no longer speak using words, because the words he wanted to use were not the kind that could be said in his mother's presence. As soon as he finished fluffing her pillow and opening the windows to get a breeze going, he stormed back down the stairs, preparing to unleash a verbal blitzkrieg upon his dickwad houseguest.

Lore stood up when she saw him barreling across the room. "What's up?"

"Burgundy Shit-for-Brains tried to fry my mom alive. Let's go kick his ass, shall we?" He opened the door to the basement and stood there panting, his snowy-white chest puffing up and down in a barely contained rage.

She joined him at the top of the stairs. "Your nostrils are flaring."

"Good."

They pounded down the stairs to find an empty sofa. Rumpled snack bags were strewn about the floor, and the owner of some hair salon was screaming on the television. From the crack under the storage area door, a sliver of light poured out, along with a rousing chorus of *"Jeff, the Gooorton's Fiiishermaaannn . . ."*

Max tried the door. It was locked.

He looked at Lore. She nodded. "You gotta do it, man."

Max nodded back. With a deep breath and a reminder that this day had already been so embarrassing there was no point in stopping now, he reared back, raised his leg, and kicked at the door with all his puny quad muscle might.

The door exploded open. Granted, the thing was basically a piece of particle board, and his heroic display would have been a lot more impressive if the door had been made of a solid chunk of mahogany, but still. The door was open and he, Max Kilgore, had kicked it open. With his foot. HIS MIGHTY FOOT.

He stopped to shoot a triumphant look at Lore, but she'd already stepped into the room, unmoved by his tremendous display of plywood butchery.

Max's secret projects had been relegated to the far corner of the table. In the center was a mess of his modeling plaster, with big, gloppy drips leading up to where Burg was sitting.

Burg turned in his seat and promptly burst into laughter. "Check out Snow White over here!" he screeched, nudging Lore and pointing at Max's chest. "Next time, warn me so I can put on my sunglasses —"

"*What* . . . are you doing?" Max asked.

Burg wiped his hands on a towel. Sitting before him were two perfect plaster replicas of his own horns — every stubby, ragged inch. "Thought I'd make some models of my own fine specimens. Why should Carmine get all the glory?"

"Who's Carmine?"

Burg pointed to the far end of the table, where the model of the fossil from Ugly Hill lay. "The original owner of that horn over there. Well, the *real* horn, not your sucky fake one."

"Wait — the fossil is *a devil horn?*" Max asked, forgetting for a moment that he was supposed to be blindingly furious at the guy.

"Yep. Recognized it immediately. Ole one-horned Carmine Sassafrass. Was up here, oh, back in the 1700s, I think? He's a legend back home. Got into a tiff with a local mob and lost, breaking off his horn on the way back home. But not before taking out the better part of the village."

Max looked at Lore, who'd gone pale. "Well, thanks for the history lesson," he said, "but don't mess with my stuff anymore. Why did you come in here in the first place?"

"I was *booored,*" Burg said, sauntering back into the den and plopping down on the sofa. "You have, like, *two* video games."

Max put his hands on his hips. "Oh, and cranking up the heat to unbearable levels wasn't enough fun for one afternoon?"

Burg chuckled to himself. "Well, yes, that *was* fun. But I required more."

"Well, guess what?" Max towered over Burg, blocking his view of the screaming hairdresser. "You are officially evicted! We found you a house, and you're moving in tomorrow!"

Burg looked at his fingernails, seemingly uninterested. "It's not a trailer, is it? Because I specifically requested a full-fledged house. With a hot tub."

This stole the words right out of Max's mouth, so he just stood there for a moment, huffing and puffing in a holding pattern. "How did you know it's a trailer?" he eventually said.

Burg let out a groan. "Ugh! I knew this was going to happen. This is exactly what Verm had to go through, isn't it?" he said to Lore. "Well, *I'm* not a pushover like he is. *I'm* not going to settle."

Max looked at Lore. Her face had gone translucent. "What's he talking about?" he asked her. "Who's Verm?"

Burg looked back and forth between the two. A smile doused with pity slipped onto his face. "Oh, sweetheart," he said to Lore in a cloying voice. "You haven't told him?"

"Shut up!" Lore shot back, panicked. This was the most emotion Max had seen out of her since — well, since they met. "I'm not doing this again. Not for some lard-ass douchedonkey —"

Max loudly cleared his throat and grabbed Lore by the elbow. "Lore? A word?"

He pulled her up the stairs and closed the basement door behind them, resisting the urge to kick it shut with his mighty foot. "What is he talking about? And what are *you* talking about? You're not doing this 'again'?"

Lore extricated herself from his grip. "You have no idea what you're getting into here, Max." Her voice was getting louder. "He's just going to keep lying to you, manipulating you, and using you, and before you know it, someone's going to get *really* hurt—"

Max threw a nervous glance at his mother's bedroom door. "Lore, shh—"

"Don't you get it? This is what they do. They get everyone else to do their dirty work, then drag even more people in, make them complicit—"

His mom was going to emerge any moment, he knew it. "Come here," he said, grabbing Lore's hand. He led her outside and into the backyard, where she stopped in her tracks. Everyone always stopped in their tracks when they saw what was back there.

"Why is there a killer whale in your yard?" she asked.

Max sighed. This explanation never got any saner. "It came with the house. The previous owners were big on antiques, and they got it from an old water park that had gone out of business. My mom thought it was charming and insisted we keep it. It irritated some of the neighbors, which made her want to keep it even more."

"She wanted to keep it?"

"Collecting random nonsense is kind of her thing."

The orca flashed a big fiberglass grin back at them. In one of its flippers was a cartoony-looking fishing pole, which really didn't make much sense when you thought about it. The paint had chipped in some places, but overall it really did look as if Shamu had been frozen in time and unceremoniously dropped from the sky into a suburban backyard.

Max climbed on top of the life-size creature, balancing himself with its dorsal fin. "Here." He opened up a port on its back. "Step into my blowhole."

"Ew."

"Don't worry, it's clean," said Max, pulling her up. "Mom sanitized it long ago. It was my playhouse when I was a kid. Like a tree house, but . . ."

"But a whale."

"Right."

Lore lowered herself into the belly of the beast and sat on the floor. "Cozy."

Max joined her. "Wait, it gets better." He reached up and pulled the blowhole closed. Sunlight from outside streamed in through the dozens of tiny rusted-out holes in the structure, creating a planetarium effect.

She looked so entranced, Max almost forgot that five minutes ago she had been ripping him a new one. But then he thought about what had just transpired in the basement, and he remembered he was supposed to be suspicious/confused/mad at her. "Why do you know so much about this stuff, Lore?" he asked. "About breaking and entering? Why do you own a crowbar and know how to use it? Why—" *Do it. Ask her.* "Why did I see a streak of black ash on the side of that green trailer?"

Lore spun her head toward him, her ponytail dancing across the wall. In the low light, her eyes looked even harder than usual. "What did you say?"

"It's the same as the one on my hand," he said, holding it up to illustrate. "I just don't get it. I mean, have you been there before?"

Lore bit her lip, her face pained.

"I live there."

Max blinked.

"Not in the green trailer — in the yellow one, the one with the patio lights," she said. "The green one was . . . *his*."

"Whose?"

She sighed and started to stand up, but that didn't work out too well. She sank back to the floor. "I lied to you, Max. Or — not lied, exactly. More like I left something out. A really big something."

She looked up at him. "I did the same thing you did. I summoned a devil."

"*What?* How?"

She dug her fingernails into her hand, then laid her hands flat on the curved inside of the whale, as if to steady herself.

In a small voice she said, "I told a lie."

"What kind of lie?"

"That doesn't matter. I just did, okay?" She twisted her lips, her mind only half present. "He came up out of that old well near my house. Vermillion Wackersham. He made me find him somewhere to live, too. He was fine with the trailer, but otherwise he wasn't as easily satisfied."

"Lore —"

"His Vice was beer," she pressed on, as if stopping would hurt.

"Couldn't get enough of the stuff. He made me steal it for him, just like Burg makes you steal snacks. And let me tell you, alcohol is a lot harder to steal than Doritos. I had to raid my dad's supply, then I had to go to a bunch of hateful senior parties just so I could sneak some into my bag, and finally I didn't know where else to get it, so . . ."

Max wasn't catching on. "So?"

She picked up Russell Crowebar and made a burgling gesture.

"Get out," said Max. "*You're* the Booze Hound?"

She nodded miserably. "He didn't give me a choice! I broke into all the liquor stores in and around Eastville, then had to keep having to find new ones farther and farther away, had to sneak out, secretly borrow my dad's car. Not that he ever noticed," she muttered.

Max was at once horrified and in total awe. "But the devil's not here anymore, right? So you know how to get rid of him!"

"Well, there's the kicker," she said with a look of despair. "You *can't* get rid of them. All you can do is keep them happy until they go back to hell. If you don't, they get mad. And if Burg gets mad—"

Max sighed. "I know, I know. He'll kill me."

"No." Her hands were shaking. "He won't kill you. He'll kill someone else."

"What?"

"Think about it, Max. Has he ever threatened you directly? Or just other people, like Audie and your mom?"

"I—" A sour taste gathered on his tongue. "I don't know. I just assumed . . ."

She shook her head. "He won't go after you. He'll go after the ones you love, and then you'll have to live with the guilt. That's your 'punishment for dealing in devilry,' or so Verm liked to say."

Max jumped to his feet, ice freezing in his veins. "Then we have to get rid of him. *Now.*"

He ran back into the house, clomping down into the basement with all the grace of an ornery hippo. "You are moving into that trailer," he informed Burg, who was watching TV. "So pack up your snacks. Tomorrow, you're GONE."

With a loud *whoosh*, Max felt his feet leave the ground. He didn't realize he was soaring through the air until suddenly he wasn't anymore, crashing into the wall and denting it soundly.

At the same time, despite all the writhing and moaning he was doing, he could hear his mother upstairs, well into the throes of a coughing fit.

He looked up at Burg, who calmly crossed his legs atop the coffee table.

"House," he said in a firm voice. "Hot tub."

Max scrambled to his feet and raced upstairs, practically knocking Lore aside in his haste. His mother was doubled over in her bed and holding a tissue to her mouth.

"Mom? Are you okay?"

"Yes, fine." She gave her chest a tap and looked sheepish. "Yikes. Don't know where that came from. The heat caught up with me, or the humidity—"

"Here." He grabbed a half-empty glass of water from her nightstand and shoved it into her fingers.

She took a few sips and nodded. "Thanks, hon. I'm fine, really."

Once he'd determined that she really, definitely, positively was fine, Max left her room. He walked past Lore as if in a daze.

"We have to find a house," he said, his voice devoid of hope.

Lore began to say something about researching real estate listings, but her voice receded into the background as Max sank into the living room sofa and put his fists to his eyes. A kaleidoscope of colors burst onto his eyelids as he pressed his fingers harder, but all he kept seeing were the splotches of blood on his mom's tissue.

• • •

Max's stomach gurgled as he approached the parking lot of the Gas Bag, yet another location that struck fear into the heart of his very being. Just like home. Just like school. His life had turned into a giant haunted house, each room holding more potential terror and destruction than the last.

Spotting the top of Stavroula's hair bobbing above the shelves as she restocked the ramen noodles, Max darted behind the counter and threw on his vest. He checked his watch. Only an hour and a half late.

Roula, strangely, did not say anything — though her subsequent sneeze did sound a bit like "headaches and scoundrels." She peeked out from behind the shelf, gave him a curt nod, and went into her office.

This didn't make Max feel any better. It only put him more on edge. Once the after-work rush of customers subsided, Max opened his crossword puzzle book and stared at the jumble of words swirling before him. They didn't make any sense. The stress of the day had robbed him of his wits, gnawing away one neuron at a time.

My brain is broken, he thought, staring dumbly at clues he could normally answer in his sleep. *Damaged. Ruined. Uh . . . shit. Only two synonyms?*

He closed the crossword puzzle book, dropped it into his backpack, and decided to henceforth tackle only the sorts of tasks his enfeebled mind could accomplish. He counted the pennies in the penny tray. He counted the Slim Jims. He started to read the ingredient list on a pack of mints, but it had too many big words.

When the door jingled open around six, he jumped — but it was only Paul. "Hey, Paul."

"Hey yourself." He started to root around the gum display, which Max had to imagine was a terrible idea. There wasn't a gum on earth that wouldn't get caught in those bear-trap braces of his. "I heard you ditched school after lunch and went smoking in the woods out back."

Oh, crap. Had people seen him and Lore skip out? "That second part isn't true," Max said. "Rumors of my juvenile delinquency have been greatly exaggerated."

"So have mine," Paul muttered. "Have you talked to your boss yet about hiring me?"

The guilt stung. Max had not talked to Roula, and he did not plan to. He *wanted* to help Paul, but he was on thin ice at work as it was; given the chance, Roula would almost definitely hire someone else, someone who wouldn't keep showing up late, or not at all.

"She's . . . not hiring," Max said, the words caustic in his mouth. "But —"

He almost gasped as the idea came to him. It was perfect.

"But *I* am!" Max finished.

Paul stared at him, mouth agape as always. "Huh?"

"Maybe you can help me out with something," Max said, hoping this didn't sound as if he were making it up on the spot, which he absolutely was. "I was digging up on Ugly Hill the other day —"

"Looking for the Super Fossil?"

"If that's what you want to call it, sure. But —"

"Did you find the Super Fossil?"

"No. I ran into a problem. See, I went kind of nuts and ended up digging a big hole. Like, a *really* big hole. So big, a forest ranger caught me and told me that if I didn't fill it back in, they were going to close the area down, and we'll never be able to dig there again."

Paul made a weird snarfing sound. "Oh no!"

"Right?" Max made an incredulous face, which was easy, because he couldn't believe Paul was buying a word of this. Ugly Hill was not part of a state park and therefore would never be patrolled by a forest ranger. "I've been meaning to get back up there to fill in the hole, but I've been working so much lately, I haven't had the time."

"*I* have the time!" Paul exclaimed.

"You do! So here's what I'm thinking: You go up there and fill the hole for me, and in return I'll give you a cut of what I earn here at the store. You'd really be helping me out. Actually, not just me. *All* of us." He paused for dramatic effect. "One small step for man, one giant leap for paleontology."

Max felt that this would have been a perfect moment for the *Jurassic Park* score to swell up beneath his stirring speech, but Paul had been won over without it. "Deal!" he said, pumping Max's hand. "I'll go tomorrow after school!"

"Awesome. And speaking of school—let's not talk about it there. In fact, let's not speak of this at all unless we're completely alone." When Paul looked confused, he added, "In case any rival paleontologists are listening in."

What appeared to be a twinge of understanding passed over Paul's face. "Right," he said, nodding. "Good thinking."

He was almost at the door when Max thought of something else. "Oh, and Paul? If you see anything weird up there, let me know."

Paul hesitated at the door. "What do you mean, weird?"

"Just, like, strange sounds or smells. Anything, really. It's important to document all our findings. You know. For science."

"For science!"

Paul gave him a strange salute and bounced out of the store.

Max couldn't believe that a positive development had just . . . developed. Who would have thought that he'd find an unwitting savior in Paul the goofball?

Once the giddiness of his success subsided, though, the guilt crept back in. Nothing would happen to the guy, right? He was *filling*, not *digging*.

Yeah, he'd be fine. Probably.

Hopefully.

But as the hours wore on, Max felt worse and worse about what he'd done. The risks were too great; there were too many unknowns at play here. Paul was innocent. He didn't deserve to get roped into this.

Next time I see him, I'll tell him the deal's off, Max resolved. *In fact, I should call him right now.*

He looked at the phone but couldn't will his hand to pick it up. Fantasies flew through his head, thoughts of his healthy mom laughing, eating dinner over at the Gregorys' the way they used to.

He'll be fine.

• • •

At eight o'clock, with two hours left in his shift, Max heard Stavroula's office door click open. She sidled up to the counter and stared him down.

"What is going on with you?" she asked.

"Nothing," Max answered in a high voice.

"Problems at home? With your mother?"

"No, she's fine. I mean, considering."

She tapped a lacquered nail on the counter and looked at him. Max swallowed.

"I know about the cat," she said quietly.

Max went still.

"Security camera." She pointed at the ceiling. "I see everything."

A curious combination of feelings began to flush and swirl around inside Max, the human toilet. He counted the emotions as they drifted by: shame, guilt, fear, and that same overwhelming sadness he'd felt at the top of Ugly Hill the night he dug the hole.

And then Max did something he hadn't done since that night when he was fifteen, when his mom got real bad and had to be rushed to the hospital, drifting in and out through the revolving door of uncertain death for an agonizing twelve hours.

He put his head down on the counter and started to cry.

It was too much to deal with. Paul, Mom, Lore, Burg, Audie, this. He couldn't shoulder all of these burdens on his own, couldn't handle the possibility that every move he made was the wrong one, the ax balancing precariously over his head, ready to fall at any moment and destroy him, destroy his mom, destroy every effort he'd made to keep their small, broken family together and give them some semblance of a normal life —

And all because of a stupid plastic cat.

Through his quiet sobs, Max could tell that Stavroula had gone very still. Her hesitation was palpable — he felt her lightly touch his shoulder, then immediately draw back, unsure about what she was supposed to do in this situation.

"Is okay," she said after a moment, patting him on the head. "Don't cry, *pethaki mou*."

Max looked up at her, his face tear-streaked and red. "I'm sorry, Roula," he said haltingly, hiccups jumping between each word. "I'm sorry I stole the cat. It was for my mom. I thought she'd like it, but I couldn't afford it. I just — I made a mistake, and I understand if you need to fire me, but please don't. Please. I need this job. I don't know where else to go."

At this last admission, one that seemed to sum up the mess his life had become in the past couple of days, another sob escaped from somewhere deep and blubbered out of his mouth. He was a quivering, wretched mess. If this had happened at school, he never would have heard the end of it.

Thankfully, there were no witnesses. Though Max had a feeling that even if there had been, he wouldn't have cared. This thing stirring inside him had been a force of nature, a twisting, feral serpent nipping at his throat. He couldn't have stopped it if he tried.

Stavroula was still rubbing his hair. "I no fire you," she said.

"You work overtime. No other teenagers work overtime. Trust me, I look."

Max sniffed and raised his head. "Really?" he said. "I'm not fired?"

She gave him a rare smile. It looked strange on her face, like food that had splattered there without her knowledge. "No," she said. "No, you good boy."

She said it with such conviction that Max nearly believed her. He'd always thought of himself as a good person, but with everything that had happened lately, he'd started to feel that that wasn't true anymore. Or maybe it had never been true to begin with.

Because just as soon as the relief had rushed in, it rushed out once again, faster than a rip tide.

Because the thought he was now thinking wasn't: *Yes. Yes, I am a good person.*

It was: *I must have miscalculated the angle of the security camera.*

I won't make that mistake again.

FAIRY-TALE BEGINNING

STAVROULA LET HIM OUT OF WORK right then and there. Immediately he rode over to Just Glue It, parked his bike, and walked into the store. It remained unchanged from the last time he'd been in there to buy modeling plaster, months ago. Maybe a year.

"May I help you?"

He looked up from the potholder loom kits. "Lore. Hey."

A few seconds' pause.

"Can I interest you in one of our brand-new sparkle bead sets?" she said flatly, dusting a languid hand over a display of boxes. "They come in two styles, Glitterific and Dazzlicious."

"Uh, no. Listen, I got out of work early, and I was hoping we might be able to go do a little more house hunting tonight."

"Glitterific it is." She picked up a box and headed for the cash register, giving her head a sharp nod to get him to follow.

"I get off in a half-hour. Meet me out back," she said in a low voice as she rang him up. "That'll be five dollars and eighteen cents," she said, louder.

He fumbled in his pocket for some cash, but she waved for him not to. Instead, she bent down, picked up a bunch of papers, and shoved them into his hands. "Here," she whispered. "I already did some research."

"Honeybrook Hills?" He looked at the map on top. "That fancy-schmancy neighborhood up in the hilly part of the woods?"

"Yes. Cash or credit?"

"Uh, cash." He lowered his own voice. "This is awesome," he said with genuine gratitude. "Thank you, Lore. Seriously. And, uh, thanks for the beads."

Lore handed him the bag. "Have a Glitterific day."

• • •

A half-hour later Lore emerged into the alley behind the store. "Why'd your boss let you out early?" she asked Max.

"I don't know, I guess she could tell that I was stressed. She gave me the next few days off, too." That last part was true. After the crying incident, Stavroula had insisted that he take a break. The words "nervous breakdown" may have been bandied about, but he wasn't about to tell Lore that.

As they rode, Max caught only bits and pieces of what she was saying, but he thought it went something like this:

"The urgency of this situation requires one thing that, heretofore, we have not considered."

"Heretofore?"

"Strategy," she said. "We can't go at this thing all willy-nilly, just picking houses at random. We need a plan of attack. We need to do our research."

"Research?"

"There an echo out here?" She rode up closer to him. "Yes, research. Real estate listings." At the edge of the development, she pulled off to the side of the road. "Now," she continued once Max came to a stop next to her, "under the cover of darkness, we are going forth to investigate said real estate listings. Sound good?"

"Sounds amazing." Max was looking at her with such admiration, he almost pictured some cartoon hearts floating up from his head. "I can't believe you did all that for me."

"I'm neck-deep in this now too. So it's not just for you."

Tom Hanks would have grabbed her around the waist, dipped her down low, and planted a big one right on her lips. But Max was no Tom Hanks. And that sort of intricate choreography was just a tad beyond his grasp at the moment.

They stashed their bikes behind the flowery, elaborate Honeybrook Hills sign that may as well have said ATTENTION: RICH PEOPLE LIVE HERE. Max clicked on his keychain flashlight, which Lore immediately seized and pointed at a piece of paper that she'd produced.

"I printed out a satellite image," she said.

"Wow. Where'd you get that?"

"Google Maps."

"Oh."

She showed Max the layout of the neighborhood. The road snaked into the woods in long, wide curves, like the path of a river.

Houses were widely spaced out; so spaced out, in fact, that from where Max and Lore were standing at the turnoff from the main road, they couldn't see any at all.

They began walking down the street, making sure to stay just out of range of the streetlights. "Aren't these people going to get suspicious?" Max asked, eyeing a gigantic mansion with a sports car in the driveway. "Of two obviously not-wealthy kids scoping out their neighborhood on a night that is not Halloween? And one of them is holding a crowbar? In a menacing way?"

Lore strode on. "Nothing with googly eyes can be menacing."

"I don't know about that," Max said, walking faster to catch up with her. "Cookie Monster can get a little demented when he's jonesing for his next snickerdoodle fix."

"Snickerdoodle Fix sounds like one of those creepy educational bands for children that turns out to be composed entirely of pedophiles."

Max laughed. "You, Lore, are the best person I know at sucking the fun out of any conversation."

"You, Max, have just given me the greatest compliment I have ever received."

Max blushed, put his head down, and kept walking.

"There," said Lore after a few minutes. "That house up there, with the fountain out front. I read online that these people went broke and got foreclosed, or something."

"Or something?" Max stopped in his tracks. "Wait, we're just going to break into a house without knowing any of the details?"

"Sure."

"Do you even know what 'foreclosed' means?"

"Not really. Do you?"

Max opened his mouth, then closed it, then repeated the process.

Eventually he settled on, "Something to do with the banks?"

She sighed and pulled out a pen. "Here, here, and here," she said, marking three houses on the map. "These are the houses that are up for foreclosure sale. So these are the ones we're going to check out first."

Max gaped. "How do you know all this?"

"There's this brand-new thing called the Internet, Max. They've got it on computers and everything, you don't even have to put a nickel in the slot. It's real nifty."

Max gnawed on the inside of his cheek. He wasn't what one would call well informed on the socioeconomic issues of the day, but something felt wrong about taking advantage of people who had fallen on hard times.

Then again, something felt wrong about everything he was doing these days.

"Okay," he said with a sigh. "Let's go."

Lore determined, through various methods that Max didn't want to ask about, which of the house's entryways would be the easiest to breach: a windowless door leading into the three-car garage. "This outer door will be locked," she said, "but the door into the house probably won't."

Since the moment he'd arrived at the Honeybrook Hills sign, Max had begun to sweat in all sorts of odd places. For example, his neck. "What about the alarm system?" he asked, wiping his throat.

"The power's probably been disconnected."

"There are way too many 'probablys' in this plan of yours."

"Yeah, probably."

They were at the garage. Lore jimmied the crowbar into the gap where the door met the jamb and gave it a strong pull.

It popped open.

Max closed his eyes and shoved his fingers into his ears, waiting for a siren to decimate his hearing, but nothing happened. He opened his eyes. Lore was standing in the middle of the garage, tapping the crowbar against her open palm.

"You coming?"

Max hustled inside, clicked on his flashlight, and closed the door behind him lest any of the neighbors still left on this street were to start taking an interest in the safety of their neighborhood. As Lore had predicted, the interior door was not locked, so they easily turned the knob and were deposited into a hallway that led to a stark, modern living room, complete with bay windows, built-in speakers, and a porch leading to a sauna.

"Geez," Max said. "So this is how the other half lives."

"And this isn't even including any furniture," Lore said, drawing a finger over the spotless white walls. "Picture it with a 3D TV, leather couches, and — I don't know, a family of stuffed unicorns."

Max crossed the room and looked out onto the spacious deck. "It's definitely nice enough for Burg," he said. "Although the view isn't great —"

"Um —"

" — and I don't see a hot tub —"

"Max."

"Yes?"

"Can I interest you in a set of used needles and a ziplock bag of questionable origin?"

Max followed Lore's gaze to a pile of dirty rags in the corner, upon which was strewn a colorful assortment of drug paraphernalia.

"Oh, shit." Max recoiled, his sneakers screeching as he staggered across the hardwood floors. He looked at Lore. "We gotta get out of here."

"Are you sure?" Lore said with a teasing smile. "I think free drugs are a perk that Burg would greatly appreciate."

"Lore!"

"Ugh, fine. You're no fun."

They made a hasty exit, then sprinted up the street. The next house on Lore's map had been partially demolished; with a discouraged grunt, she drew an X over it.

The third and final house was a hulking blue behemoth with pointed spires and a few stained-glass windows. "Looks like a church," Lore said.

Max nodded. "I bet *this* one has a hot tub."

"I hope this obsession with hot tubs is just a temporary—"

"Hey!" someone yelled.

That someone was pulling up in a polished white Mercedes. Its driver's side window rolled down to reveal a pointy, face-lifted woman with fierce eyebrows and jagged red lips.

"Oh, shit," Max said under his breath. His wrists began to sweat.

"Calm down," Lore said. "Let me handle this."

The woman stuck her head out and looked the two of them up and down. Max, watching their squat, distorted reflection in the impossibly shiny car, suddenly saw them as other people must see them — Max in his ratty sneakers and old T-shirt, Lore in her bedazzled uniform for a school she no longer attended, Russell Crowebar barely hidden beneath her skirt. At best, they must have looked crazy, and at worst, criminal.

"What are you kids doing here?" she asked.

"Selling Girl Scout cookies," Lore deadpanned.

"Where do you live?"

"How many boxes should I put you down for?"

The woman squinted and pushed her head out of the window. "Lore Nedry? Is that you?"

Lore was unfazed. "No."

The woman scowled at them, clicking her tongue. "If you're not gone by the time I get back, I'm calling the police."

"Box of Thin Mints, then. You got it, ma'am! Thank you for supporting America's future!" She gave the car a jaunty wave as it pulled away.

Max looked at her. "Who was that?"

"The mom of a girl I went to Westbury Prep with," she said. "Lots of them live in this neighborhood."

Something uncomfortable occurred to Max. He wished it hadn't, but now he couldn't unthink it. It wouldn't go away until he asked.

"Um," he started, "Westbury Prep is expensive, isn't it? How did you . . ."

He let it hang in the air.

When Lore spoke, her voice was flat. "How could I afford to go there if I live in a trailer park?"

Max was now sweating out of every pore he had. "Yeah."

"I had a wealthy benefactor."

"What does that mean? You got a scholarship?"

Lore paused before she answered. "I grew up next door to a kid named Noah. We were best friends, just like you and Audie." She paused again, then continued. "He was poor like me, but then his dad developed some new software and sold it for a shitload of money. Off they moved to the other side of town, to a neighborhood even fancier than Honeybrook Hills. His parents insisted that Noah transfer to Westbury Prep, which he did, on one condition: that they pay for my tuition, too."

"Wow," said Max. "What about your parents?"

"What about my parents?"

"Were they, like, okay with it?"

"They don't give two shits where I get my education. Or if I even get one at all. Though they did raise a pretty big stink about paying for the uniform."

"Oh. Are they—"

"White trash?" She nodded tersely. "Yeah. They're white trash."

That wasn't what Max was going to ask, and they both knew it, but at least now he had confirmation that Lore didn't get along with her parents and a reason why no one seemed to care whether she was out late at night breaking into people's houses.

"Then," he said, wildly uncomfortable, "why'd you transfer back to E'ville?"

"Tuition ran out," Lore said, speaking with a finality that suggested Max drop it immediately.

So he did. "Maybe we should go," he said. "That woman —"

Lore shook her head. "She's bluffing. Come on, let's hit one more."

She marched on toward the house. Max spent so much time throwing worried glances up and down the street that by the time he caught up to her, she'd already forced her way in.

"Vaulted ceilings," she said once Max had shone the flashlight inside, elegantly indicating the walls like a seasoned real estate agent. "South-facing, plenty of light. Enjoy dazzling views of the lake from your private patio —"

Max made a face. "What's that smell?"

" — with a stereo sound system that plays soothing white noise round the clock —"

"Seriously, what is that?"

"How should I know?" She walked to the end of the foyer and into the kitchen. "Breakfast nook," she called back to Max. "Dual dishwasher."

Max followed her. "It's getting stronger, Lore."

"Stainless steel refrigerator." She pulled it open, then frowned at its emptiness. "All out of caviar. Shame."

Max investigated a cupboard. "What if it's bad food or something?"

"Electric stove, garbage disposal — ooh, this has got to be a walk-in pantry," she said, putting a hand on a doorknob. "Wanna bet?"

Max put his hand over his face. "Ugh, it's really bad right here."

"Five bucks says it's a walk-in pantry."

"Lore, don't."

She slowly turned the knob and peeked her head in.

"Ha! Pantry!" She flung the door wide, exposing a room walled with shelves. "I *told* you —"

The odor almost bowled them over. Rotten food, decaying fruit, and, on top of that, something came scuttling out between their legs, onto their shoes — one fell onto Max's head, everywhere at once —

"Roaches!" he cried.

The infestation swept out of its pantry home in a wave of solid insect. Max flailed about, throwing his arms up over his head in an amusing but ineffectual attempt to fend off the attack. He was vaguely aware of Lore screaming as well, but her cries disappeared into the background as the primal panic began to take hold. They were so fast! So disgusting!

"Outside!" Lore's voice finally rose above the din. Through his writhing, he could see that she'd opened the back door and was gesturing for him to run through it. A motion-activated spotlight illuminated the patio as they spilled into the open air, but Max could still feel the roaches crawling on his skin, under his clothes, in his hair —

Lore was just as grossed out. She grabbed his hand and dragged him onto the wooden dock jutting out over the water. "Jump!"

"With our clothes on?"

"Sorry, didn't realize you were wearing your Armani."

Max got one last look at the moonlight reflecting on the glassy surface of the water before Lore shoved him in.

The water enveloped him, a freezing rush that threatened to force the air out of his lungs and drag him by the weight of his saturated clothes down to the bottom. Max thrashed about wildly, kicking for what he hoped was the surface. Finally he burst out and took a huge gulp of the warm, humid air.

"Nice jump," Lore said. "Not quite a swan dive. More like a 'baby robin falls out of its nest' dive."

Max wheezed, swallowing a gallon of lake water. "Are they out of my hair?" he screeched.

"*Yes.* God, you're worse than a little girl."

"This could have been really dangerous, by the way," he said as they treaded water. "What if this water was inhabited by a harmful algae? Or a school of piranhas accidentally released into the lake by a rogue, embittered exotic fish importer who didn't play by the rules? Did you even stop to think about that?"

Lore didn't dignify this with a response. She paddled a little more, then stopped. "Come this way. You can touch the bottom."

Max followed her until his soggy, gross-feeling sneakers hit mud. "Weird," he said. "My feet are freezing, but the rest of me isn't."

"That's because this is a meromictic lake."

Max blinked at her. "A what?"

"It means that the water doesn't cycle or turn over like it does in most lakes. The water on the bottom always stays on the bottom, and the water on the top always stays on the top. They're really rare. Only a few in the world. Most are old quarries, like this one."

"How . . . do you know all this?"

"Why don't *you* know all this? Isn't the old granite quarry the only thing this boring-ass town is known for?"

"Um, excuse me. We also have a really good hospital. And an Ugly Hill. Why focus merely on our water features?"

Lore pushed some hair out of her face. "I like water," she said softly.

She looked so graceful. *And wet,* he thought, *and hot* —

No. Graceful.

But now she was looking at him, too. In a way that could be construed as . . . saucy. He thought about reaching out to hold her hand, but his was so wrinkly from sweat and now lake water that she'd probably think it was an eel. At least the water had deflated his hair brim, making it less baseball cap and more floppy sun hat.

But before he could make a move or even point out how much he resembled a beach-going flapper, she started to splash back to shore. "Come on," she said, paddling toward a small muddy alcove. "We can start fresh tomorrow."

"Yeah, I gotta go home and make sure Burg hasn't impaled my mom with a—" He broke off as something in the woods caught his eye. His skin tingled into goosebumps. "Lore, wait a sec. Come here."

She swam back to where Max was floating, squinting as droplets of water bounced up into her eyes.

"Look." He pointed to a massive wooden structure half hidden by trees. Its peaked roof poked out over the canopy, and moonlit reflections from its windows glinted through the leaves.

"Is that a house?" Lore asked.

"Looks kind of rundown," Max said, fumbling for his flashlight — which was waterproof, naturally, as a true scientist always came prepared. He still couldn't see much, but he was at a slightly better angle now. "See, there's a canoe with grass grown up all around it. And I think one of the windows is broken."

Lore squinted. "Hard to tell. It looks like a log cabin. One of those rustic dealys. Rustic things always look dilapidated no matter what."

"But still — you think it could be abandoned?"

Lore frowned. "It certainly *looks* abandoned." She reached into her pocket, pulled out the sopping-wet map, and unfolded it carefully so it wouldn't tear. Max clicked on his flashlight as Lore oriented the map to face in the right direction. "Oh, that place. Public records said it belonged to some guy named . . . O'Cooper? O'Connor?"

"O'Connell?" Max said, going pale. "As in the O'Connell Quarry? And the O'Connell wing at the hospital? And O'Connell Stadium?"

Lore paused. "What's that?"

"Our football field."

She stared at him.

"At school. Where our football team plays."

"Oh. Never been."

"It's kind of nice, if you ignore the game —"

"I don't care. What's your point?"

Max gave his head a firm shake. "If it's the O'Connell estate, we can't break in there, even if it is abandoned. Everything in this town is built with his family's money. He's a legend. The biggest cheese there is. I'm talking, like, a giant honkin' wheel of Gouda."

"Excellent."

"No, not excellent. He still lives there! I think."

"You think?"

"I mean, he'd be like ninety years old, but . . ." Max tried to remember what he'd heard about the guy. "I only ever heard rumors. Something about his son betraying him and refusing to take over the company. Once the son left, he turned into a hermit and hasn't been seen since."

"A hermit?" Lore's eyes lit up. "Well, there you go. He's probably dead."

Max's neck started to sweat again. "I don't want to break into a dead guy's house!"

"Why not? It's the best kind of house to break into."

"What if he's" — Max made a face — "still in there? Like, his body?"

"Then we'll just ignore it. Or Burg can make it into a rug. It doesn't matter. What matters is that there is a big, juicy house up there for the taking. What's the harm in doing a little more research?"

Max hesitated. This was too messy. Even if O'Connell was dead, this wasn't like breaking into some shoddy trailer. This was a Big Deal.

"You know," Lore said in a singsong voice, "a giant honkin' wheel of Gouda probably has a hot tub."

Max gritted his teeth. "I still don't think it's a good idea."

"But what does Russell think?"

She held up the crowbar. It nodded, googly eyes googling.

Lore's smirk got bigger. "Russell thinks it's worth a shot."

KERFUFFLES

MAX'S SHOES SQUELCHED AS HE SLIPPED THROUGH his kitchen door, exhausted and hardly able to believe that it wasn't even midnight yet. This day felt as if it had been a hundred hours long. Plus, the two previous sleepless nights had finally taken their toll. His plan was to microwave a can of soup, then crash.

He changed into a set of dry clothes and checked on his sleeping mom — still breathing; that was good. The bowl of chicken noodle soup was taking its final spins when a piercing shriek burst up from the basement.

He hurried downstairs, only to find Burg camped out on the couch, wearing, as expected, no pants. One hand was shoved into a bag of Cheddar Fries, and the other was hiding beneath a suspiciously cube-shaped blanket. His eyes were glued to the television, where a spiky-haired woman with large hoop earrings was screaming and telling the camera that if anyone stole her sewing machine, she'd stab out their eyes with a pair of pinking shears.

"Turn that down!" Max said.

Burg didn't move. "She didn't come here to make friends," he said around the Cheddar Fries in his mouth, gesturing at the screen. "She came here to *win*."

Max, too tired to rehash the never-followed pants rule, sat down on the arm of the couch. "Lower. The volume."

Burg picked up the remote with his cheese-powdered fingers. "It's do-or-die time. Their entire careers have been leading up to *this*."

Max looked at the TV. "And what is *this*, exactly?"

Burg gave him a *duh* look. "Duh," he said. "New York Fashion Week."

Max thought he could make out something resembling Heidi Klum beneath an arrangement of fabric that could have been either a dress or a shrunken circus tent. "*Project Runway?*" he asked, vaguely recalling his mother being obsessed with it a while back. "This show is still on?"

"It's a rerun, but *I haven't seen it!*" Burg's voice shot into a high-pitched register. "*Don't ruin anything!*"

"Calm down," Max said, getting up to leave. "I haven't seen it either."

"Then you're in luck—there's a marathon! Kick back and stay awhile!" Burg patted the empty couch cushion next to him, covering it in a fine orange dust.

"I can't, I'm too . . ." An acrid odor made him trail off. "What's that smell?"

Burg put on the guiltiest "I'm innocent" face Max had ever seen.

"Burg," he said patiently. "Kindly tell me what — oh no. No."

Max looked on in horror as Burg removed his hand from underneath the blanket, revealing the can of beer he was clutching. "Yayyy!" Burg yelled. "It's beer!"

Max yanked the can out of Burg's hand, but Burg instantly replaced it with another. Max got up and whipped the blanket off the couch like a disgruntled magician, revealing a full case of Schwill beer.

They must have been stolen, because Burg was most assuredly able to drink them. He gulped the beverage at an alarming rate, foam building up in his beard as he yelled things that sounded like "Sweet nectar of life!" and "Make a home in my belly, fizzy mistress of intemperance!"

"Where did you get these?" Max asked.

Burg switched from exclamatory remarks to run-on sentences. "Your little girlfriend reminded me that Vermillion used to haunt these parts, and where Verm went, beer was sure to follow, so I went to check out his old digs just in case maybe he left some behind, even though Verm LEAVES NO BEER BEHIND, but I guess this time he did, so I took it! I took it all!" To punctuate this victory, he poured the dregs of his current can all over his beard.

Max felt slightly nauseated watching Burg guzzle. He couldn't take the beer away—Burg would surely scream loud enough to wake the dead, and maybe even his mom. "If I let you drink these," Max said in the tone of a scolding parent, "do you promise to pace yourself? Only have a couple tonight and save the rest for another night?"

"Yeah," Burg said with a laugh. "Okay."

Max couldn't discern the degree of sarcasm in his voice, but he was too tired to expend any more discerning energy. "Okay, then. Good night."

He turned to leave, but a crumpled can whizzed past his nose and hit the wood paneling, sending a bubbly mist across his shirt.

"Where do you think you're going?" Burg bellowed.

"Um. Sleep."

"Don't you 'um, sleep' me, young man!" Burg launched himself up, threw a friendly arm over Max's shoulder, and dragged him back to the couch. "It's been *eons* since I got myself a drinking buddy. Here." He drew two more Schwills out of the box and opened them both so deftly that Max was now sure that devil hands doubled as can openers. But he didn't have time to further reflect upon this, as Burg was shoving the lip of the can into his mouth.

"Stop!" Max shouted, pushing it away and spilling some onto the table. "I don't want any."

Burg frowned. "I don't follow."

"I don't drink."

Burg thought harder. "Still not getting it."

Max spoke very slowly. "In all of my seventeen years on this green earth, not once have I imbibed an alcoholic beverage."

Burg looked from Max to the can, then back to Max, then back to the can. "Then tonight's a perfect time to start!" he crowed. "Lesson one: Schwill is the cheapest, best piss you can get. Enjoyed both ironically *and* unironically. That's really hard to do, you know? Very popular in Brooklyn. Huge fan base. That's why Verm's responsible for the whole brand."

Burg chugged the rest of the second can and moved on to a third. "Lesson two: once you start, you can't stop until it's gone. Oooh. OOOH. We can play a drinking game along with the show!" He started counting on his fingers. "One drink for every 'Make it work,' two drinks whenever someone bursts into tears at a sewing machine, three drinks every time someone is thrown under a bus, four drinks every time someone claims they would *never* throw someone under a bus, 'I will *not* stand here and be insulted by the likes of *you*'—"

"But—"

"Five drinks every time someone says 'fashion-forward'—"

Max continued to protest, but the inevitability of it all stopped him. Burg wasn't skilled at the art of self-restraint. Burg would never 'pace himself,' as Max had hoped. If Max left him alone with all of this alcohol, it was a near certainty that it would be gone within minutes, dumped directly into Burg's bloodstream, giving him all sorts of malicious new ideas . . .

"You know what?" Max said, deciding to take one for the team. The team, of course, being Team Not Getting My Mom Disemboweled by a Devil. "I think I'll join you after all."

"Splendid!" Burg put the beer down on the table in front of Max, then, spontaneously developing a taste for manners, daintily placed a coaster beneath it. "Go ahead. Taste the rainbow."

Max picked up the can and nervously squeezed it.

"This is very exciting," Burg said in a quiet, watchful voice, as if providing commentary for a golf tournament. "What kind of drunk will the lad be? A mean one? A boisterous one?"

"Maybe I'll just slink off into the corner and sob."

"Hahaha! Quit stalling."

Max put the can to his lips and took a swig. Half a second later the swig reemerged, spraying across the room and coating the television screen.

"Ugh!" Max choked. "*That's* what beer tastes like?"

"Like the feet of a thousand angels dancing the Baltimore waltz on your tongue?" Burg said. "Yessir."

"But it's disgusting!" Max had never imagined an instance when washing his mouth out with soap would be the preferable option, but here he was, casting about for a bar of Irish Spring. "People drink this voluntarily? And repeatedly?"

"Well, see, therein lies the magic," Burg said, bringing the can back up to Max's mouth. "Each sip tastes better than the last."

Max recoiled, but remembering that the alternative was the painting of the basement walls in his mother's blood, he forced himself to take another glug. It went down just as repulsively as the previous one, with twice as much gagging.

Good thing I'm never going to be able to afford college, Max thought, steeling himself for the next swig. *I wouldn't last through a single party.*

· · ·

"She's using *chiffon*?"

"She's out of her damn mind!"

"What happened to the organza swatches? At least those weren't a ghastly shade of chartreuse."

"Seriously. This pencil skirt's going to be a hot pot of *disaster!*"

Three hours, a case of beer, and countless outfits later, Max and Burg's bender had taken a strange, fabulous turn.

"Call me crazy," Burg said, clutching no less than a dozen Funyuns in his fist and gesturing wildly at the screen, "but I liked it better with the pleats."

"Are you kidding me? *Are you kidding me?*" Max, it turned out, was a loud drunk. Especially when it came to opinions about fashion, which were bold and impassioned, if not exactly educated. "Pleats are never a good choice. Never."

"They're better than embroidery."

"Nothing is better than embroidery!"

"Shhh!" Burg waved a hand in Max's face. "Tim Gunn is about to be concerned."

Max clammed up and stared at the screen, where the dapper mentor was tenting his fingers in front of his mouth, brow furrowed. The room went silent.

"I'm concerned," said Tim Gunn.

"DRINK!" Max and Burg yelled, downing the last of their beers and then smacking their empty cans together, crushing them flat into disks between their high-fived hands.

"Of course he's concerned," Max said. "She's attaching the zipper with *glue.*"

"Oh girl, you can't swing a dead cat in that studio without hitting a dress that's been glued together." Burg's eyes widened in a sudden panic. "JUST KIDDING ABOUT THE DEAD CAT!" he shouted toward the staircase.

When no offended meowing sounded from upstairs, Burg relaxed again. "You know what I think?" he drawled as the show went to commercial. "It's all gonna come down to styling. You gotta use that accessories wall wisely, bro. Too over-the-top, your look's gonna be costumey. Too cheap, and it's gonna be commercial. Then it's the Sears catalog for you, and that is the *kiss of death,* my friend."

Max looked up, bleary-eyed. "Youdon'tthinkmakeup'llmatter?" he asked, his words slurring. How much time had he wasted in his life up until now, bothering to put spaces between words?

"Well of course it will, but a smoky eye and a full lip can't save a bad design." Burg stuck a languid hand into the paper bag. "Where's the rest of the beer?"

"But Paisley's doing it all in honor of her dead brother," Max insisted, nearly moved to tears. "That asymmetrical hemline was a *tribute.*"

"Are we all out of beer?"

"He's watching down from *heaven* and giving her the *strength* to feather stitch —"

"Hey!" Burg looked downright panicked. "We're all out!"

Max looked at him blearily. "Huh?"

"There's nomore. Is allgone." Now that the flow of alcohol had ceased, the full force of inebriation seemed to catch up with Burg at once. "Is allgone," he repeated sadly.

"So?" Max gestured to the television. "We can still keep watching. The runway's coming up."

Burg was already slumping over, his lids half closed. "Beer bye-bye. Sleepytime now."

"But it's not over!" Max insisted. "Plenty of sideboob still to come!"

Burg emitted a snore-burp.

Max looked at his watch. The T.rex skeleton informed him that it was after two in the morning. "It's late. I should probably go to bed." Self-narrating was yet another one of Drunk Max's finer qualities. "I have a history quiz tomorrow. I should go study for that."

This must have struck him as hilarious, because laughter bubbled up as he stood and tottered to the stairs. "Night," he called out, grabbing the banister for support. "See you tomorrow."

"Yeah, buddy, tomorrow," Burg answered. "Unless, of course, you slipped a Mickey into my drink."

It took a full minute, but Burg's words eventually slogged their way through to Max's brain. "Huh?" he said, stumbling back to the couch. "Whadyu say?"

Burg opened one eye and looked at Max, his gaze steady and strong. "If you attempt to drug me," he said evenly, his words no longer slurred, "if you engage in any deceit or fraudulence or injurious advances whatsoever, I will not hesitate to do something very unfortunate to you."

Max had always heard that drunk people sobered up immediately in the face of trauma, but that wasn't happening for him. He was finding it even harder to concentrate; in fact, he couldn't even be sure he wasn't currently passed out on the floor, drooling and dreaming that his drinking buddy had improbably gone from hammered to evil in five seconds flat.

But he wasn't imagining it. Burg was still staring at him with that one cold, lifeless eye. A chill pounded through Max's body. *He knows.*

He knew that Max and Lore had talked about drugging him. But how?

A numbness came over Max as he staggered up the stairs, accidentally banging his elbow into his mom's bedroom door as he tried to sneak down the hallway.

"Max!" she called out in a harsh whisper.

He gave the door a shove. It opened a couple of inches, creaking quietly.

"Yeah?" he said into the darkness.

"What time is it? What are you doing up?"

A burp escaped his throat — he tried to let it out quietly, but it insisted on making its presence loudly known. "I wasjus — I hadta pee."

She didn't answer.

"Max," she said after a moment, "come here."

"Nah, I'm turnin' in. Go back to sleep."

"Max." Her voice had a sharpness to it. "Come in here. Right now."

He didn't know how or why it happened, but the stupor he'd felt moments earlier swiftly turned to rage. It consumed him, took hold of his muscles and his voice, which rose to a deafening volume. "No!" he bellowed. "Every damn day it's something else with you! *My toothbrush fell! The heat's too hot!* Can't you just leave me alone? *For five friggin' minutes?*"

When she spoke again, her voice was quivering. "Max?"

"Just shut the hell up and go to bed!"

With that, he slammed her door shut and stalked down the hallway to his room. He fell into bed, and if any thoughts of regret flickered through his inebriated mind before unconsciousness took him, they weren't strong enough to make him get up and apologize.

HOT SPOT

MAX AWOKE TO FIND that someone had replaced his organs with water balloons, his mouth with a sandbox, and his head with a train track mid-construction, repeatedly being punctured by railroad spikes.

"Guuuggghhhhhh," he moaned.

"Get up," someone said.

Max unsealed his eyes — producing, unsettlingly, a wet, smacking noise — then slammed them shut again. Whoever had done all of these terrible things to his body had also placed him in the center of a sun or a star or some other gaseous body capable of producing an unfathomable amount of light.

He fumbled with his pillow until it covered most of his head. It didn't stop the railroad spikes pounding through his brain — those workers were highly industrious — but at least the light was dimmed.

He felt a tap on his elbow. It hurt.

"Owwww," he said to verify this.

"Max, get up."

Max's stomach roiled. His skin broke out in goosebumps as a chill coursed through his body. The pungent smell of vomit wafted up from his sheets, providing Max with the strong desire to produce another batch.

He permitted a single eyelid to flutter open, seared retinas be damned. A puffy smudge of darkness sat to his left.

"Ew," said the smudge. "You smell even worse than you look."

"Audie? What are you doing here?" he asked, though it came out more like "Whayudunear?"

She was sitting on the edge of his bed and staring at him as if he were an endangered tiger, rare and dangerous. "I'm going to assume you don't remember opening your window last night around three a.m. and yelling 'That neckline is a fashion disaster!' in a German accent, but that is what happened. Since you left your window wide open, I took it upon myself to sneak in this morning to find out what's going on." She sniffed again and made a disgusted face. "And since my nose is in working order, I think I've figured it out."

"It was an accident," Max mumbled into his sheets. "I didn't mean to."

"Didn't mean to drink *an entire case of beer?*" Audie countered. "You could have gotten alcohol poisoning and died in your sleep! What were you thinking?"

Max felt as if he were processing this conversation on a thirty-second delay. "Wait, did you say I yelled out the window? Did I wake your parents up?"

"Uh, yeah, Max. You woke the whole neighborhood up."

He groaned. He tried to sift through his memories of the

previous evening, but none of them included being a public nuisance. They were all so jumbled together, with lots of holes . . . Burg was there, but so was Heidi Klum, somehow, and beer cans . . . and sequins . . .

And Mom, he realized with a lurch. Yelling at his mom. Being quite, quite rude to his mom.

He groaned again.

Audie poked him harder. "Max. What happened?"

The urgency in her voice brought him back to his senses. He sat up in bed, every atom of his body screaming in pain. "I, um —" He pressed the heels of his hands into his eye sockets, which seemed to help both with the pain and with avoiding Audie's eyes as he lied to her. "That fugue state — it was really stressful and humiliating, and I just thought I could —"

"Ease the pain with alcohol? How'd that work out for you?"

An extra-long railroad spike gleefully clobbered Max's cerebellum. "Not well."

"And I see you're still sticking with the fugue state thing. Great." She retrieved a tray from the floor; it held two mugs and a plate of steaming pastries. "Coffee, water, or Pop-Tarts?"

Just the sight of the jaunty strawberry sprinkles made Max's stomach lurch. "Oh God. Water."

She practically dumped the tray onto his bed. "Come on, Max, what's going on with you? I've never seen you like this. I mean, you're always weird, but not *this* weird."

"I know. I'm sorry." He took a sip of water, but this, too, proved to be painful. "I've just had a lot of things to take care of lately. We should hang out soon, once they're . . . done."

She gave him a sly grin. "You could come to the homecoming game on Friday."

"Sorry, still can't do Fridays. But — oh, hey," he said, attempting to inject some brightness into his voice. "I'll come to the pep rally tomorrow. How about that?"

Audie lit up. "Really?"

"Yeah. Promise."

Audie smiled widely. Though the whiteness of her teeth was making his eyes water, Max forced a grin back.

Until —

"Wait a sec," he said, trying to keep the fear out of his voice as a delayed snippet of their conversation finally caught up to him. "Aud, how did you know how much beer I drank?"

"Are you kidding me? The cans were all over the basement. You could barely see the floor."

Oh, no.

Audie was a good person. She was a good, good person, coming here at the crack of dawn to take care of him, toast Pop-Tarts, and remain relatively upbeat throughout. If what Burg said was true — that he appreciated a "challenge," relished the opportunity to ruin her future . . .

Max reeled as he realized how close she'd gotten to the guy. He'd probably just been working on his plaster horns in the next room, only that thin, propped-up door separating her from lord knows what terrible fate . . .

"Aud, listen to me." Knives slashed at Max's throat as he swallowed. "You have to stay out of the basement."

She cocked her head. "Why?"

"Because —" Max licked his lips, the taste of sick still smudged into the corner of his mouth. "Because I, uh, peed down there. On the wall, or the carpet somewhere. Gotta clean it up."

Audie stared at him.

"You're lying," she said.

Max tried to recall. "I don't think I am, actually —"

"Okay, fine, but that's not the real reason you want to keep me out of there. You're hiding something."

He looked away.

"I knew it!" she said vindictively. "I knew something was up. Something that would explain all of this. Come on, Max. Fess up. Fess up fess up fess up!"

Well, there it was. She'd resorted to the same tactics that had tricked his eight-year-old self into confessing that he'd stolen her Paleontologist Barbie. And her little plastic shovel, too.

As it had worked then, it was working now. Maybe if Max had been at a hundred percent, he could have kept up the charade. Maybe if his spleen weren't trying to force its way up his trachea, he could have formulated just one more little lie.

But he couldn't.

And hey, a nasty, foreign part of his brain added, *if you get in trouble with any of these break-ins, don't you think it would help to have the daughter of the chief of police on your side? Don't you think he'd be a little more willing to look the other way if there was a chance his daughter's bright, shiny future might be ruined?*

It was an evil thought. A devious, immoral, horrible thought . . . that sounded perfectly reasonable to Max, thanks to the vast amounts of alcohol still chugging through his system.

" — fess up fess up fess up —"

"But we're gonna be late for school!"

" — fess up — whatever, I'll tell my mom it was an emergency — fess up fess up —"

"Fine!"

Audie smiled. She won. As usual.

Pale, shaking, and woozy, Max careened out of bed and began to pace, but the room was tilting. "Wait." He grabbed the coffee from the tray and downed it all in one gulp. "Okay. Um, I don't know how to start." He folded his hands. "Please," he said charitably, "have a Pop-Tart."

She humored him with a bite. "Delicious. Go."

Max nodded, though that just angered the hangover further. His head felt like a bag of microwave popcorn, ready to pop and explode and shower the room in a lively array of brain kernels. "Okay. The other night I couldn't sleep, so I went up to Ugly Hill to do some digging. Actually, wait — the day before, I stole a cat."

"You . . . stole a cat."

"Not a real cat. A fake cat."

"You stole a fake cat."

"Yes. For my mom. And then, because I was digging up on the hill — well, really, it was just a coincidence — although *really*, he'd sort of been planning it all along, I was just the hapless victim —"

"Victim of what?" Audie was lost. "Who's 'he'?"

Max sighed. This was never going to work. She was never going to believe him.

Not without a visual aid.

Slowly, so as not to agitate the delicate brain kernels, he wobbled toward the hallway. "Stay here," he said. "I'll be right back. Eat more tart."

Unable to even look at his mother's door without reeling from guilt, he stumbled down the hallway, punting Ruckus halfway across the living room when he got underfoot. "Dammit, Ruckus — I mean, nice job, Ruckus," he said, sparing a chin scratch for the irritated cat. "You kept him downstairs. Good initiative."

Devils evidently didn't suffer hangovers. Burg was as spry as a bunny, watching *Scooby-Doo* and laughing like a lunatic. "Dude," he said, pointing at the television, "the old caretaker of the spooky mansion booby-trapped a stuffed deer head to drop onto the intruder's head, and he ran around looking like a deer until he crashed through the wall, and now there's a hole in the wall in the shape of a deer!"

"Hilarious."

"It *is,* man!" Burg said in a pitch-perfect imitation of Shaggy. And as he tipped a bag of popcorn over his face and it cascaded across his mouth, beard, and chest, Max was struck by the eerie similarity.

He gladly muted the television. He'd always hated *Scooby-Doo.* "Listen — "

"Oh hey," Burg said, "did we pee down here last night? Because I gotta tell you, this room is developing a distinctive funk."

"We did. And it is. And I'll clean it up later. But right now I need you to come upstairs for a sec."

"Come upstairs?" Burg cried, dramatically putting a hand on his chest in mock horror. "But that is a *flagrant* violation of rule number one!"

"And rule number four," Max said, indicating Burg's lack of pants, "but whatever. I want you to meet my friend Audie."

Burg sat straight up. "The next-door hottie?"

"Yes. And I am *trusting* you to be on your best behavior. She can help us get you a house, I think. Or at least make sure we don't all end up in prison once we do. But since she'll only be involved in a very tangential way, you have to *promise* not to rope her into any of this, okay? Promise me."

"Sure, sure," Burg said, turning off the TV. "I promise." He smoothed out his sweatshirt, brushed the crumbs from his beard, and, after a moment's thought, put on pants. "How do I look?"

"Sporty. Come on."

They walked up the stairs. "Audie?" Max called through his bedroom door, pausing. "I'm gonna come in. Please don't scream or anything. I don't want to wake my mom up."

He heard her say, "Uh, okay—"

"Remember," Max whispered to Burg. "Best behavior."

Burg burped. "Dude. Obviously."

Max opened the door and walked ahead of Burg into the room. "Okay, Audie. This is—"

He stopped. Audie had paused with a Pop-Tart halfway to her mouth.

"Max," she said slowly, "why did Tom Brady just walk into your bedroom?"

"Huh?"

Max whirled around. Burg had indeed transformed into Tom Brady, famed New England Patriots quarterback. He flashed Max a winning smile, then turned back to Audie and gave her a wink.

She jumped up from the couch and ran to Max's side, smacking his shoulder with each word. "You! Kidnapped! Tom! Brady?"

Tom Brady let out a hearty laugh. Then, shimmering like a mirage, he switched back to his regular Burg form, albeit a little taller, more strapping, and with a slightly more chiseled jaw. "Nah, just kidding," he said, the tips of his horns grating across the ceiling. He extended his hand to Audie. "Satan," he boomed in a robust, manly voice. "Nice to meet you."

This time she did start to scream, but Max managed to clap a hand over her mouth before it got too loud. "Calm down, Aud," he said, hugging her head. "I promised to tell you what's been freaking me out. *This* is what's been freaking me out. I think you can see why."

Wide-eyed, Audie nodded.

"Now, Burg here is going to go back down to the basement, and I will proceed to explain everything to you. Everything. Okay?"

Audie nodded again.

Burg laughed again and wiped his eyes. "Good times, good times. Ooh, Pop-Tarts!" He grabbed the plate and pounded back downstairs. "Until we meet again, sweetheart!"

Max kicked the door shut, escorted Audie back to his bed, and sat her down.

"Okay," he began. "So, Ugly Hill."

• • •

Somewhere in the middle of what had to be second period, Audie got up from the bed and handed her empty water glass to Max.

"You are so boned," she told him.

"I'm aware," Max said, hoarse from talking for a solid hour, "of my boned-ness. But that's where we're at. It's the best we've been able to figure out. Now all we have to do is find him an abandoned house, and —"

"And steal it?"

"Yeah. And I was kinda hoping that if we got caught, or if we got in any trouble, you could maybe . . ."

He trailed off, hoping she'd be able to deduce the rest of that sentence. When she did, she was not pleased.

"Max!" she shouted.

Max clapped his hands over his ears. "The shouting," he said, wincing. "Good heavens, stop with the shouting."

She reduced her volume, but not her ire. "I cannot get you out of trouble with the *police!* What kind of sway do you think I have?"

"Okay, none, but if your dad ever got suspicious of anything, you could at least try to throw him off the trail. Maybe someone calls to report a disturbance in their neighborhood, so you casually mention that you saw some big raccoons around the area. You know, poking through the garbage cans. Or maybe, like, a gust of wind or something."

"A gust of wind." She stared at him. " 'No need to do your job, Dad, it's probably nothing because I saw a gust of wind.' "

"Or whatever you want," Max said. "Be creative."

Audie rubbed her eyes. "All right. I'll do what I can. As for looking for houses —"

"No, no, no." Max held up his hands. "I don't want you to get involved in that. You need to stay as far off to the side on all this as possible. Wall, too."

"Why?"

"Because you've got better lives for Burg to ruin." Max rubbed his thumb over the ash smudge on his hand. "More dreams for him to crush. He doesn't get much fulfillment from torturing me or Lore. Our lives are already too crappy."

Audie frowned. "Max, your life isn't crappy."

"Compared to yours it is. Believe me, all your future plans—college, ESPN—and Wall's, he'll take absolute delight in dismantling them, making them disappear before your very eyes. Seriously, Aud. You have to stay out of this."

Audie's expression was one he'd never seen on her before. It wasn't jubilant, it wasn't less than jubilant, it was—upset. Worried.

"Okay," she said. "I'll stay out of it. But I'll also—I'll help you where I can."

Max sighed. "Thank you, Audie."

They hugged.

"Max?"

"Yeah?"

"Have you been sleeping with a T. rex femur at night?"

Max cleared his throat. "We're going to be late for third period."

SURVEILLANCE

MAX LEARNED MANY THINGS IN SCHOOL THAT DAY. He learned to calculate how many seconds it took to run to the nearest bathroom and position his head over a toilet. He learned that the school nurse was able to recognize the telltale signs of a hangover no matter how many granola bars one tried to bribe her with. And he'd come to the conclusion, without a doubt in his mind, that he was never drinking again.

"I'm never drinking again," he said to Lore after lunch, which he had spent not in the cafeteria, but on the floor of the men's room, hugging his new porcelain best friend. "This is agony. Is a hangover supposed to last this long?" He pressed his forehead against the cool metal while Lore dug through her locker. "I thought it went away after a few hours or so."

"Not if it was your first time and you drank roughly the volume of Lake Michigan," Lore said, stacking her textbooks.

Max moaned again, but by now it hurt even to moan. "So," he said, his voice taking on a panting quality, "are we skipping out early for more house hunting?"

This garnered a quizzical look. "You're in no shape to be hunting for anything except aspirin."

"True. But I don't have a choice. Burg is . . . not safe at home."

"Hey, you don't have to convince me to ditch," she said, slamming her locker. "Except I've got bio next and I've really been looking forward to stealing an organ from the frogs we've been dissecting. Can we leave right after that?"

Max hobbled down the hall after her; somehow over the course of the day he had developed a limp. "Yeah, sure. Fine."

She pushed a door open and was deposited into a hallway with more windows than Max was equipped to handle. Yet he plunged after her anyway, throwing up his arms to deflect the glare of the Evil Sun God. "I'm thinking a spleen would be cool," she was saying. "Or a lung. Maybe a liver, to replace the one you destroyed last night."

"Hardy-har. How about a face, because *your* face is — it's a — "

"Are you trying to zing me?"

"Yeah, because your *face —*"

"It's not happening. See you after class."

Left to his own devices, Max blinked a few more times against the bright light and made his way toward a glowing orange thing that turned out to be Paul.

"Hey, Paul."

"Hey yourself."

"Sorry I didn't come to lunch. I'm . . . not feeling great today."

"Did you eat a bad pickle? I once ate a bad pickle and the pickle returned later that very same day —"

"Stop," Max said, waving his hands. "Just stop." He lowered his voice. "Hey, did you get a chance to start filling the hole yet? Up on Ugly Hill?"

Paul stared at him, his face as expressionless as ever. "What hole?"

"Oh, right," Max said, remembering that he'd specifically instructed him not to discuss this matter at school. "Um, blink once for no or twice for yes."

Paul started blinking and didn't stop.

" . . . ten, eleven — I'm going to take that as a yes," Max said, patting him on the shoulder as he made his way in the general direction of what he thought was his next class. "Thanks a lot, bud."

He gave Paul a big, obvious wink. Paul, confused, started blinking again.

. . .

Max tapped his pen on his desk, contemplating the ridiculous futility of life itself, as people often do at 1:07 on a Tuesday afternoon. So many problems remained. He looked at the back of his hand, the ash mark still smeared across his skin. He rubbed at it again. It wouldn't budge.

Added to that, he was currently sitting in English lit. Compared with the trials of domesticating a satanic being, of course, Shakespeare should have been easy. But non-science courses weren't his strong suit to begin with, and he hadn't done the reading, *and* this was the worst possible class to slack in, for no other reason than it was ruled with an iron fist by the dark overlord known as Mrs. Rizzo.

A lot of kids called her Rizzo the Rat, owing to her small, pinched nose and the way she tended to scurry around the room as if she were sniffing out a nice hunk of cheese. Or perhaps it was because of her uncanny ability to detect insubordination even when the classroom was totally silent. She'd pause, lift her chin, twitch her invisible whiskers, and point a resolute finger at the poor sap who'd tried to pass a note or whisper to the student next to him. Out came the detention slip, and there went the kid's afternoon.

Max had never quite seen the fun in mocking the woman — she was just doing her job, after all, and he'd certainly never done anything to attract her wrath — but today her quirky habits were rubbing him in all the wrong places. Every fast movement she made caused him to jump, which wasn't exactly helping with the hangover headache. Each time she posed a question to the class, he gripped the edges of his desk, praying she wouldn't call on him — because with all the difficulties that had been piling up over the past few days, he hadn't read a single quatrain of *Hamlet*.

Is it even in quatrains? he wondered as he stared out the window, hoping to at least have something ready if she set her sights on him. *Or is it iambic pentameter? Wait, are those different things? I think they are. Unless Iambic Pentameter is a character. Oh shit, I don't know any of the characters. Except for Hamlet. Hamlet's a character, right? Or is Hamlet a place? It's another word for village, isn't it? Maybe there are no characters at all! IS THIS EVEN A PLAY?*

"Mr. Kilgore?"

Max jerked away from the window. "Yes?"

"Eyes on the board, please."

He tried to keep his eyes on the board. He tried to listen, too, but there were too many other thoughts fighting for space in his increasingly standing-room-only brain. As he reviewed the steps for the rest of his day, he could have sworn he heard static between his ears, a humming as each reminder whizzed past.

Avoid any teachers, principals, or other miscellaneous authority figures after class.

Speak to no one.

Casually pack up things from locker.

Go meet Lore outside.

BRING ME A HOT POCKET.

"Aaah!" Max shouted, spastically knocking his notebook to the floor.

That last thought had *not* been his. It had echoed through his head unbidden, as if someone had shouted it through a megaphone . . .

The PA system. It had to be. With a rush of relief, Max looked at the speaker above the classroom door and waited, expecting a rushed apology from Principal Gregory, explaining how some rascally hooligan had snuck into her office to pull a prank.

But after a couple of seconds Max realized that he was the only one staring at the speaker. Everyone else in the room was staring at him.

"Is there a problem, Mr. Kilgore?" Mrs. Rizzo asked, her lips pursed.

"No," Max said. "Why?"

"You just shouted."

"Yeah, because of the . . . the Hot Pocket thing . . ."

He looked around the room. His fellow students were staring back at him as if he'd randomly started spouting some nonsense about Hot Pockets, which, in fairness, was exactly what he had done.

"Sorry," Max said with a wave of his hands, as if he possessed hypnotic powers to erase what he'd just said. "I thought I saw a bee."

Mrs. Rizzo's gaze darted around the room. Finding no bee, she pursed her lips tighter, turned back to the board, and began to extol the virtues of someone called Horatio.

Max swallowed and did another visual sweep of the room. Had he really imagined the voice? It sounded so loud, but no one else seemed to have heard it.

Forget it. Whatever. He tried to focus on his notes, but all he'd written on the page was "Hamlet is a prince," which hardly seemed like a groundbreaking insight. He decided to listen to Mrs. Rizzo instead, jumping in just as she was saying something that ended in "ophelia," or maybe "ophilia."

Max wrote "Hamlet: possible hemophiliac?" in his notes.

Krissy Swanson was now reading aloud from the text, allowing Max a brief respite from the fear of being called on. He started to skim the pages, trying to get a feel for the characters — so it *was* a play, then —

HEY! his brain blared again. *How 'bout that Hot Pocket? These arteries aren't going to clog themselves!*

Max felt as if he'd been socked in the gut.

It was Burg. Burg was talking to him. Telepathically. In his head.

Go away! Max thought hard, with every ounce of his rapidly diminishing brainpower.

Helloooo, Burg sang impatiently. *Paging Dr. Snowychest. Dr. Snowychest, pick up?*

So Max could hear Burg's thoughts, but Burg couldn't hear his. Marvelous.

"What?" Max hissed under his breath, as quietly as he could.

Oh, there you are! Burg said. *Listen, I ate all the Hot Pockets, but I'm still having major goo-stuffed pastry cravings. Lemme try a couple of those Spicy Beef Nacho flavors, those sound dyspeptically delicious.*

"No!" Max whispered. "I'm at school. I can't leave. I can't talk."

But I'm staaarving, Burg whined. *The* Scooby-Doo *marathon is going on hour seven and I need more muuunchies.*

"I told you, I can't —"

"Mr. Kilgore? Are you paying attention?" Mrs. Rizzo was staring at him, tapping her fingers on the podium.

Max jumped. "Yes!"

Yes, you'll bring me munchies? Burg asked.

"No," Max answered reflexively.

Mrs. Rizzo frowned. "No, you're not paying attention?"

"No, I *am,* ma'am," Max said, sweat oozing everywhere. Krissy Swanson had taken out her phone and was trying surreptitiously to record his demise. He gave her a dirty look and turned back to Mrs. Rizzo. "I'm listening."

Good, said Burg. *Now, I'll also need some refreshments. Anything in the two-liter-and-up range will do.*

Max willed himself not to answer, focusing instead on the deepening crease between Mrs. Rizzo's eyes.

She scrutinized him. "Did you do the assigned reading, Mr. Kilgore?"

"Yes, ma'am."

Awesome, thanks. But stop calling me ma'am. Stick to Almighty King of the Underworld.

Mrs. Rizzo began to pace back and forth in front of the board. "Then it should be no problem for you to refresh us on who murdered the king?"

Max swallowed. "The king?"

"Yes, Hamlet's father."

"The person," Max said slowly, stalling, "who murdered the king. Hamlet's father."

Claudius, Burg answered.

Max held very still. "Huh?" he whispered without moving his lips.

Claudius killed the king.

"How do you know?"

Are you kidding me? Hell has so much Shakespeare we use it for kindling.

"Mr. Kilgore, I'm waiting."

It was worth a shot. "Cl—Claudius?"

Mrs. Rizzo wrinkled her nose in distaste, as if smelling something awry. "Cor-*rect*," she said with reluctance. "But tell me, *how* did Claudius murder the king?"

"How did Claudius murder the king?" Max parroted back to her.

Ear poison, said Burg.

Max covered his mouth by pretending to scratch his cheek. "Oh, come on, don't screw with me. What's the real answer?"

"Mr. Kilgore, are you talking to yourself?" Mrs. Rizzo asked.

"No, just, um — burping." He faked a belch. "Excuse me."

The class snickered. Mrs. Rizzo reached for her pad of detention slips. "Mr. Kilgore, I've had just about enough of this little spectacle — "

"Ear poison!"

Max could feel his face turn so red, he probably could have passed as a devil himself. The other kids in the class were tittering now, whispering to one another and thanking the gods of high school that they could say they were there for the big What's-His-Name Meltdown of Senior Year.

Mrs. Rizzo's mouth got even smaller. "Cor-*rect,*" she said stiffly.

"Really?" Max let out a puff of disbelief — then caught himself. "I mean, *really,* Claudius? Ear poison? How fifteenth century."

The class laughed again. Mrs. Rizzo, meanwhile, had been galvanized. Three decades of teaching had given her a sixth sense that could detect when a student was cheating, and Max's guilt was too obvious to ignore.

She planted herself two feet from his desk and loomed over him, arms crossed. "Claudius's advisor?"

"Claudius's advisor is . . ."

Polonius, said Burg.

"Bolonius," Max answered.

Mrs. Rizzo took a step closer, squinting as she tried to get a good look at his ears, then frowning as she failed to detect any ear-buds or listening devices. "Polonius's son?"

"Polonius's son . . ."

Laertes. What's the ETA on those Hot Pockets? Spicy Beef Nacho, remember.

"Spicy — I mean, Laertes," Max stuttered.

Mrs. Rizzo put both hands on Max's desk and leaned in, her face inches from his. "Who does Claudius send to spy on Hamlet?" she bellowed in a rush, trying to get him to crack.

"Uh, spies?"

Rosencrantz and Guildenstern, Burg said, a yawn in his voice.

"Rosenguild," Max said shakily, the pressure getting to him. "Crantzenstern."

A wicked smile began to sneak up the corners of Mrs. Rizzo's mouth. "And Hamlet's famous 'To be or not to be' soliloquy — tell me, what is it that Hamlet is contemplating?"

Hey, Shovel, I'm gonna grab a little nappy-poo while you fetch my tastycakes. Catch you on the flip side. Oh, and don't you DARE try to pull one of those Lean Pocket shitmuffins on me. I'LL KNOW.

Then, silence. The staticky humming noise faded away, though Max thought he could detect the faint sound of snoring before it did.

"Mr. Kilgore?" Mrs. Rizzo prodded. "The soliloquy?"

Max stared straight at the woman, her wrinkled eye bags jiggling with the imminent joy of exposing him for the lying liar he was.

"Well," Max said, a nervous fleck of spittle landing on his desk, "Hamlet's pretty upset, you know? About his dad dying — mur-dering — being murdered. Plus all that ear poison, that's really not something you want lying around the castle. And there's lots of danger of — of —"

He cast a glance around the room for help. A couple of kids made thrusting motions with their hands, flicking their wrists as if they were fencing.

"Lots of danger of sword fights," Max continued, "which Hamlet is really scared of, what with his hemophilia and all."

Mrs. Rizzo frowned. "Hemophilia?"

"It's a clotting disorder."

She straightened up and folded her arms. "Hamlet's soliloquy," she said, "is about suicide. Not clotting disorders."

"Yeah, but, like, couldn't it be up for interpretation?" Max said. "Isn't that what you're always telling us, that Shakespeare was a master of puns and double-entendres? That the magic of literature lies in the way it can mean something different to everyone? That maybe what *you* think is a speech about suicide is what *I* interpret as a speech about the fear of uncontrollable bleeding?"

The room was silent. Someone dropped a pencil.

Wordlessly, Mrs. Rizzo spun on her heel and walked back to the front of the classroom. "I have one final question, Mr. Kilgore," she said, taking her place behind the podium and placing her hands on its edge with all the conviction and pomposity of a cross-examiner. "How," she said, "does the play end?"

Max felt his victory slipping away. He had no idea how the damned play ended. His pores had sweated out every ounce of moisture in his body; his nerves had sizzled and burned out like the filament of an old light bulb. She'd won. He'd lost. She'd give him detention, he wouldn't be able to go house hunting, he'd fail to provide Burg with a satisfactory medley of microwavable snacks, and Burg would finally kill his mom, all because some emo Danish hemophiliac prince forgot to lock up the ear poison in ye olde medicine cabinete.

Max let out a miserable sigh. "I don't know," he said, thoroughly defeated. "Everyone dies?"

Mrs. Rizzo's face went slack.

No one moved.

The bell rang.

The room exploded in a flurry of movement and cheers. Someone gave Max a triumphant pat on the back. "Unreal!" said Krissy Swanson, leading the charge into the hallway and blocking any attempt by Mrs. Rizzo to punish him. Not that she could have caught him; he had already burst out the door, boldly snatching the pad of detention slips off her desk as he left.

ACCOMPLISHED

MAX CHUCKED THE DETENTION SLIPS into a garbage bin, grabbed his stuff from his locker, and bolted down the stairs, but he couldn't outrun his own reputation. Nor could he manage to avoid Audie's better half, who took up the better half of the hall.

"Hey, hoss!" Wall boomed as Max ran into him, bouncing off his massive chest like a pinball.

"Sorry, Mister — um, Wall," Max stammered.

"Mr. Wall?" He gave Max a staredown. "You all right? Heard you just trapped the almighty Rat."

"Oh, no, not really." Max shot a sheepish look at the students streaming by, some of whom were not-so-sheepishly staring back and giggling. "Just took a little pop quiz."

"That you knew every answer to."

Max paused in his escape attempts. "Wait, that last one was *right?* Everyone really dies?"

"Duh, hoss. It's *Hamlet.* 'To thine own self be true.'"

Max simply didn't know what to do with this previously unknown Shakespeare-quoting version of Wall. So he patted his arm — an arm that was easily as wide around as Max's torso — and said, "Indeed! Forsooth!" as he tottered away.

Mercifully, Lore was waiting for him outside at the bike rack. "Hey!" she said, holding up a small, milky sphere. "Look, I got the frog's eye. It's hard and bounces like a marble!"

"Burg can talk to me," he told her, breathless.

She put the eye into her skirt pocket. "Beings with mouths tend to be able to do that."

"In my *head,*" he said as they walked their bikes out of the parking lot. "He can communicate telepathically."

"Trippy."

"Don't you get it? This is bad. He can hear what I'm doing. He can hear who I'm talking to. He's a lot smarter than we thought he was! He knows Shakespeare!"

"Shakespeare?" At this, Lore raised her eyebrows. "Wait. Was that *you* who burped in Rizzo's face last period?"

"How did you hear about that already?"

"About two seconds after the bell, Josh Clark announced to the hallway that 'something is belchy in the state of Denmark.'"

"Inspired. Listen, this means we need to be a lot more careful about what we say to each other now. If he's listening in, he can hear our plans—"

"Our plans to what, find him a house? Do exactly what he's asking you to do? There's no harm in him hearing any of that."

"Yeah, but what about — *OH!*" He smacked himself in the head. "*That's* how he knew you were talking about slipping him a Mickey!"

"You were the one who said that. I would never say something so lame." She reached out and rapped a fist against his head. "Is he listening in right now?"

Max tried to remain still. "I don't know. I still hear a humming noise, but I can't tell whether that's him or just my lingering panic attack."

"Well, just look, then."

She held up a printout from the local newspaper's website. An obituary, dated two days earlier, accompanied by an outdated photo of an old, bloated man.

Edwin O'Connell.

"Survived only by his son," Lore said mischievously. "I called the funeral home director and found out that the house has been willed to him, but you were right, he and his father had a big falling-out. The son lives in New York City and doesn't even want the thing! He's just going to let it sit there and rot!"

Max felt a curious stirring of emotions. "It can't be that easy," he said slowly. "What if he comes back? What if he sends someone to check on it? What if —" He tensed up. "What if you-know-who *killed* him in order to get it?"

"Oh, don't drag Voldemort into this."

"I mean Burg!"

"I know who you mean. And so what if he did? The guy was old. And now we have a house." With that, she took off on her bike, leaving Max with no choice but to chase her.

"Wait!" he shouted, pedaling furiously to catch up. "What if he had a butler? What if — "

"Sorry, can't hear you!" Lore cut him off, speeding ahead of him. "Ear poison!"

. . .

Lore's prediction that the house was a "rustic dealy" was correct; Max thought there had to be a lonesome Alp over in Switzerland that was missing its ski lodge. The exterior was made of a deep auburn wood, and the roof soared up in a series of triangular gables with wide eaves. Exposed logs jutted from the corners, though it was impossible to tell whether they were functional or strictly for decoration, and a matching garage sat at the end of the gravel drive-way. A dusty old wreath made of twigs and dried berries hung on the front door, the frame of which was now being industriously chipped away by the talented Mr. Russell Crowebar.

"This is a bad idea," Max said, wringing his hands and scoping out what had once been the front yard. The forest had long since conquered and seized the land for itself, covering the overgrown grass with fallen trees and pine needles. There were no signs of peo-ple — Max and Lore had knocked, peeked in the window, and made sure they hadn't been followed — but Max still felt jumpy, cringing at the deafening screeches of the overhead birds, bristling at every small noise the woodland creatures seemed intent on making.

"Would you please stop it?" Lore hissed. "You're breaking my concentration."

"How much concentration do you need to pry a door open?"

"Burgling is an art. It takes finesse, it takes skill — " She threw the weight of her pelvis into the exposed part of Russell Crowebar, forcing the door open. She made a sweeping gesture at the house. "And it takes a hefty set of birthing hips. Now get in."

The ski lodge theme continued through the foyer and into the living room, which was so massive Max was sure it could comfortably accommodate his entire house. Thick, exposed wood beams soared up to the two-story-high ceiling, forming a latticework of trellises. Taxidermied animal heads were everywhere — several bucks, birds, a couple of moose, even a bear — all of them dwarfed by the one above the fireplace: a giant buck to rule them all, its antlers almost comically gigantic.

The cobblestone fireplace took up one wall, while another featured a sliding glass door set into a floor-to-ceiling window, providing a stunning view of the lake. A large liquor cabinet sat in the corner. Intricate Oriental rugs covered the hardwood floors, and handsome furniture upholstered with plaid fabric —

"Ahhh!" Max freaked out. "Furniture!"

Lore remained calm. "Yeah, sofas can be really terrifying. Don't get too close to that rocking chair, it'll tear your face off."

"It's just — all the other houses were empty. It feels like someone still lives here."

"With all your bloodcurdling screams about the furniture? They'd already be trying to shoot us with their obviously extensive collection of firearms." She nodded at a walled gun rack.

"True," Max said, looking up into the glass eyes of the bear.

Lore poked at one of the stuffed owls. "This one looks a little like you."

"Could you please focus?" Max was feeling queasy, and not

because he'd just been compared to a bird for the billionth time in his life. "What do we do now?"

"We pay our respects to Deerzilla," she said, saluting the big-antlered deer, "then make sure the stove works." She headed through a doorway. "Whoa, this kitchen is bigger than the Food Network! The whole network!"

"Great," Max said weakly.

"It has two ovens!" she shouted back. "Wait, no — three!"

"Great."

"There might be more. I'm investigating."

Max crossed to the massive window and rested his forehead against the glass door. Just outside, overlooking the lake from about fifty feet above it, was a gorgeous, sprawling deck. Stained a cherrywood color, it stretched out in both directions, farther than Max could see.

Though he could see one thing, something flapping against the wood out to the right. He opened the door and stepped out onto the porch. It was a green tarp that had come unfastened. Crouching down, he lifted the corner and peered beneath it.

He gasped.

He spun around and bolted back inside the house, finding Lore doing jumping jacks inside the pantry.

"I'm doing jumping jacks inside the pantry," she said. "It's so big I can do jumping —"

"Lore!"

She stopped and took in his sweating, splotchy, heaving face. "What?"

A grin replaced the splotches. "This place has a hot tub."

Lore grinned back at him. "You're shitting me."

Max shook his head in awe. "This is the one, Lore," he said, the wonder in his voice growing until he was shouting. "This is the house! We did it!" He punched a fist into the air. "Now Burg'll cure my mom!"

Lore's smile disappeared.

"What?" she said.

Max faltered. "Uh — that was the deal I made with Burg," he said. "I find him a house, he cures my mom."

Her eyes went wide. "Wait — the house wasn't part of his initial demand? It was part of a *deal*?"

Max was confused. "Well, yeah," he said. "Sort of an upgrade-type situation."

Lore stomped over to Max, grabbed him by the ear, and dragged him into the kitchen. "Explain. Explain *exactly* what transpired between you, the *exact* wording. Why you glossed over it in the first place is beyond me —"

"You were enjoying your quiche," Max said, cringing in pain. "I didn't want to bother you with tiny details."

"MAX. SPILL IT."

She let him go, and he put his hands out. "Okay, *technically*, when Burg first arrived, what he demanded was 'shelter.' I offered him a tent, which *technically* qualified. But then he kept whining about it, and I got the idea that if maybe I offered to find him a real house, I could ask for something in exchange."

"Let me get this straight." Lore was starting to pace. "This whole house-hunting deal, the torture you've put yourself through over the past couple of days, was *optional*?"

"Hey," Max said, getting mad, "in my book, a chance to make my mom better isn't optional. It's mandatory."

She stopped pacing and looked up at the ceiling, bouncing on the balls of her feet, as if she were full of some unknown burst of energy but trying desperately to hold it in.

Max didn't know what to do. He stood uselessly in front of her, his large hands floundering at his side, helpless. "Lore, what's the big deal?" he asked. "Okay, maybe I made a reckless bargain, but what was the harm in it? If I didn't find the house, he'd have to be happy with the tent. The deal would be null and void, he wouldn't cure my mom, and I'd be no better off than I was before."

"That's not how it works!"

She stormed out of the house and slammed the door, rattling the antlers of Deerzilla.

Max followed, bursting outside. The day had gotten moldy; it was the sort of heat that got caught in one's throat, that settled on the skin and didn't go away. He wiped his forehead and started down the driveway. A swampy sort of smell wafted over from the lake, biting sourly into his nostrils.

He found her near the mailbox, struggling to untangle her bike from the bush she'd left it under. Though her face was down, he could tell it was red and splotchy. She wasn't crying, though it seemed that she was on the verge.

"Are you okay?" he asked.

She looked up. "I gotta go."

"Okay." Now Max really *was* concerned. There was something going on behind Lore's eyes, some pain he'd never seen in her before. Or in anyone, really. "Um, why are you so upset?"

With one final, useless tug, Lore let out a frustrated grunt and gave up on the bike. She paced out a wild path into the yard, then reeled back toward him, her hand pressed tightly against her forehead. "I just am. I'm an upset kind of person. It's my default setting. Okay?"

"Well, you're usually a lot more sedate than this. Not as"—he waved his hands about—"emotiony."

"You want to know what's wrong?" She put a fist over her mouth as if to stop herself, but then pushed on. "I made a deal with my devil too. I got greedy too. Then he got even greedier. And you know what happened when I couldn't deliver? *He killed my best friend.*"

Max felt his legs go all wobbly.

"What?" he whispered.

When Lore spoke, it was in clipped sentences, as if each one hurt more than the last. "Verm's first demand was shelter, just like Burg's. I found him the trailer, and he was fine with that. But then he proposed a deal: offered me five million dollars to keep him in a perpetual drugged-out bliss. Christ, it sounds so stupid, right?" She looked away, tears squished into the corners of her eyes. "Nice round number like that, and I'm just the dumb, broke kid who's willing to do anything to get her and her family out of their dumb, broke life."

She blinked hard. "At first it was just beer, a case a night. Problem was, he kept drinking it as fast as I could steal it. Then he wanted worse stuff—pot, painkillers, harder drugs. It got to be too much. And the day I told him I was quitting, that the deal was off—"

She bit her lip and started bouncing on the balls of her feet again. "Noah was scuba-diving on vacation with his parents in

Costa Rica. Something went wrong with his tank. A freak accident, they said."

Max's throat felt as if it had collapsed in on itself.

Was that why she was so sad all the time?

For once, Max was put into the position of The Person Who Didn't Know What To Say In The Face of Grief, as opposed to being The Person Who Deserves All Of The Pity. Having been on the receiving end of this kind of conversation countless times because of his mom, he should have had something cued up, ready to go, ready to make her feel better.

But he knew, from being that person, that nothing anyone said ever made him feel better. So he said the same useless thing people always said. "I'm so sorry."

Her face screwed up in an effort not to cry. "Thanks."

Her eyes hardened once again. "But Verm did it, I *know* he did." She sniffed with violence. "So it was back to the substance stealing for me, more than before, because who knew who he'd go after next? My parents?"

Max couldn't gulp air fast enough. "No. No, Burg's not like that."

"Don't do that, Max. Don't underestimate him. That's what I did at first too. It's a big mistake."

"Okay, then what's your plan? It's not like I can politely ask Burg to leave and never come back. How did you get rid of yours?"

"I told you, I don't know. He was gunning so hard for all this stuff, wearing me into the ground, then one day he was just . . . gone." She bit her lip. "That's why I didn't want to help you at first.

I thought he was back, and . . ." She shivered. "I couldn't do that again. I couldn't."

"Well, maybe Burg will just disappear too."

"No." She jabbed a finger into his chest. "You can't count on that — it could have been a fluke, for all we know. Verm said devils get to come up to the surface only once a century, and from the way Burg is acting, he's planning on prolonging it for as long as he can. There's no guarantee that you'll be as lucky. So *cancel the deal.*"

Max felt as if he were drowning. He glanced at the house, then back to Lore. "I . . . can't," he heard himself say.

"Why?"

He felt the hope draining out of him. It sank through to his feet, onto the ground, and filtered out into the front lawn. Weakened, Max let it drag him down with it, collapsing his butt onto the ground.

"My mom's gonna die anyway," he whispered, his head in his hands. "Whether he kills her or her rotten heart does. It's just a question of when. So if I've got nothing to lose, why *not* ask for a cure?"

"Do you really need me to list the reasons?" Lore angrily brushed the hair out of her face. "Because he's evil! You can't trust him! He's too unpredictable!"

"That's just Burg being Burg. He's infuriating, but he isn't *that* heartless."

"Really, Max? Satan 'isn't that heartless'?"

Max had no idea why he felt the need to defend Burg, but the need was there just the same. "Hey, we found the house. Now he'll cure my mom. He'll have to."

"News flash, Max: he doesn't *have* to do anything."

"I just — I really think you're overreacting."

"And you are completely underreacting!"

He shook his head. "Sorry, but I've gotta do this. I've gotta try."

She started to back away slowly, almost as if she were scared of him. "Then that's on you," she said. "Whatever happens, that's on you."

She dived into the shrub for her bike, wrestled it out, and looked back at him one more time before pedaling off.

"You know, Max," she said, her eyes hard, "for a supposedly upright citizen, you're pretty good at being bad."

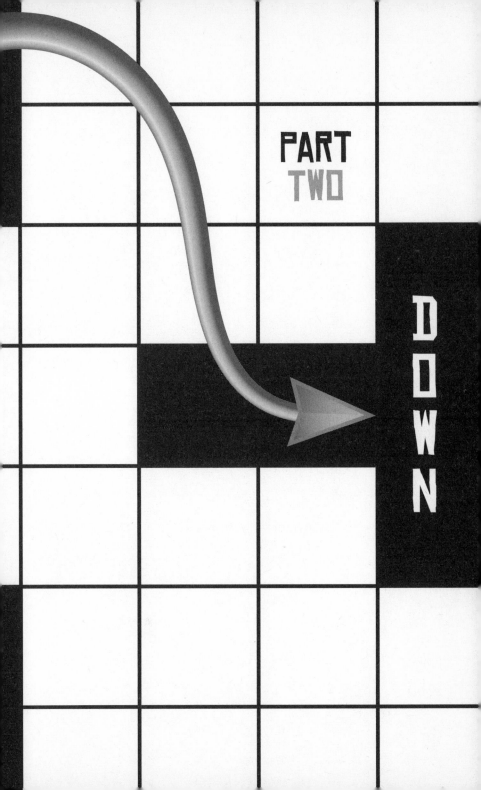

PART TWO

DOWN

THAT GIRL

MAX BIKED HOME ALONE. He stomped up the driveway. He stomped through the kitchen. He quietly stomped to his mother's room to check in on her. He was about to stomp into the basement when he glanced toward the bathroom and noticed a certain pantless demon standing in front of the mirror, squirting a tube of toothpaste into his mouth.

"What are you doing in here?" Max said, irritated.

"I had to take a whiz, then I got hungry."

"You're not supposed to eat toothpaste."

"Really? Then why do they make it so zesty?"

"Okay, fine. Whatever." Max rubbed his eyes.

Burg squinted at him. "What's the matter, Shove? You look paler and sicker and grosser than usual."

"Thanks."

Burg slung an arm around Max's shoulder and pulled him out

into the hallway and down into the basement. "Why don't you step into Dr. Cluttermuck's office and tell him all about what's bothering you." He gave him a push, causing Max to fall onto the sofa.

"Well, for one thing, you got me shitfaced last night, and now I can't consume any food or drink without wanting to hurl."

"You're welcome. But I can tell that's not what has your knickers, unnecessary as they may be, in a twist."

Max stayed silent.

Burg poked him. "Is it about school? Work? Your awful hair? A girl?"

Max tried not to react, but his eyebrow betrayed him.

"A girl?" Burg poked him harder.

Max relented. He didn't want to talk about this to anyone, especially not the one who was making his life a living . . . well, hell. But if anyone knew anything about the cruel games people could play on one another, he couldn't have found a better expert than a bona fide devil.

Burg sat next to him, rubbing his hands together in anticipation, a small wisp of smoke rising from the friction. "So . . . who is it?"

Max gave him an obvious look. "Uh, Lore."

Burg cocked his head. "Really? Her?"

"Okay, never mind," Max said, getting up.

Burg grabbed the tail of Max's shirt and pulled him back onto the couch. "No, stay, stay. I personally would have pursued the fine specimen that so conveniently lives next door to you, and not the lumpy Catholic-schoolmarm. But please, proceed with your stupid problem."

"She's so weird. She acts like she doesn't care — about, like, *anything* — but then she gets all mad at me about the decisions I make. Like the things I'm doing personally offend her, like I do them specifically to hurt her."

"So ask her why she sucks."

Max was starting to wonder if this might not be the soundest advice in the world. "I don't think that's —"

"I mean, she's probably hiding something from you," Burg said, patting him on the shoulder. "If that helps."

"How do you know?"

"Everybody lies. Your mom lies. Your history teacher lies. You lie, and like a pro at that. How many times have you borne false witness in the past twenty-four hours?"

"More than I can count."

"Well, there you have it. Liar, liar, pants on fire."

"But —"

"Fibber, fibber, baby back ribber."

"I get it."

"Perjurer, perjurer —"

"Okay, enough," Max said, though the crossword whiz in him wondered what Burg had possibly planned to rhyme with "perjurer." "You're probably right."

"Good. So strap her to a set of train tracks until she talks."

"*Or* I respect her privacy and wait until she's comfortable with telling me."

Burg burst out laughing. Then he laughed some more. Two full minutes later he wiped his eyes. "Oh, Shovel. You're never going to get laid with that attitude."

"I'm not *trying* to get laid," Max said, though admittedly it wouldn't be the worst thing. "I'm just trying to get to know her better. But how can I do that if she won't let me?"

Burg stroked his chin. "Have you *told her how you feel?*" he asked in a mocking, disgusted voice.

Max looked at his hands. "I don't really know how I feel. I like her. She's funny. She's the only girl besides Audie who's ever even looked at me. She's pretty . . ."

The skeptical look on Burg's face made him trail off.

"Well," Max said quietly, "*I* think she's pretty."

"Then knock off a florist shop and drop a rosebush at her front door. Chicks love that stuff."

"I don't think Lore would." Max massaged his temples. "I don't think she's interested in me at all."

"Well, in her defense, have you seen you?"

"Forget it," Max said with a sigh. "I don't expect you to understand what it's like to be such an oddball."

Burg was quiet for a moment.

"Actually, Shove, I kinda do."

Max knew he'd come to regret humoring him, yet he did it anyway. "Why?"

Burg scratched at the skin around his horns. "Well . . . everyone else in hell *loves* it down there. Can't get enough of the place. I mean, don't get me wrong—I love causing suffering and human misery just as much as the next guy. But you know what I love even more? This." Burg gestured to the ratty basement walls. "Being on earth. Sure, we've got anything and everything we need in hell, but we don't have — well, we don't have you. Humans. You dudes are fascinating, you know that?"

Max stared at him, his mouth slightly ajar. Burg had emotions? Burg had intellectual curiosity? Burg thought about stuff besides reality television and snacks?

"You're all so weird and squirmy," Burg said, "but complicated. You do bad things, like we do. But you also do good things, for reasons I can't fully grasp. And then there are people like you, who sometimes do a bunch of bad things in order to produce a good thing. There's something about that that's . . . what's the word . . ."

"Noble?" Max suggested. "Virtuous?"

"No, that's not it. Idiotic, maybe?"

"Ah."

"But idiotic in a riveting way. You people should be studied."

"Um. Thanks?"

"What I'm saying is, I like it up here on earth. And that makes me a total freak down below."

Burg frowned, as if surprised by what had just come out of his mouth. He sighed and put his feet up on the table, scratching his beard, thinking. Max did the same thing, scratching the skin on his chin where no whisker, he was sure, would ever dare to grow.

"You know what, Shove?" Burg said. "I think I want to stay up here for good. The powers that be won't like it, and the Moneygrubbers'll hate me — they've been trying to figure out a way to stay up here for centuries — but my mind is made up. Your world is just too fun. Your snacks are just too tasty."

Max's panic alarm went off at this, but he tried to play it off as nothing. "Okay, but—but you're not gonna, like, rain hellfire upon the earth or anything, are you?"

"Nah. Once you find me a house, I'll mind my own business. Maybe I'll get a bird."

"A bird?"

"Yeah, one of those little yellow things that can talk to you. I'll teach it all kinds of swear words. What fun we'll have! What fucking fun!"

"Well, guess what?" Max stood up and formed his body into a this-is-really-exciting stance. "I've got some good news for you. Are you ready for this?"

Burg looked intrigued. "I am!"

"I . . . found you a house!"

He lit up. "Really?"

"A really big house!"

"Really?"

"You can move in today!"

Burg slumped back down and clucked his tongue. "Mmm, no. No, that's not going to work for me."

Max almost fell over. "What?"

"I can't move in yet. I haven't packed, I haven't beat *Call of Duty*—I haven't even approved of said domicile." He put his feet on the table. "How can you expect me to just drop everything, upheave my life without even getting the grand tour first? What if I'm signing myself up for a glorified beaver dam?"

"But—it's a house!" Max sputtered. "A *mansion!* I found you a mansion, free of charge, and you're telling me you have to *approve* it first?"

Burg wagged his finger. "Buyer beware."

"Approval was *not* part of the deal."

"And now it is! Isn't haggling fun?"

There came a knock at the basement door. "Max?" Audie called. "You down there?"

"We sure are!" Burg called up to her.

Audie warily made her way down the stairs. "What's happening here?" She pointed to Burg, who on impulse had arranged himself into some unholy amalgamation of Eli and Peyton Manning.

"Hey, baby," he said to her. "Wanna—"

"No. Never. Ever." She turned to Max. "Where did you disappear to? I heard you flipped out at Mrs. Rizzo—"

"Yeah, speaking of which—" Max rounded on Burg. "Thanks a *lot* for almost getting me kicked out of school. It's bad enough that I don't have enough time to do homework anymore, but now the added voices in my head are really going to give me the leg up I need to get expelled."

"Hey! I was bored!"

"Well, it's not cool, okay? It's an invasion of privacy! How much—" Max blushed. "I mean, how much else have you listened in on?"

Burg's face was unreadable. "Nothing important."

"Well, it's rude. So stop it."

"Look, Shovel, did you get detention or not?"

Max grunted. "Not."

"Then you're welcome. Now where's my Spicy Beef Nacho Hot Pocket?"

Max ignored this and turned to Audie. "Can you do me a

favor?" he asked in a low voice. "I need to give Burg a ride to his new house, and —"

"You found a house?" she said. "Already?"

"Yeah."

"Do I want to know how . . . or where . . ."

"No, the less you know, the better," said Max. "But I need to get Burg there. As soon as possible. Can you call Wall and ask him to give us a ride?"

She shot a glance at Burg, whose face had melted into something half Manning, half Ryan Seacrest. She gave Max a look. "Well, okay. But you might want to have him change into something a little less freakish."

"Will do." He scooped Audie up into a hug. "Thank you *soooo* much, Audie."

She hugged him back, then peeled herself out after it started to go on for too long. "Don't mention it." She turned and hopped up the stairs. "I'll go call Wall and meet you out front."

"You heard her," Max told Burg. "Upstairs. Come on." He turned to leave, then Burg spoke again.

"Hey, Shovel?"

"Yeah?"

"Hold her hand."

"What?"

"That girl you like," Burg said. "Try holding her hand. Seems like your style. Slow, inoffensive. Nice guy–ish. That's your angle."

Max bit his lip.

"Thanks."

• • •

Max sat on his front stoop, uneasy and lightheaded. When he spotted Wall's car rounding the corner, he jumped up.

"Calm down," said Audie. "He won't suspect a thing."

"Yeah, relax," said Lore, remaining seated. She undid the rubber band holding her ponytail and shook her hair out. "You don't want to seem too desperate in front of the popular kids."

"Shut up, Doritos Breath. I don't need advice on how not to be a loser."

"Says the loser wearing a plastic dinosaur watch." Lore, who was really Burg in shape-shifting disguise, rearranged her hair into two buns on either side of her head. "Look at me! I'm Princess Leia!"

"Stop that."

Max gave a jaunty wave to Wall and approached the car as it pulled into Audie's driveway. "Wall!" he said. "How are ya?"

Wall gave him his trademark solemn nod. "Hey, hoss. Audie says you need a ride?"

"Yes, they need a ride," Audie said, diving into the passenger seat before Burg could.

"Yeah," Max confirmed. "We accidentally rode over a pile of broken glass yesterday, and both our bikes got flat tires. You mind?"

"Nah. Where you headed?"

"Up to Honeybrook Hills? We're working on a project for calculus" — there it was again — "with Krissy Swanson, but at lunch she told me she has to stay home and baby-sit her little sister this afternoon, so she was wondering if we could meet at her house."

Wall looked askance at him. "Krissy Swanson allowed herself to be seen talking to you?"

Max chose to take that not as an insult, but as an opportunity to strengthen his lie. "Yeah, she wasn't a fan of it. I think that's why she's 'baby-sitting,'" he said with air quotes.

Wall's shoulders heaved a mighty shrug. "Okay, whatever," he said, rolling up his window. "Get in."

"Lore!" Max called to her. "Get in the car!"

Lore-Burg, hair still in Leia buns, sashayed over to the car and bowed deeply to Wall's window. "The Force is strong with this one."

Before Wall could raise an eyebrow, Max opened the back door and pushed Burg in. "Have you even seen *Star Wars*?" he whispered, clambering in behind her.

"I've seen the *Star Wars Holiday Special*. It's a hit in hell."

Audie turned around in her seat and mouthed "Honeybrook Hills?" followed by a series of manic questions. Max mouthed a bunch of answers back. Not a word was understood by either party. Meanwhile, Burg began to fondle his own boobs.

"Stop that!" Max hissed, elbowing him.

When they got to the Honeybrook Hills sign, Max tapped Wall on the shoulder. "You can pull up right here! Thanks, Wall!" He opened the car door, shoved Burg out, and slammed it again, all before Wall could ask any perfectly reasonable questions.

Audie would throw him off the trail, Max was sure of that. Now he had to switch into upbeat real estate agent mode. If he didn't sell Burg on this house, it was back to square one, and there weren't many Combos flavors left for him to steal.

"Wait till you see this place," Max said in an enthusiastic voice as they walked. "You'll shit your pants. Should you ever choose to wear any."

"This skirt's not bad, I have to admit," Burg said, swishing the pleats. "Airy and fresh. Nice to get a cooling breeze blowing through the forest every once in a while, if you catch my drift."

"Drift caught."

Finally they came to the house. Max, sweating and out of breath, made a sweeping, grand gesture toward the front door. "This is it."

Burg took off without a moment's hesitation, throwing open the door and sprinting into the foyer. "Holy shit!" his excited cry came through the open door. "Vaulted ceilings! Parquet floors! A gun rack!"

Should I maybe have taken those away? Max thought before a wiser part of him decided, *Hey, if he wants to kill anything, he'll kill it. Gun or no gun.*

He went inside after him. Burg, back to his devilish form, had already flung himself onto the plaid sofa. "This place is so clutch," he said, smacking his lips. "Great view, big fireplace, animal carcasses — really, the full package." He got up again and stared into the glass eyes of Deerzilla. "This one's going to be my Scooby-Doo booby trap. My Scooby-Dooby trap, if you will."

"It's your house, you do what you want. Oh, and here's the best part," Max couldn't help but add. It was a point of pride that he'd managed this impossible detail. He opened the sliding glass door and ushered Burg onto the deck. "Ta-*da!*"

Burg brought a hand to his mouth. He almost seemed to be tearing up. "For me?"

He let out a squeal, then knelt down and brought his face next to the hot tub. "Hello, my pet," he cooed. "Oh, the depraved acts you'll facilitate."

"So what do you think?" Max said. "Does it meet your lofty standards?"

Max's mom sometimes watched a reality show that involved brides shopping for their wedding dresses and the hysterics naturally infused therein. It was rife with tense, dragged-out strife, all leading up to the suspenseful moment when the women decided whether they were going to take the dress or not. This was exactly like that, except with less taffeta.

"Well . . ." Burg said, expertly ramping up the drama. "Yes!" He clapped daintily. "I officially approve."

Max let out the breath he'd apparently been holding for, it seemed, three days. "Fantastic. Then we're all squared up, right? I upheld my end of the bargain, and now it's time to uphold yours?"

Burg frowned. "Refresh me."

Max remained patient. "We agreed that if I found you a house, you'd cure my mom. Well, I found you a house. With a friggin' hot tub. So you have to cure my mom."

"Absolutely!" said Burg.

"Awesome."

"Right after you do *one* more thing for me."

Max froze.

"What did you say?"

"Don't get me wrong, Shovel — the house is great. But it's so big and empty and lonely . . . how's about you fix me up with a lady friend? Your mom's single, right?"

"No," Max said, panic rising. "No, you said that all I had to do was this one thing. We shook on it! You burned my hand!"

Burg wiggled his own hand. "Gray area."

"Oh my God! OH MY GOD!" Max's fingers had assumed choking position, and they were slowly creeping toward Burg's neck. "What do you think I did all this for? You promised you'd cure my mom if I got you a house!"

"And now that I *have* a house, I'll want some company. Find me some company, and then I'll cure your mom."

Max literally saw red. He'd always imagined that expression to be a figure of speech, but bright crimson spots exploded in the outer reaches of his vision, framing the bastard in a picture of unadulterated fury.

Lore was right, he thought. *He screwed me over, just like she said he would.*

"There is no way," Max spat, "in heaven or hell that I'm setting you up with my mom."

"*I* think you're underestimating my dateability. I recently perused a magazine article that educated me on five — count 'em, *five* — new erotic zones discovered by sex scientists —"

Max wiped the sweat from his brow again. It was taking every ounce of his heavily depleted energy to stay his strangling hands in the face of phrases like "sex scientists." "You're out of your mind! Besides, what kind of woman is going to agree to go on a blind date arranged by *me?*"

This stopped Burg in his tracks. "That's a good point." He thought for a moment more, stroking his beard. "You'll have to find me someone online, then."

"NO!" Max kicked over a patio chair. "That's it. I'm not lifting another finger for you." He stalked to the sliding door and wrenched it open. "I stuck to my end of the bargain," he said just before storming out. "Now you stick to yours. OR ELSE."

Burg gave him a condescending sneer and looked out over the lake, the tips of his horns glinting. "Or else what?" he said with a dry laugh.

• • •

Max knew something was awry the moment his house came into view.

Granted, he'd just stalked all the way back from Honeybrook Hills, and the fury plus the persistent heat had lightly scrambled his brain. Plus, the sun had just begun to set, so there was a bit of a glare. But he could plainly see that the front door was open, and he knew one thing for sure: he had not left the front door open.

Cautious, he stepped inside. "Hello?" he called.

To his horror, someone answered back.

"Max?" Principal Gregory shouted from deep within the house. "Is that you?"

"We're in here!" Chief Gregory added. "Come join the party!"

What. The.

Dazed, Max headed into his mother's room. Inside was a tableau he wouldn't be able to forget for some time: Principal Gregory, seated at the foot of his mom's bed; Chief Gregory, lounging in Max's usual ratty chair at her bedside; Audie, standing stiffly beside him, mouthing "I AM SO SORRY" to Max; and, of course, Max's mom, shrunken against her pillow, looking shell-shocked, betrayed, and humiliated beyond belief.

Immediately Max swallowed and looked at the ground. He'd avoided his mother completely since he'd drunkenly snapped at her the night before, the mix of shame and awkwardness and pain too much for him to face.

And now this.

"I hope you don't mind the intrusion, Max," Principal Gregory said, "but you just seemed so agitated in my office yesterday, I wanted to come over and see for myself that everything was all right at home."

"Oh," said Max.

"Which it is, as you can see," Max's mom said, just a shade away from being rude. "You didn't have to take the trouble to come over —"

"Oh, we were just on our way out to the booster club potluck meeting, got a few more plans to finalize for the pep rally tomorrow," said Chief Gregory, "and we thought we'd stop by for a quick little visit. Just like the old days. Here, Max, have some asparagus."

He held out a covered baking dish, bending back a corner of the aluminum foil. Max robotically seized a spear of asparagus and shoved it into his mouth. He in fact hated asparagus, but given that he was too mind-blown to taste a single bite, the sky was the culinary limit.

"How was school today, Max?" Chief Gregory asked, clearly settling in for A Conversation, prompting another cringe from Max's mom. "I heard you had a bit of trouble with the ole prince of Denmark."

Max paused mid-chew. "Who?"

"Hamlet," Audie said.

Is my English class aired live on network television or something? How does everyone know about this? "Oh, yeah, him," Max said. "Yeah, I don't know what happened there. Guess I read it wrong. Shakespeare's hard sometimes." He went back in for more asparagus spears, as they were the only things in the room not judging him. Although, come to think of it, they looked a little disappointed in him, too.

"You're having trouble with your classes?" Max's mom said, now a combination of annoyed *and* worried.

"No," Max said, not wanting to hash this out in front of the intruders. "Just English. Just *Hamlet.*"

"Audie's great at Shakespeare," Chief Gregory said proudly. "Recite a sonnet, hon."

Audie dutifully recited a sonnet.

Max gave her a look. Specifically, the kind of look that said either *Who commands someone to recite a sonnet?* or *Who recites a sonnet on command?*

Mrs. Gregory sighed contently when Audie finished. "I'm telling you, sweetie, that voice of yours is meant for the stage. Broadway'd be lucky to have you!"

Audie made a murderous face. "Mom."

"I know, I know, football needs you more." She gave Max's mom a conspiratorial glance. "Can't blame a mom for trying, right?"

Max's mom gave a halfhearted smile.

The room went silent for a moment. Chief Gregory rustled the aluminum foil again.

"So, Max," Principal Gregory said in a jolly voice, in an effort to relieve the tension, "Audie tells me you're seeing somebody?"

"Mom!" Audie exclaimed, horrified. She looked at Max. "I didn't. I mean—I did, but it was *just speculation*—and it was divulged *in confidence*," she hissed at her mother.

Max wondered if it was wrong to pray for a meteor to strike the house. Not a big, Texas-size one; just a little speck, enough to rip a hole in the roof and land in the asparagus. "I'm not seeing anyone," he said hastily, and mostly to his mother. "Lore and I are just friends."

"Oh!" Principal Gregory made a cringing *oops* face at her daughter. "I didn't know!"

"Well," Chief Gregory said, giving Max a sly look, "who's to say what the future holds?"

"You *guys*." Audie dug her fingers into her scalp. "*Stop talking.*"

"Sorry!" Chief Gregory threw his hands up, innocent. "I'm just saying it'd be nice for Max to finally be able to go to the prom, don't you think? Every year, off you go with Wall, and every year, there's Max, waving the limo away with the rest of us—"

"Look at the time!" Audie burst in. She grabbed her father with one hand and her mother with the other and dragged them both to their feet. "We have to go. *Now.* Or we'll be late for the thing." She began to shove them toward the door. "Wonderful to see you, Mrs. Kilgore! Thanks for your hospitality! We'll show ourselves out! *I tried to stop them. I'm SO sorry,*" she whispered to Max on the way into the hall.

The Gregorys did their best to protest, but when Audie wanted her way, she got it. They shouted some more goodbyes and piled out of the house, and only when Max heard the door shut was he able to summon the courage to look at his mother.

Bad idea.

He flinched. He couldn't help it. Aside from the distress plain on her face, her skin looked more sallow and translucent than he'd remembered. And was her hair always that thin? He'd gone only one morning without checking in on her, but the changes in her appearance were obvious. Striking.

She looked, Max realized, undeniably sick.

She cupped her forehead with a shaking hand, her eyes swimming in misery. "That was mortifying, Max. How could you let them barge in like that? You know I hate visitors!"

"I know. I'm sorry."

"Why didn't you stop them? Where were you?"

She was really getting worked up. Max put his hands out. "Mom, calm down."

"No! I will *not* calm —"

She broke off with a gasp. Her white-knuckled hand clutched at her chest, and her eyes squeezed shut.

"Mom, what's wrong? Talk to me!"

"My chest." She opened her watering eyes and looked at him, pleading. "Get help."

WHERE THINGS HEAT UP

OUT-OF-BODY EXPERIENCES, Max had once read, didn't happen only when people encountered brushes with death. They could also occur in times of great trauma, and that's exactly what was happening to him. It was as if he were watching himself from above as the panic set in, experiencing what came next only in fragmented bits and pieces—

— scrambling for a phone, then realizing that all the lines in the house were still dead—

— grabbing the transplant beeper—but no, that only went one way—

— running outside, getting halfway to the Gregorys' house before remembering that they'd left for the evening—

— accosting a random man walking down the sidewalk, ordering him to call 911—

— riding in the ambulance, describing his mother's condition to the paramedics, holding her freezing hand—

— waiting in the emergency room lobby —

— waiting —

— waiting —

"Kilgore?"

Max stirred from the half-catatonic state into which he'd fallen, slumped against the hard plastic chair. "Yes," he said in a hoarse voice, scrambling to his feet. "That's me."

The emergency room doctor, a woman with graying hair whom Max half recognized from prior hospital visits, gave him a reassuring smile. "False alarm," she said, looking at her chart. "Your mother is fine. Well, that is to say, her condition hasn't worsened any. Her heart is still, er . . ."

"Fucked?" Max supplied.

The doctor gave him a sympathetic smile. "To put it bluntly. But it has not suffered any additional trauma."

Relief surged into Max's body like floodwater, dousing the flames of panic. He rubbed his hand over his mouth. "You said it was a false alarm? What does that mean?"

The doctor frowned. "We're not exactly sure what caused her sudden chest pains. These things happen on occasion. Could have been acid reflux, could have been . . ." A puzzled look came to her eyes. "Well, could have been any number of issues. The human body does strange things sometimes. But nothing came up on the scans, as far as I could tell, and any lingering pain has disappeared, your mother has reassured us."

"She's awake? She's okay?"

"Yes, and asking for you." She looked at the chart again. "I'd like to keep her overnight, run a couple more tests. And consult with her cardiologist—Dr. Ware, is it? But all in all, I see no reason why she shouldn't be able to go home tomorrow."

She escorted Max to his mother's room, where Max thanked her and rushed to his mother's side.

"Hey," he said. "How are you feeling?"

She gave him a weak smile. "Rotten as ever."

Max sank into the chair beside the bed and simply breathed for a minute.

But slowly, as the events of the previous evening came back to him, guilt crept up his neck. "Mom?" he said meekly. "I'm really sorry for what I said to you last night. I felt so bad after, and I wanted to apologize this morning, but I was ashamed, and—" He looked her in the eye. "You know I didn't mean any of that stuff, right?"

"Of course, hon," she said, but Max detected a false note in her tone. "We were both angry."

"Yeah, but—" He took her thin hand into his. "What I said about you being a burden—it's not true. I'm happy to take care of you. Really."

At this, her shoulders slumped. "I know, hon. You're such a good kid. But maybe . . ." Her gaze drifted out the window; then she shook her head. "Hey, wait a sec. Just because my body decides to have a freak-out doesn't mean you get off easy. What was Principal Gregory talking about? Why did you meet with her yesterday?"

He let out a hollow laugh. "It's nothing," he insisted, though even he had to admit he didn't sound very convincing. "She's just overreacting."

As is a mother's wont, she could sense something was up. "Hon? What's wrong?"

"Nothing, I—" A hard, stubborn lump was forming in Max's throat. He couldn't stop it. He had to swallow three times before he could talk. "I've just been having a little trouble at school lately. There's this, uh, bully. He's constantly making these demands and pushing me around, and . . ."

"Oh, Maxster." Her eyes filled with concern, and Max felt even worse. How could he have yelled at her like that? "Do you need me to call his parents?"

"No. No, I don't think that'll work."

"Well, did Principal Gregory talk to him? Was he in the meeting too? I can't imagine—"

"Mom, it's not a big deal. I can take care of it. Just wanted to, you know . . ." He gave her a forced smile. "Keep you in the loop."

She didn't look convinced. "Well . . . just avoid him as much as you can. Give him some space. Sooner or later he'll leave you alone—"

A timid knock came at the door, followed by an even more timid "Excuse me?"

In walked a dark-haired, kind-eyed man wearing a nice suit, shiny shoes, and a rakish fedora. "Sorry to interrupt, but the nurse said I could duck in for a second. I just wanted to make sure you were all right."

It took Max a few seconds, but he soon recognized him as the guy he'd stopped on the sidewalk, the one who'd called 911. "Oh, it's you," he said with a rush of gratitude. "Yeah, she's okay, sir. Thank you so much for—"

"I can thank him myself, Max," his mom said, sitting up a little more in bed. "Got a bum heart, but my mouth works just fine."

Dimples appeared in the man's face. "As does your smile."

For the first time in as long as Max could remember, color came to his mother's cheeks. "Well, thank you," she said. "And thank you for calling the ambulance. We don't usually do things that melodramatically, but something's wrong with our phones."

"Oh?" he said. "I happen to work for the phone company. I'd be happy to take a look at your lines, if you'd like."

She smiled. "And I'd be happy to have you over for dinner, as a thank-you."

Max's jaw dropped.

"How's six o'clock?" she added.

"Uh, Mom," Max said, searching for excuses. This felt very strange. "The pep rally's tomorrow at seven. I promised Audie I wouldn't be late."

"Oh, you won't be late," she said without looking at him, her eyes still melting into the man's. "Truly, I insist. I'll thaw my finest pan of frozen lasagna."

Max felt as though he'd fallen into another dimension. Three hours ago his mother was cowering, ashamed, in the presence of treasured friends. Then this complete stranger walks in and suddenly she's Miss Congeniality?

The man smiled again. "Well, how could I refuse an offer like that?"

Max's mom nodded firmly and held out her hand. "Wonderful. See you tomorrow, then, Mr. . . . ."

"Cobbler," he said. "Lloyd Cobbler."

They shook hands, and the man left. The whole encounter lasted less than a minute.

Max warily watched him go, then turned back to his mother. "What . . . was that all about?"

She pulled her hospital gown tighter around her, smiling shyly. "I don't know! He was just so nice, and he really helped us out, and I just—" She laughed and shook her head. "I don't know what came over me."

"Yeah," Max said, studying her closely. "Me neither."

They sat in silence.

"He was just so cute," she mused after a moment. "He even— okay, this is gonna sound nuts, but don't you think he looked a little like John Cusack?"

Max stiffened.

"I'll be right back," he said, rushing out of the room and into the hallway.

Lloyd was at the end of it, waiting for the elevator. Max grabbed him by the shoulders and whirled him around.

"Whoa!" Lloyd said with a look of shock. "What's wrong there, sport?"

"Burg!" Max hissed.

"Who?"

"Knock it off, I know it's you!"

"Sorry, champ, but I don't know what's—"

"Lloyd Cobbler? And you work for 'the phone company'? Which one?"

"The one . . . you have."

Max was so mad, he didn't know what to do with his hands, so he just let them free-wheel in the air. "How could you do this to me?"

The aura around Lloyd shimmered and disappeared, leaving nothing but Burg's lumpy, smiling form in its place. "Uh, easily. Cusack's one of my best impressions."

"No. NO. This date is not happening. I forbid it. Anything else you want, but *not this*."

Burg gave him a leering smile. "Forbid all you want, kid. And cancel the date if you must, but if you do, I can't promise your mom won't have any more false alarms."

Max stared at him, ice prickling through his veins. "*You* did that to her?"

The elevator doors opened. Burg sauntered in, turned around, and tipped his hat to Max. "See you tomorrow, Shove. Six o'clock sharp."

TORRENT

BURG IS BAD. BURG IS BAD. BURG IS BAD.

Those three little words ran through Max's head on a loop as he stalked back home. Of course he'd known all along that Burg was bad. But Lore was right — he'd vastly underestimated the degree of his badness. And now it was too late to turn back.

He burst into the kitchen, forgetting to prepare himself for the projectile cat obsessed with shredding his face. He practically batted Ruckus out of the air and headed straight for the dresser drawer in his bedroom where he kept most of his dinosaur research, away from all the dirty plaster gunk.

Wincing at the already-swollen scratches on his hands inflicted by Ruckus, he dug through his files until he found the one he was looking for: the email from Dr. Cavendish, the professor at Harvard. It was long — three printed-out pages of thinly veiled exuberance at the thought of someone finally showing interest in his work. It was clear that the guy had been a bit nutty. Max had read through the whole thing when it first arrived, but as it was clogged with so much scientific jargon he didn't understand, he hadn't been able to do much with it. At the time, he'd just downloaded the high-res photos and gotten to work on the replica of the specimen.

Now, though, he spread out the pages before him and held his breath. Maybe there was a chance that it would provide something he could work with, maybe not. Probably not a sentence that began with *Dear Max, Here's how to defeat a devil*, but perhaps something about the chemical makeup of the horn, a weakness at the cellular level.

But skimming it now, a wave of helplessness washed over him. The language was just as dense, just as hard to fathom as he'd remembered. And of what he did understand, none of it seemed particularly helpful: the specimen had not come from a particularly healthy organism (not surprising, given devils' terrible diets); it contained scant traces of the bacteria *Bartonella henselae* (also not surprising, given its proximity to the woods and all the ticks therein); and certain odd properties suggested that it might not have come from a dinosaur at all (definitely not surprising, for now-obvious reasons).

Max hurled the pages across the room in a confetti-like display of frustration. He'd never get anything from this. And it wasn't as if he could call the professor and grill him further, either. Pretty hard to get information out of a dead guy.

He melted into bed and stared at the ceiling, almost on the verge of tears. He hoped his mom was okay over at the hospital. He hoped Burg was safely tucked away inside his new home, not out causing trouble. He hoped Lore wasn't too mad at him.

I am lord of the idiots, he thought, holding his cramping stomach. *I never should have gone along with this. I should have quit while I was ahead, not gotten greedy. Now I've unleashed a juggernaut of unstoppable evil on my mom and my poor little town, and who knows how many people he's going to ruthlessly slaughter and it's all my fault and Mom probably won't live long enough for me to provide her weekly mozzarella allowance . . .*

He drifted off to a dreamless sleep.

• • •

The next morning, Max's woes continued. Because honestly, were there any rational explanations as to how he, who had gone two full school years without so much as breathing the same air as Lore Nedry, could have randomly run into her precisely when he was trying to avoid her the most?

He didn't know whether he was mad at her or in love with her, or some hopeless conglomeration of the two — but he'd felt it best to give it some time, think things through. But a closed-off staircase forced him to board one of the school elevators, a mode of transportation he'd always avoided, if only to escape awkward social situations exactly like the one he was about to encounter.

The crowd parted. Everyone got off at the first floor, revealing Lore's figure reclined against the elevator's back wall, her shirt a peppy display of cavorting rhinestone dolphins. "Oh my dammit," Max rasped, reflexively hitting the Door Open button, but the elevator gods cruelly dismissed his request and sealed him to his fate, a one-way trip to the bowels of the school basement with Lore and only Lore.

Max glared furiously at the glowing buttons. He did *not* have room in his brain for this.

"I've never taken the elevator before," Lore mused, her normal flatlined self.

Max resisted the urge to bang his head against the doors. Of *course* it was her first time, too. *What a magical set of coincidences!* he felt like shouting in hysterics. *Shakespeare himself could not have crafted a more star-crossed rendezvous!*

"Mhmph," he grumbled.

The elevator came to a lurching halt, and the doors opened. She must have been going to the art room, Max reasoned, because the only other room in the cellar was AV storage, and he highly doubted that she, too, had been sent on an errand to claim the school's sole working overhead projector.

"What are you doing?" Max asked when she kept following him.

She showed him a crumpled hall pass. "Mr. Campbell. Overhead projector."

It was too much. Max let out a booming, feverish laugh that echoed off the concrete walls of the stark basement and reverberated at triple the volume.

"I see," Lore said calmly, "you've cracked."

As swiftly as it had burst out of him, Max sucked the laugh back in. "Can you blame me?"

A hint of a whisper of something that might have been compassion snuck into Lore's expression. "No," she said, glancing at the near-identical hall pass in his hand. "I can't blame you."

Somewhere, a fan switched on in the innards of the basement ducts. A whooshing noise filled the air.

"I'm sorry about yesterday," Lore said.

"No, *I'm* sorry," Max said, wanting to shake her by the shoulders to convey how sorry he was. "*You* were absolutely right. Burg is —" He gave her a hopeless look. "Burg is evil."

He explained what had happened to his mother the night before. Lore's facial expression did not change even a little.

"So." She brought her eyes up to his. "What's the next phase of the plan?"

"Excuse me?"

"What did he ask us to do next?"

"Us? Wait, you still want to help me? I thought you hated my guts!"

"I hate all of you, not just your guts," Lore said. "But I also acknowledge that you are in a pretty big pickle, and since I have prior satanic experience, it would be morally wrong of me not to at least try and help you out of your pickle. Moral turpitude is what forced both of us into devil adoptions in the first place, so it's probably a good idea to cut back on that wherever possible, right?"

"Right. Lore, thank you so —"

"Thank-yous are nice and all, Max, but they don't do much in the realm of defense against the dark arts. So it's date night, right? What's your plan there?"

Max shrugged. "Sit in the hallway, armed with my heaviest femur — uh, baseball bat, and whack the snot out of him if he tries anything?"

"Or," Lore said, "we keep him in line the fun way."

"We?"

"You're a smart kid, Max, but you seem to have a great deal

of difficulty comprehending plural pronouns. Yes, *we*. I'll come over too. It'll be a" — and at the thought of this, even Lore looked uncomfortable — "a double date."

"Wow. I — thank you," he said yet again. "But . . . just to be clear, you need to know that I'm still doing all this in the hopes that he'll fix her. I mean, I'm also doing it to ensure that he doesn't *hurt* her again. And I'm trying to figure out whether that old devil horn fossil might show us some way to fend him off if he tries anything worse. But I'm still pushing for the cure. Otherwise all this will have been for nothing."

Lore frowned. She opened her mouth, then closed it again.

"I know it's a lot to ask," Max said. "But I'm just trying to be up-front about it. You've helped me so much, it's the least I can do. I don't want to lie to you."

Lore's eyes softened in the way one's eyes do when one is smiling without smiling.

"Throw in the overhead projector," she said, "and you've got yourself a deal."

• • •

If Max had to describe how he drifted through the rest of the day, it would be in one word: numbly. It was sort of similar to the drunken torture of the day before, but this time he was paralyzed more by fear than by the effects of a hangover. As time dragged on, he found that if one simply stopped caring about what happened to oneself, everything became a lot easier. In gym class, he let himself get pelted by dodge balls, blithely defecting from one side to the other, back and forth, back and forth. In English lit, he answered every question on his *Hamlet* quiz with "Denmark." When Audie tried to apologize for her parents' impromptu visit disaster, he just nodded and nodded, like the bobblehead cat, saying it was no big deal and he'd see her at the pep rally that evening. At lunch, he waved hello to Paul, who gave a knowing wave back. At least it seemed knowing; Paul didn't really have facial expressions like other people, so Max was left to assume.

He got a more concrete update after school, when Paul cornered him by the bike rack. "That's a really big hole up there on Ugly Hill!" he told Max.

Max cringed and looked around, but there was no one in earshot. "Yeah, I know. I told you."

"I've been filling it and filling it, but the thing doesn't seem to fill." Paul scratched his hair. "Like it's unfillable."

"Well, keep at it."

"Oh, I will! I'll fill that thing until it's filled!"

"Thanks, Paul. And you haven't seen anything strange up there, right?"

"Nope." Paul made one of his inscrutable faces. "Trust me, I'd recognize strange."

•   •   •

When Max got home, his mother was in the kitchen, looking as out of place as a bald eagle in a hair salon.

"Where do we keep the salad tongs?" she asked, digging through the gadget drawer. "Do we even have salad tongs?"

"I don't think we've ever had *salad,*" said Max. He put a wary hand on her shoulder. "Are you okay? Up and about like this?"

She put a hand on her hip and gave him a wry smile. "You know, it's the weirdest thing — or maybe it's all the drugs they pumped into me — but when I woke up in that hospital this morning, I felt better than I have in ages. Maybe that whole thing last night was just my heart jump-starting itself. Maybe I was touched" — she put a dainty, dramatic hand on her chest — "by an angel."

Max snickered. And deep down wondered if this was Burg's doing. Was the cure starting now that he'd secured a date with her? Was she getting better already?

Maybe, but best not to push his luck. "Why don't you relax and let me handle everything? You shouldn't be running around like this."

She waved him off and began pulling things out of the pantry. "If the doctor said I was healthy enough to take a cab ride home, I'm healthy enough to throw together an impromptu dinner."

"Yeah, about that," Max said. "I was wondering — would it be okay if Lore came too?"

She paused with a box of oatmeal in her hands. "The calculus project girl?"

"Yeah."

"I thought you were just friends."

"We are. But, um —" *I need her there for moral support. I need her because we're having dinner with a devil. I need her there in case Burg unhinges his jaw and tries to consume us all.*

His mom gave him a wise smile. "Ah," she said. "But you want to be more than friends."

"Um — sure." If that's what she wanted to think, fine.

And it wasn't exactly *un*true.

His mom sighed and studied the pile of food she'd lumped onto the counter: a pan of frozen lasagna, a box of spaghetti, a bottle of sauce, a can of olives, a jar of peanut butter, and two shriveled peaches. "This is . . . sad. Can I send you to the grocery store?"

Max didn't think he could risk showing his face at the Food Baron these days. "I'm sure this will be fine." He doubted that Burg could eat this stuff anyway, since none of it was stolen.

"But what if he's a picky eater?"

Max reached into the pantry and grabbed three cans of Pringles. "Here," he said, handing them to her. "Barbecue, ranch, and something called Screamin' Dill Pickle. Three well-balanced courses of hyperbolic paraboloids."

She crossed her arms. "Max. We can't serve the nice man potato chips for dinner."

"Oh, I assure you," Max said, "we can."

ADVENTURER IN SURREALISM

THE CROSS-GENERATIONAL HUMAN-DEVIL Double-Date Dinner: cute title, terrible idea.

All four of them sat awkwardly around the dining room table, a piece of furniture that had gone unused for as long as Max could remember. Dusty place mats had been unearthed from dusty kitchen drawers, silverware hastily washed and arranged in uncertain settings, and leering creepily at all of them was a Popsicle-stick turkey centerpiece that Max had made for Thanksgiving when he was six.

Max's mom had never exactly been blessed with a gift for entertaining.

"So," she said, nervously fingering the napkin in her lap, "where do you live, Lloyd?"

Burg-Lloyd took a sip of water and gave her a charming, irresistible smile. "On the other side of Main Street, not far from here. Just a hop, skip, and a jump home after a long day at the bank."

Max kicked him under the table.

"Phone company," Lloyd corrected himself.

Max grimaced. The Popsicle-stick turkey looked on.

"And you, Lore?" his mother continued, to Max's further dismay. He appreciated that his mother was trying to take an interest in Lore — really, he did — but when he saw how uncomfortable Lore was, he wanted to call a helicopter taxi and airlift the poor thing out of there.

"Um, I live over in Paradise Fields," Lore said timidly, picking at her soggy lasagna.

"Oh? I haven't heard of that. Is it a new housing development?"

Lore slouched deeper in her seat. "Yeah. Sure."

Max's mom struggled to come up with another way to engage her sullen guest, but finally she had the sense to abandon this pursuit. Her other guest, though, was even more puzzling. "Are you sure you don't want any lasagna, Lloyd?"

As expected, Burg-Lloyd had gone straight for the Pringles, arranging them in an artistic spiral on his plate and completely forgoing any of the dinner-type food on the table. "Nah, I'm good. So tell me, what did you do for a living before you started modeling full-time?"

Max's mom giggled and blushed. Max strangled his napkin.

"I was a nurse," she said.

"Mmm," he said, nodding. "That must have come in handy around Halloween."

She cocked her head. "How so?"

"Well, you're all ready to go with a slutty nurse costume —"

"Mom!" Max interrupted, frantic. "Why don't you show Burg — uh, Lloyd — some baby pictures of me?"

But she was lost in his Cusack-y eyes. "Oh, no one wants to see those, Max."

Max grunted. Years ago, she couldn't pull out those things fast enough. Now some guy waltzes in, bats a few eyelashes, and she forgets she ever had an adorable naked baby boy with a bubble-bath beard.

"Tell me, Lloyd," his mother said in a sultry tone Max had never heard before and never, *ever* wanted to hear again, "is there a Mrs. Cobbler?"

"Not since—" Burg-Lloyd paused, as if he were choking up. "Not since she passed a few years ago."

This earned a compassionate coo and a comforting pat to the hand, both of which Max watched with unbridled hatred. He shot a look at Lore, who was looking quite ill. He mouthed to her, "Help, please."

"Phones!" Lore shouted. Everyone jumped and stared at her. "Wasn't . . . he going to fix the phones?"

"Oh, yes," Max's mom said hesitantly, "but surely that can wait until after dinner—"

"I'm done!" said Max, tossing his napkin onto his plate.

"Me too," said Lore, doing the same.

Max's mom looked at Lloyd's plate, on which nothing remained but a couple of Pringle crumbs. "Well, look at that. I guess we *are* done . . ."

"Phone lines are out back," Max said, grabbing Lloyd by the elbow and dragging him away from the table.

"This is going really well," Burg whispered to him as they walked. "I'm gonna be your new daddy!"

With an infuriated grunt Max deposited him outside the kitchen. "Good luck, *phone genius*."

When he returned to the dining room, his mother smacked him on the head. "What is *wrong* with you?"

Max scowled and took her aside, out of earshot of Lore. "Mom, I don't like this guy. I don't think he's right for you."

She was scowling even harder than he was, but all at once, her face relaxed. "Oh, Max," she said, putting a hand on his arm. "Are you just uncomfortable with the idea of me dating?"

"No. No, that's not it —"

"Because that's totally understandable, honey, especially since I screwed the pooch so badly with your father. But it's been so long since I — "

"I know," Max interrupted, not wanting to hear the end of that sentence. "Just — not this guy. Anyone else."

"We barely know him, Max. At least let me socialize a little before you so summarily dismiss him." Her face brightened. "I have an idea. Why don't we split up for a little while — you and Lore can be alone, and Lloyd and I can be alone. To talk."

Max grunted. "Fine. But your overprotective son doesn't want you out of his sight."

She glanced at Lore. "And your responsible parent doesn't want you out of hers. You stay here in the dining room, and Lloyd and I will go sit on the couch."

"And we'll both agree not to" — he felt squeamish — "do . . . anything."

"Ew, Max. What do you take me for, a slutty nurse?"

The kitchen door opened and closed. "Phones are fixed!" Lloyd said, swooping back into the dining room.

Max scoffed, but he grabbed the cordless out of its base and hit the Talk button. A dial tone sounded from the earpiece. "It works," he said in amazement, retrieving the Beige Wonder from the junk drawer where he'd thrown it. It lit up, working and somehow fully charged.

"All in a day's work," Lloyd said, winking at Max's mom.

She giggled (again with the giggling!) and started backing up into the living room. "Care to come join me on the couch?"

Burg-Lloyd scampered over to the sofa and they sat down together, talking in hushed tones while Max plopped back into his seat at the dinner table. "Can you believe this?" he said to Lore.

"No," she said. "Especially not that your mother thought this lasagna would be edible. How long has this lived in your freezer?"

"Since the Cryogenian period." Max picked up his fork and absent-mindedly dug through the now-cold spaghetti. "Here, have some of this."

She started picking through the pasta. "You know what I wish we had for dessert? One of those cookie cakes. You know what I mean, those giant cookies with frosting that you can get at the bakery section of the grocery store?"

"Yeah. I've never had one, though."

"Really? Oh man, those things are so good," she said, slurping up a noodle. "My mom used to get them for my birthday. They must have been, like, the equivalent of forty cookies, but I didn't care. I ate the whole friggin' thing. I still would."

"That's adorable," Max said.

"What is?"

He reddened. "I don't know."

He really didn't. He just knew there was something cute about Little Lore eating a giant cookie, or maybe it was Now Lore not being embarrassed about eating a giant cookie, or maybe Lore was adorable even when there *wasn't* a giant cookie involved. Whatever the case, he'd just made a case for adorability. Out loud.

He dove back into the pasta. The Popsicle-stick turkey looked on.

"So what should we do while the kids have their fun?" Lore asked, graciously ignoring his dysfunction. "Watch a movie?"

"Nah," Max said. "I watch enough bad movies with my mom. I have a bunch of board games, though. Got any favorites?"

"Nope."

"What?"

"We don't own any."

Max gawked at her. "Not one? Not one single board game?"

"I think we have a deck of cards somewhere."

"Wow. Okay."

"Oh, how shocking, I don't share your interests. What about you? Got a stash of yarn at your house, any half-finished knitting projects?"

"No."

"Not one? Not one single ball of wool?"

"Okay, point taken." He scratched his chin. "So . . . we need to find a common hobby. How about video games?"

"Negative. Jigsaw puzzles?"

"Yuck. Model dinosaurs?"

"If you mention model dinosaurs one more time, I'm going to throw you in a time machine and feed you to an actual T. rex."

"T. rex doesn't want to be fed," Max said. "He wants to *hunt.* Can't just suppress sixty-five million years of gut instinct!"

Lore stared at him. Max goofily grinned back at her.

"It's a line from *Jurassic Park,*" he explained.

"Ah."

You know, Shovel, dinosaur movie quotations are not the panty-droppers that all your paleontology heroes would have you believe.

Max flinched, then glared into the living room. "Go away!" he hissed under his breath. When Lore looked startled, Max pointed at his temple. "Sorry, it's Burg. He's in my head."

"Oh. Weird. Well, tell him to vamoose."

Max laughed.

"What?" Lore asked, grinning.

"Vamoose. You're funny."

"Am I?" Lore looked dubious yet pleased.

"Yeah."

Ugh, **Adultery Cove** *is more stimulating than this,* Burg scoffed. *Here. Watch and learn.*

"I like jazz, myself," he heard Lloyd say. "In my opinion, nothing on earth is more sublime than a good saxophone solo."

His mom sighed in admiration.

"Stop it," Max whispered. *"Just stop it."*

Not gonna happen.

"I'm also a volunteer fireman," Burg droned on, "though sometimes that conflicts with my schedule of delivering toys to impoverished — argh!"

Burg had recoiled to the other side of the couch.

"What's wrong?" Max's mom asked as Ruckus nestled in her lap. She ran her hand down his furry orange back, prompting his butt to pop up in the air, his tail wiggling with pleasure. "You don't like cats?"

Max shouted, "That's a real deal breaker, right there!"

"Max!" his mom shot back. "Be nice!"

"No, no," Lloyd said with a dashing yet forced grin. "I *love* cats." He held out his hand and gave Ruckus's head an unconfident tap, as if he'd never petted an animal before. "Here, kitty. Here, Undisputed Lord and Master of the Universe."

Max's mom raised an eyebrow at him as Ruckus jumped away. "No need to stand on ceremony. 'Ruckus' is fine."

Burg shot her a smolder. "*You're* fine."

Max started to stand up, but Lore pulled him back into his seat. "Max, look at me." He turned away from the gurgling couple and looked at Lore. She pointed her fork at him. "Don't get mad. That is the key to this operation. When you get mad, you don't think straight, and you need to be thinking as straight as you can. So ignore him. Eat your pasta."

Incensed, Max stuck his fork into the noodles, and gradually, through the soothing power of carbs, began to calm down. Lore plunged her fork into the same bowl, spurring Max to hope for a *Lady and the Tramp* moment, where one single, strong, determined strand of spaghetti would venture its way into both their mouths, and as they slurped each end, their lips would get closer and closer —

"Ever seen *Lady and the Tramp*?" Lore asked.

Max chomped down on his strand in surprise, causing it to break and jettison a gob of sauce at his chin. "Yeah," he said, willing his voice not to squeak. "I was just thinking about that."

But Lore wasn't looking at him. She was looking at the floor, and her smile had disappeared. She put down her fork.

"Max," she started, then stopped, then started again. "If I tell you something, do you promise not to — well, I don't really know what I want you to promise. I guess I just don't want you to be weird about it."

"Uh, okay."

"I just mean — I've never talked about it much. You're really the only friend I've had since I transferred back here."

Max felt his heart crack like the Liberty Bell when he heard the word "friend" and all that it implied, but he nodded and did his best to look concerned. He *was* concerned. "Sure. You can tell me."

"It's about Noah," she said to the tablecloth. For a moment it seemed that she'd changed her mind, but then she started talking much faster than before. "Um, the thing I sort of left out about Noah was that even though he was my best friend, I was also sort of in love with him, and I was going to tell him, but then the devil thing happened and then he died, and I never got a chance to."

Max blinked. "Oh."

"That's —" A flush went up her cheeks. "That's the lie I told, the one that brought Verm up. Instead of telling Noah how I felt about him, I told him that the girl he'd been seeing was cheating on him. Which for all I know she *was*," she added defensively. "But he was heartbroken. And I felt awful."

She rubbed her eyes. "I don't really know why I'm telling you this, except — well, I guess it's because —"

"Hang on," Max said, unable to stop himself from glancing into the living room.

"Max, are you listening to me? I'm kinda trying to say something here."

Max nodded, but the bulk of his concentration was devoted to shooting glowers at Burg-Lloyd, who had put his hand on his mother's knee. "Yeah, totally —"

"Max!"

"What?" He whipped back around to Lore. "What is it?"

She screwed up her face, then stood up, her chair loudly scraping across the floor. "Nothing. Forget it."

With that, she stormed out through the kitchen. It happened so abruptly, Max didn't get up and run after her at first. By the time he stumbled over to the kitchen door, she was already flying down the street, hair streaming from beneath her bike helmet.

Max scratched his head. Confused and exhausted, he sat back down at the dining table. "What was that all about?" he mused aloud.

The Popsicle-stick turkey looked on.

• • •

For the next half hour Max sat in an armchair in the living room and watched as Lloyd and his mother canoodled. It was disgusting.

It was infuriating. And it made Max want to claw his own eyes out with salad tongs, if only they owned a pair.

Finally, *finally,* his mother did the one thing she could always be trusted to do: she fell asleep. With her head on Burg's shoulder.

Max snapped his fingers at Burg. "Leave," he said, pointing to the door.

"But she's sleeping!"

Max rushed forward, gently took his mother's head off of Burg's shoulder, and switched it to the arm of the couch. "There," he whispered, yanking Burg to his feet. "Out. Now."

Burg made his way toward the front door. "Should I leave my number?"

"Go!"

Once he was sure that Burg had reached the end of the driveway, Max shut the door and locked it. He'd collect on the cure later that night, after the pep rally. For now, all he wanted was for that guy to be out of the house.

And for his skin to stop crawling.

• • •

Despite his mother's insistence that he would be on time, Max was late for the pep rally. Though the sky was dark, the huge, powerful lights of O'Connell Stadium lit up the field. The air had cooled a little, but it was still pretty warm for a September evening; instead of hats and blankets, the crowd sported shorts and flip-flops and drank cold lemonade rather than steaming cups of hot cocoa.

Not that Max would have known what the norm was; he

couldn't remember the last time he'd been to a sporting event that didn't take place inside his Xbox. Way out of his element, he sat at the top of the wooden bleachers, next to the announcer's booth so that Audie could duck out every so often to chat. But between commemorating alumni, introducing the seemingly endless series of montages of the team's greatest moments on the Jumbotron, and the abundant raffle announcements, she didn't have much time to make the weird nerdy kid feel at home among the throngs of cheering sports fans. There wasn't enough time in the world, really.

Besides, her side of the conversation was peppered with so many comments like "Did your devil friend happen to mention if I'm in mortal danger today?" that Max finally had to insist, for the first time in his life, that he'd prefer to talk about football over anything else, especially devils.

"Ugh, fine," she relented, plopping down onto the wooden bench next to him. "Are you having fun, at least?"

Truth be told, he'd gotten distracted by a bird's nest under the bleachers for the past twenty minutes or so, but she didn't need to know that. "Absolutely."

Audie laughed and tousled his hair. "I'm glad you came. If you're half as miserable as you look, I take it to be a remarkable honor that you're sticking it out."

"I'm not miserable," he said. "I'm enjoying the great outdoors without the danger of a sunburn. I'm appreciating the statistics you've been announcing. And that lady over there took pity on me and gave me half of her giant pretzel."

Audie rolled her eyes. "There *are* cheerleaders, you know," she said, pointing at the bouncing pyramid of flexible girls. "It's your civic duty as a teenage boy to ogle them. Look at their short skirts! Behold their perky bosoms!"

Max furtively adjusted his pants. "Uh, Wall looked pretty good in that montage," he said, his voice cracking. "Knocked a lot of people down. Caused an impressive amount of spinal injuries, from where I was sitting."

"Yeah." Audie smiled, as if this talent for imposing pain were one of the things that made her fall in love with him. "Recruiters are coming to the homecoming game on Friday. From Alabama."

"Wave Power?"

"Roll Tide."

"Right."

"He's pretty nervous about it. It's kind of cute."

"I'm sure he'll crush more than enough vertebrae to impress them."

"That's the dream."

Someone inside the booth shouted for her to come back, so she jumped to her feet. "Gotta go. Have some *fun,* okay?"

"I'll try. There were some kids in the marching band who tripped and lost their hats. I'm on the edge of my seat waiting to see if they found new ones."

Audie made a dismissive noise and disappeared into the booth. Max tried to focus his attention back onto the field, but he was distracted by the image that had just flashed onto the Jumbotron: Edwin O'Connell's wrinkled, puffy face, along with a few words about his recent death, lifetime generosity, and the fact that the homecoming game would be played in his honor.

Max looked away.

In doing so, his nose caught a whiff of cotton candy. Nearby, a mother fed the fluffy pink stuff to her two small children, who were laughing and pinching their sticky fingers together.

A wave of urgency threatened to bowl Max over, knocking him clean off the top of the bleachers. His mom. The cure. What was he doing here? Why hadn't he insisted that Burg fix her right then and there in the living room? He'd been so focused on getting rid of him that he hadn't been thinking clearly.

It was enough to make him stand up to leave. He prepared to pound his way down the rickety bleachers when the cotton candy caught his eye again.

But it wasn't the kids who stopped him dead in his tracks. It was the tall, bearded, tracksuit-wearing gentleman they were feeding it to.

Max bounded across the bleachers so fast he practically became airborne. "Hi." He grabbed Burg by the shoulder, forcing a smile onto his face so as not to scare the kids. "There you are, Uncle, uh, Lance." Lance? Where did Lance come from? "I've been looking all over for you."

"This stuff is mind-blowing," Burg said, stuffing the fluff into his mouth. "Is it food or is it insulation? No need to choose!"

He licked his fingers, then grabbed another handful of cotton candy out of the little girl's hand. Her lips were starting to quiver.

"Where did your mommy go?" Max asked her.

The little girl pointed at the concession stand. "To get napkins."

"And ruin the sticky fun?" Burg cried. "That witless cow!"

Before the children could start crying, Max pushed Burg to the uppermost corner of the bleachers, as far away from other spectators as he could get. He threw him down onto the seat, the creaky sound screeching all the way down the length of the bench to a group of parents, who turned to stare.

"What are you doing here?" Max demanded in a low voice.

Burg slapped on an innocent face — a face, Max noticed, that was not red, but rather a normal human skin tone. "Rallying my pep."

Max spun around to make sure no one was watching them, then faced Burg again. "You have to go," he said. "Now."

"Why?"

"It's too dangerous!"

"I'll say. These bleachers are a million years old. I almost broke my neck getting up here."

Max had to bite his tongue to keep from saying that this would have been a wonderful development. "I mean it's too dangerous for other people. There are little kids!"

Burg waved a dismissive hand. "Ah, kids love me."

"Seriously. Go."

"Come on, let me stay," Burg said, kindly pretending that Max had any real control over whether he stayed or not. "I've never been to one of these before. And *Madden* doesn't replay any of the gruesome injuries. Would you really deprive me of the chance to witness a compound fracture on the Jumbotron?"

"I don't think they put those in the montages," Max said, but he thought about this for a moment. A happy Burg might be more apt to finally live up to his end of the bargain. Plus, how much damage could he do, all out in the open like this?

"Fine," he told Burg. "You can stay, as long as you don't remove your pants."

"Shovel, the pants go where they want."

"And as long as you agree with me that I did what you asked. I got you a date with my mom. Did I not?"

"You did."

"Would you agree that I have more than upheld my end of the bargain?"

"I would."

"Then will you *please* cure her already?"

"Can't," Burg said, popping more cotton candy into his mouth. "Our original bargain has been invalidated."

Everything around Max fell silent, or at least it felt that way. "What do you mean?"

"I mean the house. You haven't secured me a house."

"Yes, I did! You moved in! It's all yours!"

"Not anymore," Burg said with a smarmy grin. "The owner came home."

• • •

Max biked furiously up the streets of Honeybrook Hills, sweat pouring down his face. Lore pedaled alongside him. He'd immediately decided to call her, but since he didn't have her number, it was the Beige Wonder to the rescue. Because it was a phone designed for seniors, an operator had been standing by to connect him, though she did seem surprised to hear the voice of someone under the age of seventy.

"Hey," he said as they rode, still feeling weird about the semi-fight they'd had after dinner, "about earlier —"

"Forget it," she said, focusing straight ahead. "This is more important."

Yes, this. This awful thing that he could *not* believe was happening. They'd checked! They'd scoped out every room of that house, and Max was positive no one was living there. Granted, they'd been there only about twenty minutes before giving it the green light, but the beds hadn't been slept in, there was no food in the kitchen, no car in the garage . . .

Max tried the door. It was locked.

He knocked. No one answered.

He rang the bell. No one answered.

Lore, ready with Russell Crowebar, jammed it into the door and popped it open, re-splintering the wood they'd demolished the day before. They fanned out into the living room and looked around.

"Looks the same as yesterday," Lore said. "I'll check the kitchen."

Max rechecked the bathroom and the closets. "I don't get it," he said. "There's no one here. And the owner is *dead*. Why would Burg . . ."

Lore emerged from the kitchen holding a milk carton. "Okay,

so this is kind of weird," she was saying. "I opened the fridge and found some stuff in there. Did Burg go shopping?"

The milk carton exploded in her hand.

As the mist of airborne dairy cleared, their eyes flew to the foyer. Standing there was a man with salt-and-pepper hair, aiming a rifle.

ESCAPES INJURY

"DON'T MOVE," SAID THE MAN.

Max did his best to obey, though he was sure every organ in his body had simultaneously liquefied. He tried to look at Lore out of the corner of his eye, but all he could make out was that she was relatively still, not shaking the way he was.

"What are you doing here?" the man asked.

Max tried to speak, but his mouth was too dry to work properly. He tried a second time. "We're sorry, sir. We — um, we got lost, and —"

"We broke into your house," Lore said casually. "Sorry."

"I called the police," the man said. His aim was still trained on Max. "And you're going to sit down on that couch and wait until they get here."

Max speedily uttered, "Yes, sir," and scooted his butt onto the plaid sofa. Lore, on the other hand, yelled "Run!" and plowed right toward the man, knocking his rifle aside as she ducked around him and sprinted out the front door.

Max watched her go, baffled.

I have chosen poorly.

The man threw one last look at the open doorway through which Lore had made her escape, grunted, and aimed back at Max.

Furniture turned out to be just as terrifying as Max had initially thought. He clutched the fabric with clawed hands, trying to squeeze all his fear into it — yet he still had enough left over to ooze out of his sweaty pores. Blood pulsed through his ears in a steady hum. The man sat across from him in the rocking chair, gun pointing directly at Max's head.

"Sir, is there any chance you could just forget about this and let me go? I won't come back, I swear."

The man shrugged. "Already called the police."

Max slumped further into the sofa and looked at his hands, pale and lifeless beneath the stark black ash mark.

Ask him who he is, Burg thundered.

Max inhaled sharply.

"What's wrong?" the man asked, tensing up.

"Nothing," Max said evenly. "Just . . . scared."

The man relaxed. "You should be. Some hard jail time will do a punk like you good."

Max had been called many things in his life, but "punk" had never been one of them.

Go on, Burg urged. *Ask him. The house belonged to that old guy, right? Maybe you're just encroaching on something that this guy already stole.*

Max swallowed. Could that be possible?

"Beautiful home you've got here," he said. "I like all the" — he gestured helplessly at the glassy-eyed animal heads — "death."

The man snorted. "It's my father's place. *Was* my father's place."

Shit.

"Oh?" Max said shakily.

"All he left me was this goddamn eyesore of a cabin." The man spat onto the floor. "Soon as I sell it, I'm outta here."

"You're selling it?" Max repeated for Burg's benefit.

"What'd I just say? Listed it last week."

For a brief, insane moment, Max was hopeful. *He can sell it to me!* he thought. Then: *Wait, I don't have enough money to buy a mansion.* Then: *Even if I did, I'm only seventeen.* Then: *And it needs to be stolen, not bought.* And finally: *I really have to pee.*

Max started fiddling with his hands again, tearing up hangnails until he bled. He wondered if Lore was off getting help. But what could she say? That she'd broken into a house and the owner had the gall to call the police and report it? Lore wasn't that brainless.

Make a run for it, Shovel, Burg said with — was it concern in his voice?

Max faked a cough. "No way," he whispered in the midst of it.

What's he going to do, shoot you? No one's going to buy a house with bloodstained wood floors. He's just trying to scare you.

Max felt sick. Was Burg right? If the man had shot that carton of milk, he could have picked off both Max and Lore, real quick and easy. If he was going to shoot Max, he would have done it by now.

If he wanted to kill you, Burg confirmed, *he would have done it already.*

It still seemed like a risk. Max would have to be fast, graceful, and coordinated, three things he had never been all at the same time.

I'll talk you through it, Burg said. Max had never heard him sound this serious before. *Listen carefully. Stand up fast, like you just remembered you have to be somewhere.*

Max jumped to his feet, his body so wound up it couldn't sit still anymore. The man stood up just as fast. "What are you doing?" he demanded.

"Sorry," said Max. "Leg cramp."

Now inch slowly toward the deck. He should match your movements, like you're circling each other. You want him right in front of the fireplace—that's the best spot for him to be when you bolt, since the coffee table will be in his way.

Max inched another centimeter to his right.

The man inched another centimeter to *his* right.

Is he in front of the fireplace?

"Yeah," Max whispered.

There were a series of grinding noises.

Then a loud *twang.*

Max watched in shock as the large deer head above the fireplace came crashing to the floor, taking the man down with it.

For a moment, everything was still.

Then a groan sounded from the floor. Carefully stepping around the sofa, Max held his breath until the man came into view.

He was flat on his back. A dark stain slowly blossomed out from his chest, where Deerzilla's antlers had sunk in deep. His unseeing eyes stared up at the ceiling.

Oh God.

Max had never in his life been so utterly horrified. He trembled — his whole body shook, a chill furiously working its way up his spine, then back down again.

Did it work? Burg asked gleefully.

It took Max a few seconds to respond. "Did what work?"

My Scooby-Dooby booby trap!

Max just stood there, stunned. It was impossible. Then again — if Burg could telekinetically lift Max and throw him across the room, why *couldn't* he do something like this?

Did it land on his head? Burg asked. *Did he run around in a comical manner looking like a deer?*

Max balled his hands into fists. "No!" he yelled. "He got impaled by the antlers!"

Burg paused.

Well, damn, he said eventually. *That's not comical at all.*

"No! It's not!"

Don't worry, I'll pull it off next time. The hardware probably just needs a few tweaks.

With that, the buzzing in Max's head went silent.

Swallowing the strangled lump in his throat, Max knelt down and felt for the man's pulse. Nothing. He put his head on the floor, careful to avoid the pooling blood, and tried to look beneath the body. The antlers had skewered him all the way through, poking a hole in the bearskin rug.

Max got up again and began pacing.

Oh my God. Oh my God. He's dead. A man is dead and it's all my fault.

Well, the other side of his brain said, *not completely your fault.*

But Burg never would have been in this house if it weren't for me!

And, a smaller, meaner chunk of his brain said, *the police are coming. If all they find is you standing next to a dead body, that's kind of a dead giveaway, isn't it? And even if you leave, they'll know someone was here — the door was broken into, your fingerprints are all over the place . . .*

But, sniveled another, more sinister slice of his brain, *now Burg can stay in the house indefinitely. Everyone will think that this guy decided to keep the family home instead of selling it. That he took after his father and became a hermit, a solitary person who never went into town.*

Because the house, said the scabbiest, worst part of Max's brain, *is the key to it all.*

No house, no cure. No anything.

You need to keep this house at all costs.

HIDE THE BODY.

Max was breathing harder and harder now. He felt like he was going to pass out.

Police sirens sounded in the distance.

He had to make a decision.

For Mom, all parts of his brain chanted in unison, repeating it like a mantra as he dragged the corpse across the floor. *For Mom, for Mom, for Mom.*

SNARE

THE DOORBELL RANG.

Max unclutched his hands from the plaid sofa and stood up. He willed himself to stop shaking. Assured himself that the blood underneath his fingernails looked very plausibly like his own, as if it had come from a ripped hangnail.

He opened the front door, the very picture of calm.

Chief Gregory frowned. "Max? What are you doing here?"

Max let out a charming laugh. "Funny story, Chief G."

Max proceeded to weave a tale of great deceit. He didn't even have to try. The words flowed from him as if preordained, as if he'd memorized an Oscar-winning script. He'd run into Mr. O'Connell Jr. at the pep rally, see, and the man had asked him for help because the moving company he'd hired had fallen through. It seemed Mr. O'Connell Jr. had a bad back, so he offered Max a hundred bucks to help him move some of his father's things out of the house.

Chief Gregory chuckled. "Well, you've always had strong arms," he said. "All that digging."

"Seems it's finally paying off, sir," Max said humbly.

Chief Gregory's brows furrowed. "But the call we got from O'Connell was about someone breaking in. And the —" He twisted around in the rocking chair to look back at the foyer. "The doorjamb *is* chipped. Consistent with the use of a crowbar."

Max shrugged. "I don't know anything about that, sir. I've been upstairs hauling boxes."

Chief Gregory tapped his hat against the arm of the rocking chair. "Where'd you say Mr. O'Connell went again?"

"Hunting, he said." Max indicated the empty space on the gun rack. "I came down for a glass of water and he was getting ready to leave. To be honest, sir, he seemed a little . . . well, drunk. He rearranged all the carpets, for some reason." Max pointed at the series of Oriental rugs that now formed a trail to the deck, hiding the bloodstains. The bearskin rug, of course, was stashed in the basement, along with Deerzilla himself. "And when I went to pour myself a glass of water, I saw an empty whiskey bottle in the trash. It's still there, if you want to check," he said, neglecting to add that he'd flushed the actual whiskey down the toilet.

Chief Gregory looked at the open liquor cabinet, which Max had artfully arranged to look as if it had been raided. "Still," the chief said, drumming his fingers. "It's an oddly specific call."

"You don't think he was going to try to frame me for something, do you?" Max said, mock horror on his face. "Calling you about a trespasser, then here I am, and he's gone?"

"Why would he do a thing like that?"

"I don't know. Like I said, he was hammered."

Chief Gregory scratched his chin. "Odd ducks, the lot of them," he said. "Threw a lot of money at the town, but they weren't the nicest people around." He glanced at the gun rack. "Haven't seen the son in years. Hope he's not staying long."

"Long enough to make a fake call and waste the police's resources, sir."

The chief laughed, then stood up. "All right. We'll chalk this one up to idiocy and call it a night. I'll stop by tomorrow to check up on everything and give O'Connell a piece of my mind."

"He'd be lucky to have it, sir."

Chief Gregory walked to the sliding glass door, squinting outside. "On the other hand, maybe I should track him down. Out there at night, under the influence — could hurt himself."

Max held his breath. The man's body lay outside on the deck, not ten feet from where they stood.

Chief Gregory's phone rang.

He took a few steps away from the door and answered it. "Hello? Hey, sweetie. No, I'm on a call — actually, Max is here —"

He listened for another few seconds, during which Max could hear Audie bubbling excitedly on the other end; then he said, "Sure, I'll be there in a few." He hung up and looked at Max. "Audie wants me to pick her up from the pep rally, says she has some exciting news."

Thank you, Audie, Max thought. *Thank you thank you thank you.*

"Bah." Chief waved a hand and turned away from the window. "I'm sure O'Connell will be fine. What's he going to do, freeze to death? It's eighty degrees!"

Max smiled.

The chief put his hat back on. "You need a ride home?"

"That'd be great, sir."

They rode without speaking, with Jimi Hendrix generously stepping in to fill the silence. Chief Gregory spoke only once, at the turnoff for Honeybrook Hills. "Little late for a jog, buddy, don't you think?"

Max, who'd been staring at his knees, looked out the window. A bearded figure in a velour tracksuit ran past the car, in the direction of the O'Connell house. He gave Max a smile and a small wave.

Heading to the slammer, Shove? he piped into Max's head a moment later.

"No," Max whispered under his breath, covered by the music.

Oh. Was he disappointed? *Well, good. That means you can bring more snacks tomorrow. Hey, how'd that guy pull through?*

The road blurred through the windshield as the cruiser shot around a bend. "He's *dead*," Max said, barely moving his mouth. "You killed him!"

Oh. Oops.

Max didn't say anything. He just felt cold all over.

Oh, come on, Shove. I didn't mean to. It was an accident!

"You expect me to believe that?"

You believe what you want to believe, kid.

Max's vision swirled. He put his head against the glass of the window and stared outside, trying not to gag at the reeling landscape. "How did you even do it?" he asked, breathless.

He could almost hear Burg smiling.

Just knocked a few screws loose.

Outside the stadium, Audie skipped over to the passenger side of the car but stopped once she saw Max's ghostly face within.

"I'll explain later," he mouthed to her.

Confused, she continued on to the back seat and hopped in.

"Hey, baby!" Chief Gregory boomed as she put on her seat belt. "How did it go?"

"Amazing!" she bubbled. "Guess what, guess what: The recruiters who are in town for homecoming were there, and one of them wanted to talk to me about their sports journalism program! Like, they were *interested* in me! And it's *exactly* what I'm looking for!" She heaved a contented sigh. "I'm still floating. I can't believe it was real."

Chief Gregory let out a loud whoop while Max turned around in his seat. "That's great, Aud," he said, trying to conceal the hoarseness in his voice. "You deserve it."

Her bubbliness reduced itself to a simmer. "Where did *you* run off to?" she asked with a hint of irritation.

Before Max could answer, Chief Gregory said, "He was up at the old O'Connell place, helping move boxes around."

Max made a pleading face at her.

"Oh, right," she said carefully, holding Max's gaze. "You said . . . you were doing . . . that."

"Not sure you should keep hanging around that guy, Max," Chief Gregory said. "You don't want to get mixed up in something you can't get out of."

Max turned around in his seat and stared out the window, gripping the car door handle so tight his hand went numb.

Five minutes after he'd kissed his mother good night and three minutes after he threw up, Max heard a knock at the kitchen door.

He opened the door but didn't see anything. He took a few steps out into the yard, and there it was, that spiky, palm-tree hair. "Max?" Audie said, stepping out into the light of the back stoop.

"Hey, Aud." His voice seemed, to him, strangely cold.

"Why'd you come home with my dad?" she asked.

Her scared brown eyes looked up at him — they'd remained unchanged all those years, looking the same as they did when they were little kids chasing after fireflies.

His, he surmised, were much different now.

"Audie," he said, taking care not to let his voice tremble, "whatever happens from now on, I need you to not ask any questions. It's better if you don't know."

"Don't know what? What happened, Max?"

He squeezed his eyes shut. When he opened them again, he focused on the ground, only the ground. "Don't ask me that, okay? If you don't ask, I can't lie to you. And I'd have to lie. You can't know anything about what happened. It wouldn't be safe for you."

Resolving not to say another word, he pushed past her and went back into the house. Audie stayed behind, reeling.

"Max!" she called after him, stepping toward the house as he started to shut the door. "What — "

"I said don't ask!"

The door slammed in her face.

CAN'T STOMACH

OVER THE NEXT TEN HOURS, Max left his bed sixteen times.

The first time, he pulled down every blind in the house and locked all the doors.

The second time, he removed a pile of leftover lasagna from the refrigerator, snuck into his mother's room while she was sleeping, and placed it onto her nightstand.

The other fourteen times, he went to the bathroom to vomit.

• • •

"You okay, hoss? You look terrible."

"Terrible" didn't begin to describe the state Max found himself in when he rolled into school around eleven. "Repugnant" was far more accurate, or possibly "subhuman." Or whatever the word was that described the sort of person who hid another person's body under the tarp of a hot tub.

"I'm fine," Max said to Wall before he could ask any more

questions. Then he crumpled up the yellow principal's office slip sticking out of his locker. *Sorry, Principal Gregory,* he thought. *Not gonna happen.*

In English lit, he bent his head low and kept his eyes on his quiz, which was full of words that didn't make any sense, questions that danced before his eyes, and names that burned holes into the page. He didn't know who Horatio was. He didn't give a single distinct fuck who Horatio was.

He turned in the paper, blank except for his name at the top. When Mrs. Rizzo called after him to come back into the classroom, Max ignored her and kept walking past the other students, immersing himself in the crowd until he got to the safe haven of his locker, which he opened and put his head inside. He closed his eyes, savoring the cool, muted darkness.

Only five more periods to get through. He could do this.

• • •

"I can't do this," he said to the school nurse. "I need to go home."

She raised an eyebrow at him. "Hung over again, are we?"

"No, I'm not. I swear." He pulled his shirt out from his chest, puffing some air into it to fan his skin. "I'm sick. One of those twenty-four-hour bug things."

She put a hand to his forehead. "You don't have a fever."

"But I—" *I can't eat,* he wanted to say. *I can't sleep. I can't function.*

I'm dying, slowly and arduously, of guilt.

"You're fine," she said. "Get back to class."

• • •

Max now knew how a zombie lived (or unlived). It was as though someone had taken a belt sander to his senses, dulled them down until they were nothing but wisps of their former selves. He saw the world through dead eyes, barely feeling the touch of other students as they brushed past him in the hall, hearing everything around him as a vague, generic noise from which no distinct sounds could surface. In chemistry he stood over a flask of sulfuric acid for a full minute before the teacher shooed him away, astonished that he hadn't passed out from the fumes.

He was sure that every person with whom he came into contact could tell what he'd done, could read it on his face. Their stares would linger a little too long, or they'd pause and glance at his dirty fingernails, beneath which O'Connell's stubborn blood was still caked. But then they'd just smile and move on, and Max would exhale with relief.

At lunch he shoved food into his mouth without tasting it. He sat alone, facing the wall, at a table in the far corner of the cafeteria, where he'd arranged open textbooks around him to make it look as if he was studying too hard to be disturbed.

It worked. No one approached, not Principal Gregory, not Mrs. Rizzo, not even Paul. Max stared at the wall, chewing his cold, unmicrowaved Hot Pocket like cud.

"What happened?"

Max twisted his head. Lore had sat down at the table behind him, her back to his.

"No, don't look at me," she scolded. "Look straight ahead. Pretend we're not talking."

"We're *not* talking. I have nothing to say to you."

She paused. "Don't be like that. Don't blame me because I made a smart move and you didn't have the sense to follow."

Max gripped the edges of the table. He didn't know what his hands might do if he let them fly of their own accord. "You left me there," he said through clenched teeth. "*You left.*"

"I told you to run!" she hissed. "Why didn't you?"

"Because he was pointing a gun *at my head!*"

"Shh!"

"What was he doing there, anyway? I thought you said he was just going to let the house 'sit there and rot'!"

"Well, lesson learned: funeral home directors aren't the most reliable sources of information."

"*You think?*"

"Max, keep it down," Lore said, her voice dropping.

"No." Max swiveled around to look at her. "I am done taking instructions from you. It was a huge mistake to bring you into this. Every time you try to help, things get worse. *You're* the one who insisted we break into a house. *You're* the one who dragged us up to Honeybrook Hills —"

"*I'm* not the one who keeps treating my mother's life as a bargaining chip," she shot back, turning around to glare at him. "And *I* didn't dig up the bastard in the first place, so maybe you should stop wasting your time on blaming me and start using it to figure out how to save your own ass!"

Max angrily flared his nostrils as he breathed, but she was right. This was his responsibility, even if he'd brought her onboard. *Especially* since he'd brought her onboard.

"Tell me what happened," Lore said. "After I ran out. Which

I *am* sorry about. I hid in the garage and waited until the cop got there. I saw him leave with you. And since you were smiling and not wearing handcuffs, I knew you were okay."

"Okay?" Max let out a bitter laugh. "Guess you didn't hear the crash."

"Crash?" For once, she sounded concerned. "What crash?"

Max told her the whole story. He relayed it calmly, in a detached manner, as if reporting the news. As if it had happened to someone else and he'd merely heard about it secondhand or watched it on *CSI*.

Lore was quiet as he spoke, her eyes wide, terrified.

"He's . . . dead?" she said. "Burg killed him?"

"He says it was an accident," Max said. "But who knows if he's telling the truth. Not that it really matters at this point."

She was silent for a moment. When she spoke again, her voice was a whisper. "Do you believe me now, Max? That you're never going to beat him — that he's going to keep manipulating you and getting you into deeper trouble? Or are you still trying to figure out a way to keep that house, still pushing for that goddamn cure?"

He gave a helpless shrug. "What choice do I have? I've come this far."

For a moment Lore looked crestfallen. Then her face hardened, back to business. "Where's O'Connell now?"

"Still on the porch, I assume."

"Okay. I doubt Burg's going to do anything about it himself. So we go there after school. We —"

"I can't. I'm supposed to be back at work today."

"Then we skip out early again. We go to the house. We clean up the mess. We assess the situation. And we move on from there."

"Move on?" Max said. "How so?"

"Well, O'Connell left the city to come up here and sell the house, right? So it's not like anyone back home will notice that he went missing."

"But what are people going to think — that he had a change of heart and decided not to sell it?"

"Uh, yeah. That's exactly what they'll think."

Max frowned. "But he already listed the house. There have got to be real estate agents involved, people who will be trying to get into contact with him. What if —" A sudden fear rose in his chest. "What if they're showing the house to prospective buyers?"

Lore turned around, her back to his. "Like I said, we go there after school," she said. "And we clean up the mess."

• • •

As he'd ridden home in Chief Gregory's cruiser the night before, Max had sworn to himself that he was never going to set foot on that property again. And here he was, fifteen hours later, doing just that. With two bags of stolen snacks in tow.

Lore turned the doorknob — Chief Gregory had left it unlocked, "in case O'Connell returns too drunk to find his house keys" — and carefully stepped inside. Max followed her, putting every ounce of his concentration into not blacking out.

The house was just as he'd left it, with the exception of Deerzilla, which Burg had restored to its rightful position above the fireplace, proudly displaying its red-stained antlers. Max cowered under its watchful glare as he made his way inside. The bathroom door was slightly ajar, releasing the sounds of a streaming shower and of Burg's voice belting *"Gimme a BREAK! Gimme a BREAK! Break me off a piece of that KIT! KAT! BAR!"*

Lore crossed the living room to the sliding glass door and turned to face Max. "Aren't you coming?"

Max hugged himself tight and looked at the rugs, beneath which lay approximately three pints of Mr. O'Connell.

Lore opened her mouth to protest, but she reconsidered when she followed his gaze to the floor. "Okay," she said, stepping outside. "I'll take care of it."

Once she closed the door, Max busied himself with little things. He pulled the rifle out from where he'd stashed it under the couch and put it back on the gun rack. He swept up a few more crumbs of rubble that the deer had knocked off the fireplace; he'd thrown out the big chunks the previous night, before Chief Gregory got there. He headed into the kitchen, which, as Lore had attested, was enormous. A huge granite slab, probably mined from the family quarry, formed an island in the center. Wooden cabinets and pantries lined the walls, their surfaces stained the same shade as the deck. Two stainless steel refrigerators begged to be opened, but Max ignored them. Seeing the man's food would make him more human, more real, and Max needed to run in the opposite direction when it came to that stuff.

The man was no longer a man. The man was an obstacle that needed to be overcome. A problem that needed solving.

He looked through some drawers but found nothing other than silverware, kitchen gadgets, and old clipped recipes. No address book, no phone numbers. No family photos, for which Max was supremely grateful. Seemed the O'Connells, both Junior and Senior, weren't especially beloved. With luck, no one would miss them.

He leaned against the island and scratched his scalp. He'd showered after Chief Gregory had brought him home, scrubbing until his skin turned pink and raw, but it still felt as though insects were crawling all over him. His lips were chapped, bloody from his near-constant biting and picking.

Burg, meanwhile, had moved onto yet another verse of the Kit Kat jingle. *How many verses does that song have?* Max thought, annoyed. It wasn't fair. Why was Max the one who had to go through all of this, do all these deplorable things just so that asshole could have a nice house to lounge in and sing commercials?

Max sighed and accidentally looked at the refrigerator again. Reflexively, he started to look away, but he ended up doing a double take. Something sat in the upper-right corner, a magnet —

He heard the glass door slide open. "Max?"

"In here."

Lore entered the kitchen, face pale and hands shaking. She looked at Max, then quickly lowered her eyes and put her elbows on the counter. "It's done. I took care of it."

"You . . . took care of it? What'd you do?"

"I got rid of the body."

"How?"

Still not looking at him, she held her hand up above her head, then swooped it downward, as if miming a dive.

He gaped. "You threw him off the balcony?"

"Did you have a better plan? There aren't any beaches for him to wash up on. The water is super deep. Plus, it's a meromictic lake, remember? The water doesn't turn over, so there's almost no chance of any evidence surfacing. No one will find him."

"Well, great. Science saves the day."

But despite his sarcasm, Max had to admit it was a decent plan. Icky, unnerving, and disrespectful, but a decent plan.

"Next, we have to clean up the blood." Lore opened the cabinet beneath the sink and began to remove cleaning products.

"No, the blood can wait. Actually, Burg would probably prefer if we left it where it was."

She dropped the sponge in the sink and crossed her arms. "All right. Then what do *you* propose we do next?"

Max crossed to the refrigerator, unpeeled the magnet, and held it up for her to read. "We call Flossie Powell, Eastville's Most Recommended Real Estate Agent."

WENT BERSERK

THERE WAS SOME DEBATE about the best way to proceed.

"Can you do an impression?" Lore said. "Like, imitate his voice?"

"I don't know," said Max. "He didn't say much. I can't really remember what he sounded like."

This was patently untrue. Max remembered exactly what he sounded like. It was seared so deep into his memory, he doubted it would ever fade.

But he couldn't have done it convincingly; O'Connell's voice had been deep and gruff, while Max's was nothing of the sort. "What if we got one of those voice modulation things? Like serial killers use in movies to talk on the phone?"

"Yeah, 'cause the more associations we can draw between us and serial killers, the better," Lore said dryly. "And where would you propose we get such a thing? Is there a spy store on Main Street that's so covert I've never seen it?"

"No, but online . . ." Max frowned. "Would take too long. For-get it." He drummed his fingers on the granite. "Maybe I can just call as me. I already told Chief Gregory I was helping him out. It's plausible that he'd ask me to make some calls for him."

Lore twisted her mouth as she thought. "I don't know. Adults don't usually rely on kids to handle things like, you know, selling property."

"True." And Max knew it probably wasn't a good idea to recon-nect his presence back to the scene of the crime. Better to create as much distance as possible, take himself completely out of the equa-tion . . .

"Why," Lore asked, narrowing her eyes, "are you looking at me like that?"

Max picked up the kitchen phone and handed it to her. "How good are your acting skills?"

• • •

"Eastville Realty, Flossie Powell speaking."

Max and Lore huddled around the phone, which was set on speaker. It sat on the granite countertop, growling "Hello? Hello?" and glowing impatiently.

"Say something!" Max mouthed.

Lore grimaced. "She sounds like my chain-smoking grand-mother," she whispered.

"Talk!"

Lore steeled herself and pinched her nose between her fingers. "Yes, hello?" she chirped in a nasal, secretarial voice. "Is this Flossie Powell?"

"Yes. Can I help you?"

"Oh, Flossie, I *do* hope you can," Lore drawled in a thick accent. "This dang house is fixin' to be quite the hair in my buttermilk biscuit!"

Max covered the mouthpiece. "Why are you southern?"

"I don't know!" Lore whispered, flicking her hands. "It just came out that way!"

Flossie was too busy hacking up a cancerous-sounding lung to hear them. "Which house? Who's calling?"

"Oh, forgive me, this is . . ." Lore looked around the room, as did Max. Panicked, he pointed at the nearest cookbook, and Lore, equally panicked, read the title aloud. "Betty. Crocker."

Max ducked from the roll of paper towels she threw at him. "Sorry!" he mouthed.

"I'm Mr. O'Connell Jr.'s secretary," Lore continued.

"Oh, of course, of course!" A pause. "Mr. O'Connell has a secretary?"

Lore giggled, a high-pitched blubber. "That's me!"

Flossie grunted. "Didn't know Home Depot employees had it so good."

Lore slapped a hand over the phone. "He works at a Home *Depot?*"

"I didn't know that!" Max whispered. "I thought he was rich! But I guess . . . if they had a falling-out, then maybe his father cut him off . . ."

Lore scowled, practically blowing steam out of her nose. "Well," she droned back into the phone, "it's on a trial basis. If it goes well, maybe *all* the hardware professionals will get one!"

"Oh," Flossie grumbled. "I guess they do things different in the city, eh?"

"Indeed!"

"So, Miss . . . Crocker, what's this in regards to? Would Mr. O'Connell like to start showing the house? I can bring some prospective clients by this afternoon —"

"NO!" Lore screamed. She put her hands flat on the granite. "No. In fact, that's why I'm calling, in fact. It's the darnedest thing — Mr. O'Connell has decided not to sell the house!"

Now it was Flossie's turn to yell. "Why not?"

"Well, see, he's taken quite a shine to life in the countryside. The view, the privacy. *Loves* the lake." She cringed. "It's a far cry from the hustle and bustle of the city, and he's fallen noggin over toboggan in love!"

Flossie muttered something that sounded like "son of a bitch." "Are you sure?" she pressed. "Is he sure?"

"Yes. Positive."

"Son of a bitch!"

Flossie then went off on a hacking, emphysemic rant, during which Max made big sweeping motions with his arms.

Lore shrugged, lost.

Max made the motions bigger, adding little hops for emphasis.

Lore jutted out her jaw in irritation. "Three syllables. Sounds like —"

"Tell her not to bring anyone over here!" Max shouted.

"What was that?" Flossie demanded.

The finger Lore gave Max was delightfully incongruent with the honeyed voice that came out of her mouth. "Sorry, darlin'. Seems this house has a bit of a pest problem. I was just saying, please make absolutely sure to cancel any appointments with prospective buyers. If you bring anyone 'round here to look at the place, Mr. O'Connell will be mad as a wet hen, I can tell you that!"

"*He's* mad?" Flossie made a noise that might have been a cough. "That place could have sold for well over a million."

That certainly explained why O'Connell was willing to put his daddy issues aside to sell the thing. "Oh, but you can't put a price on happiness," Lore said into the phone, gritting her teeth. "Anyway, thank you for taking the time to speak with me. You've been a huge help. Mr. O'Connell sends his thanks as well."

"Yeah, well, he can thank me himself when he comes down to the office to terminate the contract."

Lore blinked. "The what now?"

"And to pay the withdrawal fee. Couple hundred dollars, give or take. Tell Mr. Fancypants to come on over, we can get it taken care of by the end of the day."

"Um —" Lore looked to Max for help, but he was plumb out. "Today's not great for Mr. O'Connell."

"Well, I'm leaving for Boca Raton tomorrow. How's the week after next?"

Max gave his head a vigorous shake. "It can't wait!"

"Then we'll . . . take care of it today!" Lore blurted, while Max chanted *Shit, shit, shit, shit* to himself.

"Splendid," Flossie hacked. "Goodbye."

"All right, darlin', thank you *so* much again for your — she hung up." Lore hit the End button on the phone and threw it into the kitchen sink. "Goddammit. Now what?"

Max leaned his back against the island, sank to the floor, and buried his head in his arms. "I don't know. Where are we going to get a couple hundred dollars, give or take?"

"I think our bigger problem is figuring out how to get a dead guy to terminate a contract. Any thoughts?"

There was a knock at the door.

They both froze, as if the visitor might go away if they stayed still long enough. Finally Lore broke free of the trance and went into the living room. "Uh, Max?" she said, peeking out the window. "It's the police?"

Smacking himself in the head, Max joined her at the window. "Shit, shit, shit! Chief Gregory said he was going to stop by. I completely forgot!"

She crossed her arms and glared at him. "You forgot."

"Sorry."

"See, this is one of those things you want to write down on a sheet of paper and *staple to your forehead.*"

"Just hide, okay?"

Lore ducked behind the curtain with a grunt while Max got into position at the door. He took a deep breath and opened it, trying not to react when a piece of wood splintered off the doorjamb, courtesy of Mr. Crowebar.

"Chief Gregory!" he exclaimed with all the jolliness of a shopping mall Santa Claus. "Hello!"

Chief Gregory raised an eyebrow. "Max? You're here again?"

"Yes, well, Mr. O'Connell offered me some more work, and I couldn't pass it up." He made a sad, pitiable face. "You know, because of my mother."

But the chief wasn't buying it. His eyebrow bent at a more skeptical angle. "Don't you already have a job at the gas station?"

"Yes," said Max, nodding vigorously. "Yes, I do."

"And don't you work there after school?"

"Right again!"

"Then why—"

"Because I'm paying him double," answered a gruff voice.

Mr. O'Connell, wet and naked except for a towel wrapped around his waist, appeared in the doorway. He propped his elbow up on the wood and sneered at Chief Gregory. "Afternoon, Officer. Anything I can help you with?"

Relief visibly washed over Chief Gregory's face. "Just following up on the call you made yesterday. When you reported an intruder?"

O'Connell held up his hands and let out a good-natured laugh. "Guilty as charged, Chief. It's a little embarrassing—turned out to be a really big squirrel. Got into the heating ducts, made all sorts of noise. Chased it up onto the roof, but it jumped into a tree and I lost it."

Chief Gregory looked at Max, who made a dubious face and a glug-glug motion at his lips.

The chief shot him a conspiratorial wink and looked back at O'Connell. "If you say so. Glad to hear all is well. You two have yourselves a good day."

"You too!" said O'Connell. "And hey, if you catch that squirrel, you give him the chair!"

All three of them laughed. With gusto.

Only once the door was shut and Chief Gregory was well out of hearing range did Max switch from laughing to yelling. "What was that?" he demanded.

"That was me saving your ass," said O'Connell, shimmering back to Burg. "For, like, the thousandth time."

Max began to sputter. He sputtered so much he couldn't get a word out, giving Lore time to emerge from behind the curtain and give him a good smack. "Hey. Snap out of it."

"But I—he—"

"Just provided us with the answer to our problems."

Max stared at her.

Lore pulled him aside. "Mr. O'Connell needs to go down to the real estate office and terminate the contract," she said slowly.

"Yeah . . ."

"And if Burg can do a serviceable impression of Mr. O'Connell . . ."

"Then Burg can terminate the contract!" Max exclaimed.

"Yes. Very good."

Max wiped his clammy hands on his jeans. "If he even agrees to do it."

He turned to make his proposal, but Burg had already begun to wander into the living room. Upon discovering the bags of snacks that Max had brought over, he gasped. "Cheetos! Fritos! Doritos! Tostitos!"

Max beheld his handiwork, a symphony of snack foods laid out across the coffee table like a buffet. "All yours." He looked at Lore, who wordlessly urged him forward. "If," he said, "you do one thing for me."

He explained what they'd learned from the phone call

with Flossie Powell, Eastville's Most Recommended Real Estate Agent.

"Oh sure, I know who that is," said Burg.

"How?"

"Her ad kept popping up on the Jumbotron at the pep rally. She seems highly recommended."

"Ah," Max said. "So here's where you come in. And trust me, I've looked at this thing from every angle, and if there were any other way to do it that didn't involve you—"

"Let me guess. You want me to assume the form of this O'Connell guy and go into the office in person to sign off the paperwork. Right?"

"Um . . . yes. That's exactly right."

"Sure, Shove. No problem."

"Really?" Max felt weird. This was too easy. "You literally have *no* problem with that?"

"Nope." Burg straightened up and popped open the bag of Fritos. "I mean, doesn't make a difference, really, whether I help you out or not. Either way works out in my favor."

"What do you mean?"

O'Connell's cell phone, which Max had placed on the fireplace mantel, rang.

"Oh good!" Burg said, picking up the phone. "More practice!"

Max froze. It could be anyone on the other line. Did O'Connell have a wife? Friends? *Kids?* "No, no, don't answer that—"

Burg closed his eyes and appeared to be centering himself. "Shh. I need to get into character."

"Burg, don't!"

"Yyyyello?" Burg crooned into the phone.

Max grabbed his hair and held it, motionless as Burg listened to the caller, frowning. "Mmm-hmm. Mmm-hmm. Well, it's not *my* fault the fertilizer didn't get restocked. You're the ones who can't move shit!" He put a hand over the phone and paused to laugh at his joke. "Get it?" he said to Max. "Shit?"

Max nodded.

Burg went back to the call. "Well, you can tell Fernandez to — no, as a matter of fact, I *won't* be in tomorrow — no, *you* go to hell! You can't fire me—I quit!"

He clapped the phone shut and tossed it to Max. "That's called acting. Check it."

"Good . . . job," Max said, letting out a huge exhale with each word. He couldn't even remember what normal breathing patterns felt like. Surely a chronic lung condition was in his future. "So can we go down to the real estate office right now?"

"Sure!"

Max looked at Lore and knew she was thinking the same thing he was: Burg seemed just a bit too eager to go out of his way to do something nice for them. But they were stuck between a rock and Boca Raton, and if Burg was willing to do this before Flossie left on vacation, they had to do it immediately.

"We'll have to swing by my house first," Max said. "I'll grab a few things — my Xbox, a few games, maybe some of my mom's jewelry — and then we can hit up the pawnshop."

Lore produced a set of keys. "I'll drive."

Max ogled. "Where did you get those?"

"They were hanging in the kitchen. Come on, let's go."

"You're going to steal the guy's car?"

"He's not using it! Besides, it's a friggin' Beamer. How many chances am I gonna get to drive one of those in my lifetime?"

Burg looked at him. "She makes an excellent point."

Max sighed. "All right. Everyone into the dead man's pillaged vehicle."

DRIVING AID

AS LORE CAUTIOUSLY STEERED THE CAR through the winding roads of Honeybrook Hills, Max turned around in his seat and looked at Burg.

"You should change into O'Connell," he said. "People might get suspicious if they see his car driving around without him."

Burg shrugged out of his own skin and into Mr. O'Connell's. Max was still freaked out by the process — one body blurring into the other so seamlessly he truly didn't see the transformation. When Burg was finished, from the neck up he looked exactly like the unfortunate heir.

From the neck down, he was still wearing that dreadful velour tracksuit.

"You can't wear that," Max said.

"Why not?" Burg hung his arms out in front of him. "It looks good on this body. Thinner. More svelte."

Max shivered. The gravelly voice was dead-on. He turned to Lore and muttered in her ear, "This. Is. A. Complete. Horror. Show."

"I know. Just get through it."

Max set his jaw. "You have to change," he told Burg.

"Into what?"

Max looked at Lore. "Do you remember what he was wearing?"

"Jeans," she said. "And heavy boots. And a plaid shirt."

"Oh, come on!" Burg said, exasperated. "Plaid?"

Max stared him down.

"Fine," he said, shimmering out of his tracksuit and into the requested outfit.

"Neat party trick," said Lore, watching in the rearview mirror. "Now do a gorilla suit."

"We do not have time for a gorilla suit," Max said. "It's already four o'clock. I don't want to miss Flossie."

"I do," Lore said. "That woman sounds like a yeti."

Burg frowned. "Really? I thought you said she was attractive."

"I never said that."

"Said it, implied it, same thing. With a name like Flossie, how could she be anything but a thong model?"

Max massaged his temples. This was going to be a challenging afternoon. "Okay, how about I owe you a bottle of tequila as a non-model bonus?"

"I accept this generous offer."

"Wonderful. Now, just to review, you're going to tell them you're Edwin O'Connell Jr. You're there to terminate your contract and pay any outstanding administrative fees. Make sure there is nothing left that they could possibly need to contact you about. We need a clean break. And that's *it*."

"Yeah, yeah. Now, this tequila you speak of — we talking gold, or aged, or —"

"I don't know. It's a surprise." Max whispered into Lore's ear again. "Are we making a huge mistake with this?"

"Yep," she said. "Off we go."

Max turned to face the road again, but he frowned as Lore pulled down a dusty road. "Where are you going?" he asked her. "This isn't the way to my house."

"I know," she said. "It's the way to mine."

"Why —"

"Stay here," she said, throwing the car into park and getting out. "I'll be right back."

Max threw a glance at the PAR DI E FI L sign. "You don't think leaving a BMW parked outside a trailer park isn't the least bit suspicious? Lore?"

She slammed the door and walked off.

"Geez," Burg said.

"Yeah." Max ran his hands through his hair.

"Chicks, am I right?"

"Please stop talking."

The Beige Wonder rang. Max frowned and flicked it open, praying that it wasn't his mom. "Hello?"

"Max, it's me," said an audibly distressed Audie. "*Please* tell me what's going on. Dad said you're back up at that house —"

"Sorry, wrong number," Max said, flipping the phone shut.

The car went awkwardly silent. Burg began to whistle the Kit Kat song again.

Moments later Lore returned from the trailer and got back into the car. "Um . . ." Her eyes went squirrelly. She dropped a ziplock bag onto Max's lap. "Here."

"What's this?"

"Four hundred dollars. For the administration fees. Take it."

Max stared open-mouthed as he pulled out crumpled-up bills of every denomination. "Where did you get this?"

"It's my life's savings. But it's not like I'm saving up for anything in particular, so . . ." She shrugged. "I want you to have it. Hopefully it's enough."

Max just sat there, the money limp in his hand. "Lore, I can't."

"You have to. I broke my piggy bank. No turning back."

He wanted to hug her. He wanted to kiss her. He wanted to proclaim his love through song and interpretive dance.

But all he did was sigh. "Thank you. So much."

"You're welcome," she said, starting the car. "*Now* we can go."

• • •

Next on the day's agenda: frosty chocolate milk shakes.

Lore and Max sat at a booth in Uncle Scallo's Diner, an Eastville legend that just so happened to be located directly across the street from the office of Flossie Powell, Eastville's Most Recommended Real Estate Agent.

Lore looked out the window. "Uncle Scallo still alive?" she asked, pointing at the ESTABLISHED 1904 sign.

"I don't know," said Max. "Never met him."

"Does his family still run this place?"

"Possibly."

"Or maybe there never *was* an Uncle Scallo."

"Can you be quiet?" For the millionth time he looked out the window at the office that Burg had entered roughly half an hour ago.

He glanced back at Lore. She looked hurt.

"I'm sorry," he said.

"No, you're cranky. Here, finish your milk shake."

Max shook his head. "I can't really handle dairy at a time like this."

She shrugged and stuck her straw into his glass. "Fine. More for me."

Max dropped his head into his hands. "Ugh, I'm sorry," he said. "Thank you for coming with me. Thank you for the money. Thank you for sticking with me through all of this. You didn't have to."

"No," she said between sips. "I didn't."

"But I'm —" Max licked his lips. "I'm glad you did. You're . . . a real pal."

Lore snorted. "A real pal?"

"Um. Yeah."

"Gee willickers, Max. What a swell thing to say."

Max gave a resigned shrug. There'd never be a time he wouldn't be hopelessly inadequate, and that was that. "You know what I mean."

She looked at him for a moment, something foreign in her eyes. "Max —"

"There he is!" Max pointed out the window. "He's done!" He reached into his pocket, but Lore threw some bills onto the counter before he could grab his wallet.

"This one's on me," she said. "Pal."

.   .   .

They waited for him in the Food Baron parking lot a few blocks away.

"How'd it go?" Max demanded when Burg got into the car.

"Easy. Just knocked a few screws loose, and done." He flung a piece of paper at them. "There's a copy of your contract, plus the termination, plus a receipt for two hundred and forty-six dollars in administrative fees."

"Where's the other hundred and fifty-four?" Lore asked.

"In my pocket. Care to fish it out?"

Lore made a face. Max leaned forward. "But — there were no problems? She didn't fight you on it? Or suspect anything was strange?"

"If she did, my wiles and charm were sufficient enough to distract her." Burg made a kissy face into the mirror.

"So she wasn't a yeti after all?" Lore asked.

"Nope. Stone-cold fox. See?" He handed them a business card with Flossie's photo.

A haggard old woman with a bowl haircut, giant sunglasses, and yellow teeth sneered back at them.

"Egh," Lore said.

"So no problems at all?" Max asked again. He wanted to be very clear on this.

"Nope! Flossie was a consummate professional."

"Huh," said Max. "Guess she really is Eastville's best agent."

Burg gave a thoughtful nod. "I'd recommend her."

• • •

The drive up to the O'Connell house was celebratory.

"And I get a free Beamer!" Burg shouted, bouncing in his seat. "Jackpot!"

When they pulled up the driveway, Burg jumped out of the car and ran into the house like an excited puppy. Lore approached the door, but Max lingered in the yard. "You coming?" she asked.

Max hugged himself. "I don't want to go in there again. This house and I are never, ever, ever getting back together."

Lore gave him an understanding look. She ducked into the house, then reemerged a moment later with Burg's ear pinched between her fingertips.

"Unhand me, woman!" Burg shouted.

"Not until you square up with Max," she said, letting him go.

Burg dug around in his pocket and gave Max the remaining hundred and fifty-four dollars, even more crumpled than before. "Here!"

"That belongs to her," Max said.

"No it doesn't," Lore said. "I gave it to you. Use it for any other 'administrative fees' that pop up. I don't want it."

Max shoved the money into his pocket and turned back to Burg. "The house is one hundred percent officially yours. And I one hundred percent officially set you up on a date with my mom. Which means there's only one thing left to do."

"Set up the sex dungeon?"

"Nope, that's all you. I'm referring to the terms of our deal."

"Dude, I'm already on it! One healthy mom, coming right up."

"No, not coming up! Now!"

"Shovel, healing is an *art*. It'll take me a day or so to get everything set up."

"What about that ficus? You fixed that instantly!"

Burg waved his hand. "Oh, I just replaced that with a different ficus."

Bewildered, Max looked at Lore. She shrugged.

Max jutted out his jaw. "You're not going to replace my mom with another *mom*, are you?"

"Of course not," Burg said. "Besides, I work better under pressure. Don't worry, Shove, I promise I'll do it."

Max stepped right up to Burg. "You're not messing around with me, are you?" he said, almost growling. "You *swear* you'll cure my mom?"

Burg smiled from horn to horn.

"I swear, Shove."

With that, he tore off into the house. Max watched as the door swung slowly shut behind him, not quite lining up with its broken frame.

"Hey," Lore said, poking him. "It's done. You did it."

"Yeah. I guess."

"Then loosen up. Celebrate a little."

He pointed a finger into the air and whirled it around. "Woo-hoo."

"Better, but not quite. Here."

She grabbed his hands and began to swing him around like two little kids on a playground. And then, magically, Max did start to loosen up, as if the Charlie Brown–like cloud of unease that had settled over him for the past week slowly began to dissipate. As they swung, he began to feel lighter, free. Euphoric. He didn't even care how ridiculous they looked. Mom was going to get better, he was going to get his life back, and all of this unpleasantness would soon be a distant memory.

He stopped whooping long enough to perk his ears to a strange sound: Lore was full-on laughing.

"Don't look at me like that," she said, giving him a shove after they stopped twirling.

"Careful, Lore. You're getting dangerously close to expressing a happy emotion."

She rolled her eyes. "Okay, I'm human. You got me."

Her face was inches away from his, and for a brief, terrifying moment, Max thought she was going to kiss him.

But then the front door banged open. "Hey," Burg said. "One more thing."

Max deflated. He and Lore had been having A Special Moment, and now it was most assuredly fizzled.

"What now?" Max asked, irritated.

"All my friends are gone."

"Your . . . friends?"

"Captain Morgan, Jim Beam, Johnny Walker, Jack Daniels. Who's the guy in the commercial who fights a sea monster to get his whiskey back?"

"Huh?"

"No, that's not it — Jameson! There were a bunch in the liquor cabinet, but they seem to have mysteriously disappeared."

Max sighed. "I poured out all the alcohol to make it look like O'Connell was drunk —"

"You POURED!" Burg cried. "OUT! The ALCOHOL?"

"Well, I'd get you some more, but I *have* to go to work today, even if it's only for a couple of hours. Or I'll get fired for real," Max said. "You'll have to make do without them for a night."

"MAKE! DO! WITHOUT?"

Max's hands were forming into claws again, but Lore stepped forward. "I'll take care of it," she told him. "I've got a bunch of stolen booze left over from when Verm was around. I don't have to work today. I'll just swing home — in the BMW of course — and come back here to drop them off."

Max frowned. "I don't want you coming back here alone."

She reddened. "Well, as gallant of you as that is, Max, I can take care of myself. But thanks for your concern."

"Well . . . okay," Max said, biting his lip. "Just come by my house after work so I can make sure nothing cataclysmic happened to you."

"Okay," Lore said. "It's a date."

Max and Burg watched her go, her ponytail swinging.

"You two banging yet?" Burg asked.

"Shut up."

SORT OF JERK

MAX'S TIRES SKIDDED ACROSS THE PAVEMENT. He dropped his bike against the side of the Gas Bag and ran inside without bothering to lock it up.

Stavroula was behind the counter, arms crossed, wearing an expression reminiscent of those in paintings of Vikings.

"You're late," she growled. "*Very* late."

Max looked at his watch. He was supposed to have arrived two hours ago. "Sorry, Roula —"

"No excuses!" she shouted, which was a relief to Max. Somehow he didn't think *I'd have been here sooner, but I had a little murder to tidy up* was an acceptable explanation. She pointed a finger into his face. "I forgive you for cat burgle. I give you days off. And still, you late." She shuffled back to her office, shaking her head. "You're on last straw! Five strikes and you out!"

Lack of baseball knowledge aside, Max took that cryptic last part to mean that he was very close to being unemployed. He put on his vest and took his place behind the counter, catching a glimpse of his old crossword puzzle stashed beneath the register. Something tugged inside him. What he'd give to have that be the most pressing issue of his day, how many puzzles he could solve in a shift.

Okay, technically he was still solving puzzles. They'd just increased in difficulty and proximity to corpses.

• • •

Max managed to duck into the Food Baron just before they closed. He made a big show of paying for each and every one of his items. He made a series of terrible jokes to the cashier so that she'd remember him. He even spoke to a manager about Paul in a last-ditch effort to get him his job back.

When he got home from work, he presented dinner to his mother as if it were as fancy as lobster topped with caviar stuffed with filet mignon.

"A supermarket rotisserie chicken complete with drippings!" she cried, clapping as he put the tray down.

"I didn't even bring utensils," said Max. "So you can tear into it with your bare hands, just the way you like it."

She'd already ripped off a drumstick. "Thanks, hon."

"How was your day?"

"Oh, fine." She sounded a little disappointed. "Lloyd said he'd call, but . . . whatever. Guess it was just a fun little fling."

"Like I said: you're too good for John Cusack."

She laughed and wiped a bit of gristle from her cheek. "What have you been up to today?"

Oh, just a little theft. Fraud. Some light murder.

"Same old, same old."

"You sure? You look tired." She squinted at him. "Is it that bully again? Still giving you a hard time?"

"A little." He ran a hand through his hair. "But I think I may have finally gotten rid of him."

She put the drumstick down, still concerned. "Seems like you're under so much stress lately, hon. School, work—and *I'm* certainly not helping matters." She wrung a napkin through her hands. "You know, I've been thinking . . . maybe it's time to get a little help. You're getting older, you've started dating, you'll be going off to college next year—"

Max let out a soft laugh. "We can't afford college, Mom."

"Well, you might get a scholarship. Either way, you're young and free and shouldn't have this huge responsibility bearing down on you all the time. It's not fair."

"It's not about what's fair—"

She took his hand and leaned in. "Max. This isn't the life I want for you."

He stared at her.

"I so appreciate what you've done for me," she said, squeezing his hand. "You have no idea how much I appreciate it—I thank God every day that I have you, and I'll keep doing so all the way to my grave. You're the best thing my life has produced. And I love you too much to see you cooped up here all the time, me selfishly keeping you all to myself."

"But—"

"No 'buts.' Before I left the hospital yesterday, one of my colleagues offered to set me up with a visiting nurse. She'll feed me and dress me and get a good look at my sad, bony ass, and it'll be miserable and embarrassing, but I've been mulling it over, and I think it's what I want. Really."

"But we can't afford a nurse."

"She made a good offer. I think we can squeeze by."

Max shrank. "I don't know what to say."

"Don't say anything. Do you have any idea how happy I am that you turned out the way you did? I didn't know the first thing about how to raise a child, but I guess somewhere along the way I must have done something right."

O'Connell's pale, blank face swam across Max's vision, the blood on the floor, so much blood . . .

Max shuddered, then stood to cover it up. "Thanks, Mom."

Maybe it'll all be worth it, he thought as he watched her crinkling eyes. *Maybe all these awful things I've done really will add up to something extraordinary.*

"And hey," he said with an easy smile, "you never know. You might get better. Might bounce back completely. Maybe we won't need that nurse after all."

She gave him a placating smile. "Maybe, hon. You never know."

Max heard a quiet, secret knock at the kitchen door. He kissed his mother good night and told his heart not to thump out of his chest when he opened it.

It thumped anyway. "Oh, good," he said with a melodramatic sigh of relief that was, in truth, not that exaggerated at all. "You're alive."

"So it seems," said Lore.

He let her into the house. "Was he satisfied with the booze you brought?"

"For now. We'll see how long it lasts. Why are you grinning like that?"

He led her into the dining room. On the table, beside the DVD of *West Side Story* that had arrived in the mailbox that afternoon, sat a flat, round item covered with a dishtowel. "I got you something from the Food Baron."

"Is it stolen?"

"Nope. Paid in full."

He lifted the towel.

"Whoa!" Lore said, her eyes growing as round as the platter. "A cookie cake!"

"Yeah. As a thank-you."

She squinted at the frosting. "Why does it have footballs on it? Why does it say 'Go Team Go'?"

"Because it was the only one left that wasn't covered in flowers. And because the cake decorator had already gone home for the night, so I couldn't get anyone to write 'For Lore, almighty Satan warrior.'"

She smirked. "Can we eat it in the whale?"

Max almost kissed her right then and there. "I — yes. Of course."

They went outside and lowered themselves, then the cake, inside. Light from the full moon streamed in through the open porthole.

"Crap," Max said. "I didn't grab silverware. Should I go get some?"

"No. I forbid you."

"Then how do we eat this thing?"

"Like this." Lore dug her hand into the gooey, half-baked dough, rolled it into a disgusting-looking ball, and held it up in the air. Max did the same, making a mental note to encourage more Mom-Lore bonding, since they seemed to share a fondness for utensil-free eating.

They clinked the blobs together as if they were champagne flutes. "Go team go," Lore said.

She shoved the abomination into her mouth, then proceeded to moan with delight as she chewed. Max took a more modest bite, but had the same reaction. "Oh, man. That *is* good."

"Glad you agree."

"Hey, does loving cookie cake count as a common interest?" Max asked.

"I don't think so. I think it just means we're both pigs."

"Okay. Well, we should keep looking, then. I still think you should give model dinosaurs a try."

"You are aware of my feelings on model dinosaurs. Want another glob?"

"Yes."

Lore scooped up another clawful and plopped it into his hand. "Now, here's an important question: You're committed to finishing this whole cake, right?"

"Absolutely. We deserve every single calorie."

She snorted. "Like you have to worry about calories."

"And you do?"

"Uh, yeah. Duh."

Max's heart thumped double time. Dead Noah or not, he knew what he was going to say. He was powerless to stop it. "Well," he said carefully, "I think you're perfect."

Lore was quiet for a moment. The cicadas swelled and faded, swelled and faded.

"You know the moon?" she said out of nowhere.

"The . . . one in the sky?"

"That's the one."

"I've heard of it, yeah."

"So . . . like . . ." She waved her hands around, casting about for the right words. "You think you know the moon pretty well, right? It's big and white and circular, or sometimes half or crescent. You know?"

"Sure."

"Well, there was this one time—" She paused to grab more cookie off the plate. "I went with Noah's family on vacation to Cape Cod a couple of years ago. And the town we were staying in had fireworks on the beach every Friday night. So we went down to the beach and sat on our blanket, and even though it was summer, it was cold at night, you know? So we were huddled all together on the blanket, and I was digging my feet into the sand, and we were waiting for the fireworks to start."

She took a big bite of cookie, so her mouth was full as she spoke. "But instead of looking at the spot on the beach where the fireworks were set up, everyone started to look out at the water. Because the ocean was starting to . . . glow. A weird red color, just on the horizon. There were some clouds, so it was hazy. But then it got stronger and brighter. It looked like a nuclear bomb had gone off and we were witnessing a genuine mushroom cloud, and then, just when it looked like it couldn't get any brighter, a light pierced through the clouds. It was the moon. A full moon, rising right up over the ocean."

Her bit of cookie was gone, but this time she didn't reach for more. "And like I said — I thought I knew the moon. But turns out, I didn't know the moon at all. I'd never met this version of the moon. Because this one was red, then orange, then gold — this furious, unstoppable gold that was pissed it never got to be seen. And it was *huge.* You know how sometimes you see the sun at sunset and it seems really big? The moon was even bigger than that. It was enormous. It lit up the beach. And everyone just sat there in awe. The kids stopped waving their sparklers. The adults stopped drinking their wine. Everyone stopped to watch the moon."

Max's chest got tight. He loved her so much right then, he couldn't trust himself to speak.

"Max?"

"Yeah?"

"I like you."

"I like you too."

"No, I mean — well, in the words of your average seven-year-old, I *like you* like you."

Max's heart thumped triple time. "Oh."

"And you like me like me too, right?"

Max swallowed. His throat was dry.

"Yes," he said. "How could you tell?"

"It's kinda obvious."

"Oh. Sorry."

"Don't apologize."

"Okay. Sorry."

"So I like you and you like me."

"Correct."

"But I still really miss Noah."

"I know."

"So we'll have to take this very slow."

Max felt lightheaded. "Okay," he said.

Hold her hand, Burg had said.

So he did, slipping his gooey fingers into her gooey fingers.

"How's that?" he asked.

A pause.

"Perfect."

CUT SHORT

FOR THE FIRST TIME IN A WEEK Max got a full night's sleep. He woke up feeling as fresh as a daisy (the friendliest flower, according to *You've Got Mail*). Everything seemed to exude a rosy glow; his teeth seemed whiter, his nose seemed smaller, even his hair seemed to resemble a hat that *didn't* have a brim.

He buoyantly skipped into his mother's room to wish her a good day, though he had a strong inkling that she'd be having one regardless. "How do you feel?" he asked, way too earnestly.

She gave him an odd look. "Uh, fine. What's with you?"

"Nothing," he said, grinning like a hyena. "Just checking in." His fingers sprang out to her wrist. "How's that pulse? Feeling any stronger?"

"Doubt it. Same old pitter-patter of a three-legged kitten it's always been."

"Well," he said, winking, "who knows? Miracles can happen."

She frowned. "Max, did you eat some expired meat?"

After assuring her that he was perfectly sane, he biked to school. And so began the Great Apology Tour of First Semester, wherein Max proceeded to beg amnesty from every teacher who had scolded him, berated him, or flunked him over the past week.

"I've been having trouble at home," he said, which technically wasn't untrue.

In most cases his plaintive tone — plus the masterful way he was able to blink back watering eyes — earned him a "Well, just do better next time" or a "I'll let it go just this once" or, the most painful, "I'm disappointed in you, Max. Don't let it happen again." He'd thank them profusely and sit upright at his desk, taking copious notes and asking thoughtful questions. He attended every one of his classes on time, with the utmost studious aptitude. He raised his hand so much some teachers politely asked him to stop.

He even poked his head into Principal Gregory's office to personally apologize for blowing her off. By the end of the day, he was convinced he'd undone most of the damage Burg's presence had wrought.

The only snag was Mrs. Rizzo. Once the room had cleared after class, he approached her podium and formed his face into the expression he'd come to think of as the Heartbreaker.

"Mrs. Rizzo, can I talk to you for a sec?" he asked, biting the inside of his lip until a tear sprang to his eye. "It's about the past week. I've been having some trouble at home, and —"

"Spare me."

"W-what?"

She crossed her arms, unmoved. "I've been a teacher for thirty-three years, Mr. Kilgore. I know your kind. The innocent, meek students who think that a solid track record is enough to fall back on once senioritis hits. Or who think that they can make up sob stories, spinning tales of woe and sorrow and five or six dead grandmothers. Or maybe you're one of the ones who think that teachers are just plain idiots."

She vaulted herself forward and towered over him. Max had never realized how tall she was.

"I'm not an idiot, Mr. Kilgore. I will not be changing your grades. You made some unfortunate choices. No matter the circumstances, you made them. And now you will have to live with the consequences of your actions."

Max's hands started to shake. She was only talking about grades, of course. But her words resounded much deeper within him. The unease that had so lightly flitted away began to creep back in, more insidious this time, seeking out newer and smaller capillaries in which to hide.

"There will be a final test on *Hamlet* next Monday," she said, going back to her desk. "I suggest you study."

"I will," Max said. "I'll be better now, I promise."

But his words felt hollow.

•   •   •

He delivered the same song and dance to Stavroula when he got to work after school, but she'd just chased off another gas-and-dasher and wasn't in the mood.

"I'm not in the mood," she huffed. "Probably same hooligans who steal snacks, throw off inventory. Headaches and scoundrels! Why I even bother?"

Max felt bad. Bad enough to slip some of the change from Flossie's administrative fees into the cash register when she wasn't looking.

"Well, *I* think you look ravishing today," he told her, gesturing at her hair, which seemed poofier than normal.

"Is fake," she said, but Max could tell she was pleased. "Something called weave. They say the kids wear it, but I no spring chicken! Bah." She waved her hand and disappeared into the office.

That afternoon was one of the busiest shifts Max had ever worked at the Gas Bag, with an endless stream of customers coming in to stock up on supplies for the homecoming game and the tailgating parties that would precede it. By the time the sun went down, they'd already sold out of hot dog buns, frozen hamburger patties, and red plastic cups.

It was so crowded Max almost missed Paul's braces as they poked their way up to the counter. "Paulie boy!" he cried. "How's it going?"

"Good." Paul gave him an odd wink. "The turkey's in the bag."

"Huh?"

"The eagle is in the nest."

"Paul. In English. Without bird metaphors."

Paul stared at him. "Uh, the hole. I filled it all up."

Max could have kissed him. "You have no idea what this means to me, Paul. Seriously. Here —" He dug through his pockets and pulled out more of Lore's money. "Here's a hundred bucks. That seem fair to you?"

Paul gawked at the bills on the counter, but as his mouth was in a constant state of gawking, it was difficult to tell the difference. "Um, *yeah*."

Max was in such a good mood, he reached out and arranged the bills into a little dinosaur-shaped wad. "Here," he said. "To the Super Fossil."

"To the Super Fossil!"

And Max, no longer able to contain his gratitude, lunged over the counter to hug him.

• • •

Not five minutes after that, Lloyd Cobbler walked in.

"Oh! Hey!" Burg-Lloyd said as Max stared at him. "Didn't realize you still worked here. Shouldn't you have gotten fired, like, days ago?"

Max's previous jubilation all but disappeared. "What are you doing here?"

"Just came to load up on some supplies. Look the other way, would you?"

Reluctantly, Max pretended to bend down to tie his shoe. When he straightened up, all the Slim Jims were gone.

Max concentrated hard on not looking up at the security camera. "How's the house?"

"EPIC. You would not *believe* what that hot tub can do. I already had to clean out the filters twice."

"Well, there's a lot of information I didn't need."

They stood awkwardly for a moment.

"So I guess this is goodbye, huh?" Burg said.

Max wanted to grab him by the throat and pull him in close, but he settled for giving him a dark look. "Except my mom's heart still isn't fixed," he spat. "When are you going to pencil that in?"

"*Soon,* I promise. Did I forget to mention that devils are notorious procrastinators?"

"Burg, I swear to God —"

"Kid, don't sweat it. I'm a man of my word! You helped me out, and . . ." He trailed off and looked at the floor, his voice taking on a more contemplative tone. "You really did help me out."

He rubbed his sculpted chin. "I want you to know that I'm grateful for all the things you did for me. I know they weren't easy for a simple-minded mortal like you, and sometimes I wish things could be different . . ." He looked out the window, then back at Max. "But they aren't. So thank you. Is what I'm trying to say."

"You're welcome. Just fix my mom, all right?"

Burg smiled harder. "Already on it." Energized, he exited the store, dropping a couple of Slim Jims.

Max watched him go, then picked up his old friend the crossword puzzle book.

He finished ten in three hours, a new record.

•   •   •

He biked home through empty streets. He didn't even see another human being, except for Mario the pizza man. It seemed as if every single citizen in Eastville was at the game, crammed to the gills inside O'Connell Stadium.

Except, of course, for the Kilgores. "Hey, Mom?" he asked, pushing her bedroom door open. "Do you feel pretty?"

"Oh so pretty!" she cried, screeching when he held up the *West Side Story* DVD.

Max opened the pizza box, and she sniffed after it like a coke fiend. "Ooh, that prancing bucktoothed guy is gonna die so hard. *So hard.* How opposed are you to rewinding it and replaying it so we may enjoy his demise in a never-ending loop?"

Max snickered. "Whatever you want, Mom."

The only thing Max's mom loved more than mocking romantic movies was mocking romantic movie musicals. Jazz hands really got her goat.

"*I* think she looks like a guppy," she said as they watched. "And he's a singing woodland creature with a bad Jersey accent."

When Tony finally bit the big one, they both started laughing so hard they cried. Or crying so hard they laughed. It was somewhat difficult, this time, to figure out which was which.

Exhausted from too much chuckle-sobbing and pizza, Max sank back into the armchair and watched, amused, as his mom had her rewinding fun. "Alive chipmunk boy, dead chipmunk boy," she chanted. "Alive chipmunk boy, dead chipmunk boy."

Max smiled and let his drowsy head fall to the side. Just before he fell asleep, his eyes landed on the glittery plastic cat, the one that had started this whole mess. It smiled back at him, still hideous.

•　•　•

The night before, Max had enjoyed a deep, dreamless slumber. He'd completely blacked out, dead to the world, waking up hours later with no recollection of what had transpired in his subconscious, if anything at all. Blissfully unmemorable.

The same could not be said of Friday night.

He tossed and turned, hurling his body around the small armchair, yet unable to fully wake up. He was fuzzily aware of his surroundings, part of him insistent that he should get up and go to his own room, but the nightmares kept pulling him back under: swirling blurs of the bloodstained floor — of O'Connell's bloated, waterlogged face looking up from the bottom of the lake, screaming futilely for help — of gunshots pounding, exploding, relentless — police sirens, a whole squadron arriving to arrest Max — Lore being led away in handcuffs — Max shouting for her to be let go — Burg's grinning face, burning red as fire — more sirens — more sirens —

Max woke up in a haze, bewildered. That noise — it was real. Continuous, shrill, steady. Loud. Max looked down.

The transplant beeper.

"Mom," Max said in a shaky voice. "Wake up."

OK PLACE

THE AMBULANCE ARRIVED AT THE HOSPITAL in a dazzling array of lights. "I can't believe it," his mother kept saying as the attendant wheeled her through the emergency room doors. "I can't believe it."

"Mom. Believe it already." Max squeezed her hand as they bustled through the halls, his shoulder bumping into people left and right. He was so focused on her, he became completely ignorant of his surroundings; for some horrible, irrational reason, he felt as if she'd die if he took his eyes off her.

Stupid movie, he thought. *Stupid chipmunk Tony.*

They arrived at the cardiac ward and were whisked into something called a family room, a big, welcoming den with ample seating that Max, being a very small family indeed, would never be able to fill. The transplant coordinator plunked down a stack of paperwork on a table in front of Max's mother and instructed her to start filling it out. The doctor would be in shortly to go over the procedure.

Max's mother sighed. "This might take a while, hon," she told him. "Why don't you run down to the cafeteria and get a snack or something?"

"No, I'm fine," Max said, taking a seat across from her. He was so nervous, anything he ate would get puked back up anyway.

It seemed like hours later, but the doctor finally arrived to explain everything, going into what Max thought was way too much detail about the rib cracking and the heart stopping and—

At some point he stopped listening, retreating into himself and wondering how on earth they'd arrived at this moment. Was this Burg's work? It had to be. The timing was too perfect for it to be a coincidence. But it hadn't gone exactly the way Max had anticipated. He'd expected . . . well, he didn't really know what he'd expected. Maybe he thought the heart would simply heal itself? It sounded silly, now that he thought about it. And Burg *had* said that he'd only replaced that ficus plant, not revived it—

"Max?" his mother was saying. "Are you coming?"

He snapped back to attention. "Coming where?"

"We're taking her into prep," the doctor said. "You can either come with us as far as the OR and hang out in the waiting room there, or stay here. If I may be so bold, I recommend you keep this room. Sofa versus hard plastic chairs, no contest."

Max started to get up. "But I want to come—"

"Max, stay," his mom said. "You baby-sat me enough for several lifetimes. I'll be fine. Get some rest, okay? It's a long surgery. And who knows how long it'll take for the staff to subdue me once I've got my unstoppable new ticker. I can't promise I won't punch through a wall or two."

"Well . . . okay. If that's what you want."

Her hands curled nervously around the arms of the wheelchair. "Come here, hon."

He bent down to hug her. And as she lifted her thin arms into his embrace, as he felt the ribs poking through the skin on her back, it dawned on him —

He regretted nothing.

He'd bought the health of his mother by lying, stealing, and covering up the murder of another human being. They weren't the right things to do, but they sure as hell weren't the wrong ones either.

"I love you, Mom," he said, trying to keep his voice from wobbling. "I'll see you soon."

"Love you too, Maxter."

The doctor wheeled her out of the room and closed the door behind him. Max stared at it for a moment; then, restless and uncomfortable with being so alone, he sank into the sofa.

And waited.

• • •

"Sweetheart?"

Max curled into a tight ball at the woman's touch. Lore's face jumped into his head. He smirked, picturing her ponytail swirling like a lasso.

"Max?"

He opened his eyes. It wasn't Lore. It was a nurse dressed all in green, shaking him awake.

She was smiling.

• • •

Max's mom was covered in so many bandages and tubes and wires, he couldn't be sure there was a person under there.

He rushed to her side. "Mom?"

"It'll still be a while before she wakes up," the nurse explained. "I just wanted to bring you to Recovery as soon as she was out of surgery. You two seem so close."

He gave her a weak smile. "We are." He pointed to the tube going down his mom's throat. "Will she be able to talk?"

"Not until we take the ventilator out. But I can grab a pad of paper for her to write on, if you like."

Max imagined that his mom still had some choice words for Chipmunk Tony. "That'd be great, thanks."

He squeezed her fingers again — and it was then that he noticed that the ash mark had disappeared from his hand. He brought it up to his face, rubbing his thumb over his skin.

It was gone. Really gone.

"What happened there?" the nurse asked, pointing at his hand.

"Excuse me?"

"All those scratches?"

"Oh," Max said with a weak laugh. "That. I have a really mean cat."

The nurse clucked her tongue. "Better keep him away from your mom. That bacteria's no good for immunocompromised patients."

"Don't worry," said Max. "I'll . . ."

He trailed off. *Bacteria*. Why was that ringing a bell? A very loud, insistent bell?

"What kind of bacteria?" he asked.

She put her hand on her hips, thinking. "*Bartonella henselae*, I think? The one that causes cat scratch fever. It's what makes the cuts go all red and puffy so quickly."

Max's bones felt as if they were trying to leap out of his body. *Bartonella henselae.* He knew where he'd seen that before. He knew where he'd read that before.

As his brain raged on, Max watched the nurse leave. She merged effortlessly into the never-stopping stream of people rushing down the hallway—doctors, nurses, family members, Wall—

"Wall!" he called out.

Wall overshot the room, then retraced his steps, slowly peeking through the door. "Max?"

"Wow, did word get out that fast?" Max said, getting up, shoving the bacteria thing to the back of his brain for the moment. "I didn't even tell anyone."

But Wall didn't look happy to see him. His face was drawn and pale. "What are you doing here?"

"My mom," he said. "A donor heart opened up. She got the transplant."

Wall stared at the tubes.

Max gave him a playful shove. "It's a good thing, Wall!"

He shook his head. "Yeah, I mean—" He frowned. "It *is* a good thing."

"So let's celebrate! The nurse says it'll still be a while before she wakes up. Care to join me in the cafeteria for a couple of juice boxes?"

Wall didn't seem as though he was hearing him correctly. He just kept staring at Max's mother, his giant hands shaking.

Max frowned. "Wall? What's wrong?"

As he moved in closer, he noticed that Wall's eyes were bloodshot. And there were dark stains on his football uniform.

Why, Max slowly wondered, *is he still wearing his uniform?*

"Wall. What's going on?"

He looked down at Max, his eyes watery and scared.

"You haven't heard?"

666 – 15

THE ELEVATOR DINGED. GROUND FLOOR. Max didn't want to know what he'd see when the doors opened, but he forced himself to step over the threshold and into the waiting area of the emergency room.

It was packed.

His stomach clenched shut like a bear trap. Eastville was not a big city; there was no reason for its hospital to be this crowded this late at night.

Clumps of people were sitting on the hard plastic chairs, some of them huddled together and crying, others pressing gauze into bleeding wounds. Every time a doctor came out of the emergency room, faces turned upward, hopeful, then darkened when no news was given. Red streaks painted the floor. Gurneys lined the sides of the corridors. Some of them held moaning patients. Some of them were covered with white sheets.

Max stared at one such gurney, at the small hand poking out

from beneath the cloth, the skin covered in something sticky. Cotton candy.

He tore his eyes away, dragging his gaze back into the waiting room. It landed on two people sitting in the corner. Tense in their chairs, they stared straight at the door to the emergency room, nothing else. Principal Gregory threaded a wrinkled Kleenex through her fingers, while her husband's hands gripped the armrests.

The room spun. Max reeled, reaching out to grab the wall, unable to go any farther. "What —"

"The bleachers at the football stadium." Wall's voice was gravel. "They collapsed."

Max took in each word, one at a time, his throat closing as he realized where his mother's new heart had come from. From whom, he didn't know — didn't want to know, would never want to know. Wall was still talking, something about "Fourteen dead . . . dozens wounded . . . Audie critical . . ." but all Max understood was: The bleachers. Football stadium. Collapsed.

Just knocked a few screws loose.

• • •

Max ran.

He'd arrived at the hospital via ambulance, which left him without a bike. So he had no choice but to sprint. The only sounds breaking the air were of his sneakers pounding against the pavement, his ragged breaths, and the continuous wail of sirens echoing in the hills.

When he arrived at his destination, he didn't need a crowbar. He could have torn the door off his hinges.

But it was unlocked. As if he were expected.

Thick, smoky air stung his nostrils as he stormed into the foyer. A fire roared in the fireplace. Glasses of alcohol dotted various surfaces and end tables, and seated on the plaid sofa, staring into the flames and sipping a brandy, was Burg.

Max stalked up to him. He wanted to rip those horns right out of the guy's skull. He wanted to tear him limb from limb. He wanted to grab a rifle off the wall and shoot him in the gut, throw him over the balcony into the lake, and watch him drown, slowly.

But all he said was, "Why?"

Burg looked at him. Multiple emotions were at war on his face; Max could tell that he was struggling to control them, to banish the kinder, more human ones. Eventually a sneer wormed its way to the surface and stayed there, his eyes gone cold.

"Your mother needed a new heart." Burg took a sip of the brandy. "I got her one. Shouldn't matter how I did it."

"You killed innocent people!" Max shouted.

"So did you."

Max slapped a hand over his mouth; he felt sick, sicker than he ever had before, as if his guts were instantaneously rotting.

"I warned you," Burg said quietly. "I told you not to get greedy. I warned you not to go down this road. It's not a nice road, Max."

Max let out a whimper. "But I trusted you."

"That was your first mistake."

"I did everything you asked."

"Second mistake."

Max forced himself to look Burg in the eye. "How could you do this to me?"

Burg's face tensed. He held Max's gaze, then looked back into the fire.

"A devil doesn't change his horns," he said softly.

Max sank to the floor. His knobby knees came down hard, pounding like hammers on the bloodstained wood floor. After that, there was nothing but his muffled sobs, the crackling of the fire, and silence.

Until something caught Max's eye. A crumpled-up wad of money sitting next to Burg's brandy.

"Where did you get that?" he asked, standing up to get a better look at the bills. Except they weren't in a clump — they were in the shape of a dinosaur.

Burg picked up the glass without answering.

"No," said Max. "No, I gave that to Paul —"

The blood drained out of Max's face as it dawned on him. The buzzing in his ears when Paul told him he'd been fired. How they only ever talked about it in private after school, or at the Gas Bag — never in public. And that the real Paul never would have bought gum, not with all those braces.

"*You* were Paul."

Burg calmly sipped his drink.

"And let me guess," Max said, his voice hollow. "You didn't fill the hole."

"Sorry, did you say 'fill'?" Burg said, tipping the remains of the brandy down his throat. "I heard 'dig.'"

Just then Max noticed a glint of something outside, a tiny ball of yellow light floating on the balcony.

A lit cigarette.

Max stared into the darkness. The light began to move to the right, traveling toward the hot tub, until it was no longer in view.

He approached the sliding glass door, his brain recycling bits and pieces of what Burg had said to him over the past week and spitting them up in random splotches . . . *any act of evil can bring up a devil . . . the big ones exert the strongest pull . . . murders are very popular . . . the Moneygrubbers have been trying to figure out a way to stay up here for centuries . . .*

He slid open the door and stepped onto the balcony, bracing himself for what he was about to see. But he could have been bracing for weeks, steeling himself for this all his life, and he still wouldn't have been prepared for what awaited him in the hot tub.

Fourteen devils, one for each of the dead — naked, drinking, and cackling like madmen.

SECRET WEAPON

MAX RAN SOME MORE.

All the way to the top of Ugly Hill. There he stood, gulping air as he ran his flashlight over what he desperately hoped were figments of his imagination.

But they weren't. They were there, carved right out of the earth, identical to the one he'd accidentally opened up a week ago.

Holes. Everywhere.

• • •

More running.

Down the hill. To his house.

To retrieve his last-ditch Hail Mary secret weapon.

• • •

One final sprint. Back up Ugly Hill.

Max stared into the holes, lowering his backpack to the ground in awe. So many of them. So, so many of them.

It was nothing personal, Shove.

Max clapped his hands over his ears. "Get out of my head!" he shouted.

WHOOSH.

Max turned around, then fell on his butt, blinded. A massive column of flame had erupted from one of the holes, like a flame-thrower shooting up from the center of the earth.

Burg walked out from behind it. "Sorry," he said as the whooshing died down. "It was nothing personal, Shove."

Max held up his arm to block the light. Heat pulsed out from the flames, which receded to a height of about twenty feet, like a huge bonfire.

It was so hot Max wanted to cover his face — he could feel his skin scorching, like a bad sunburn — but he kept his eyes on Burg, alert, like a cornered animal. He stood up and took three steps closer.

"When I asked you to pose as O'Connell," Max said evenly, "when I asked you to sign the paperwork at the office, you said it didn't matter whether you helped us or not."

"Yeah," said Burg. "So?"

"Tell me why it didn't matter."

Burg shrugged and picked up two dried-up shrub branches from the ground. "The way I saw it, you guys had two options." He held up one. "Either you enlisted me to help you secure the house, thereby guaranteeing my continued domesticity there, thereby keeping me happy, thereby keeping up your end of the deal, thereby earning a cure for your mom." He held up the other branch. "Or, you hung me out to dry. You decided that enough is enough, you canceled the deal, and you let the house slip away. Problem with that one is —"

"You kill my mom."

"No!" Burg shot him a don't-be-ridiculous smile. "No, that's the great part, Max! Your mom gets to live! *You,* of course, get arrested for murder once I tip off the police to the fact that O'Connell's body is perforated and lying at the bottom of the lake, thereby prompting an investigation that'll reveal your fingerprints all over the house, thereby nicely depositing you out of the picture, thereby giving me the freedom to move *in* on your mom!"

Max stared at him, shell-shocked.

"So it's like I said." With a vindictive grin, Burg held up both branches. "Win-win situation for old Burgy."

He tossed them both into the hole, instantly doubling the height of the flames.

"Of course," he said, taking a step closer to Max, "once she's good and healthy, I see no reason *not* to proceed with Plan B. Though I suppose, as a courtesy, I could allow you to continue operating under Plan A — continue to do stuff for me, get me snacks, keep me happy, miscellany and so forth. Then, if you decide to get rebellious, I'll simply invoke the Plan B protocol."

Max was no longer looking at him. He wasn't looking at anything. Eyes open, but not seeing. Just staring at the space before them, the world a blur of blacks and grays and eye-searing yellows.

I'm trapped, said his brain.

A bird let out a lonely, strident call.

No, you're not, said another part.

You heard the guy, rational brain said. *He's right. Either we don't help him and get arrested, or we do help him and become his slaves. We're totally screwed.*

. . .

Not if we take the third option.

"Or," Max said in an eerily calm voice, taking another step forward, "we go with Plan C."

Burg grinned. "Okay, Shove," he said, playing along. "What's Plan C?"

Max flashed him an expression he'd never sported before, a hint of a smile mixed with a hint of a snarl.

"I send you back to hell."

And with a mighty, pectoral-muscle-filled push, Max shoved Burg into the flames.

They burst into an impossibly bright fireball. Max shielded his eyes, staggering away for a moment before looking back — and scowling at what he saw.

Burg lazily looked up at Max. He appeared to be floating in the fire, bobbing up and down as if it were nothing more than a kiddie pool.

He was laughing, too. Cackling. "Really, Shove? *That* was your plan? To throw me into a fire? To give me a good shove into — OH MY STARS AND GARTERS, your *nickname* is Shove! It works on EVERY SINGLE LEVEL!" He exploded with a new burst of laughter, his cries carrying into the clear night sky.

Max bent down and unzipped his backpack.

Burg was now doing laps around the perimeter of the fire.

"Not as soothing as the hot tub. No bubble jets. But it'll do in a pinch. Care to join me?" He swam up to the lip of the hole and propped his elbows on the ground to hold himself up. "You know—"

He abruptly broke off. It was hard for Max to see, since the flames raged behind Burg, throwing his face into shadow, but he knew that Burg's eyes had gone wide.

Wide with terror. Riveted on what came out of the backpack.

Max dropped it to the ground. It darted out from between his legs and began weaving through the piles of dirt, tearing back and forth, zigzagging, an orange blur—

Into the fire it flew, landing right on Burg's face.

"Aaaaaggwwwwmmmffff!" Burg let out a shout, which turned into a muffled growl, which turned into a gargled groan. Which turned into a piercing scream.

Eventually he managed to maneuver his hands into the gap between Ruckus's razor-sharp claws and his shredded face, tossing him like a basketball into the air. Ruckus landed on his feet and sat on his haunches, daintily wrapping his tail around him. He licked his front paw, uninterested in the entire spectacle.

Burg's face, now crisscrossed with red, raised bites and scratches, was furious. "What the fuck, Max?" he said in a raspy voice.

"*Bartonella henselae.* Found it in the Super Fossil, which— remind me again? Belonged to a devil, correct?"

Burg said nothing. The point of his beard began to sizzle.

"And when Lore and I checked out Vermillion's old trailer, there was a cat in there, too. Verm's vacation was cut shorter than he expected, wasn't it?"

Ruckus took another swipe at Burg's face. He let out another howl.

"Guess you were right," Max said with a grin. "Cats *are* evil."

Burg's wounds got redder, puffier, angrier. They began to split, spilling beams of a blood-hued light into the sky like a horrific laser show. Then, suddenly, they went out.

Burg shot Max a grumpy, resigned look. "Aw, hell."

And with that, he dropped into the hole.

The fire disappeared.

All was silent.

Max inched up to the rim of the hole but saw nothing inside except dirt. He tossed a rock into it and started to count how long it took for it to hit bottom.

But he didn't get very far. The rock fell only about ten feet.

Max raked his hands through his hair and looked out on the town of Eastville. It sat below, glittering and quiet, an occasional siren breaking the silence. The football field was still lit up.

Max hugged himself tight. The night had gotten cold.

Ruckus rubbed up against his ankles, purring.

"Good kitty," Max said, giving him a pat.

EPILOGUE

MAX TIED HIS SHOE, then double knotted it. His mom was always reminding him of stuff like that now, the little things she'd neglected in her motherly duties for so long. "Don't trip and fall down the stairs and require a heart transplant," she'd say. "They hurt like hell."

"But they work," he'd remind her, patting his chest.

She'd pat hers back.

He cracked his knuckles, the way Audie would before creaming him at *Madden*. She'd probably obliterate him even more epically now that she'd had a couple of months to hone her skills. Recuperating from a crushed pelvis, it turned out, scored you a lot of quality video game time.

Then he pulled the fishing rod out of the whale's flipper. He affixed to the end of the line a briefcase conspicuously overflowing with dollar bills and walked around to the front of the house, placing the bait atop a prominent mound of snow.

Finally he returned to the backyard, took his place behind the whale, and waited.

A few minutes later he spotted Lore jogging down the street. Vapor was puffing out of her mouth, and money was streaming out of her bag. She darted into the backyard and plopped down next to Max.

"Ready?" she asked, out of breath.

Max nodded and handed her the pole. "Ready."

"Same as last time, okay? I'll reel him in, you drop the payload."

"I know, I know. I'm getting pretty good at this, remember?"

She leaned in and kissed him. He kissed back — a passionate, artless thing. It had become a sort of tradition of theirs to kiss right before bagging their prey.

Also, they just really liked kissing.

They finished up, wiped off the slobber, and nodded to each other. Lore removed Russell Crowebar from her waistband. Max pulled out the secret weapon.

The Moneygrubber came sniffing around the corner, picking up each bill that Lore had dropped. As soon as he came into view, she began to reel in the fishing line. He sniffed after the briefcase, ratlike, following it all the way to the whale and scuttling inside with a *thump.*

Max took a moment to grin at Lore, then dropped Ruckus through the blowhole. She slammed the port shut and jammed the crowbar into its handles to lock it, grinning back at him.

"I'm so glad we found a common interest," she said.

They flopped back into the snow, their fingers entwining as the whale rocked fiercely back and forth, the devil's wails echoing in the clear winter sky.

Crossword Puzzle

Grid answers:

Row 1: H O T · · D I G
Row 2: E V I L · R A S E
Row 3: R E D O · A L O T
Row 4: · N E A T N I K ·
Row 5: · · T E A ·
Row 6: · S C H E M E D ·
Row 7: C O R E · O N C E
Row 8: A D O S · K I L N
Row 9: T A P · · D I D

Across

1. Stolen
4. Excavate
7. Malevolence
9. Demolish, variation
10. Start over
11. Frequently (two words)
12. Obsessive-compulsive type
14. Kind of party
15. Devised a plan
19. Center of the earth
20. Fairy-tale beginning
22. Kerfuffles
23. Hot spot
24. Surveillance
25. Accomplished

Down

1. That girl
2. Where things heat up
3. Torrent
4. Adventurer in Surrealism
5. Escapes injury (two words)
6. Snare
8. Can't stomach
9. Went berserk (two words)
13. Driving aid
15. Sort of jerk
16. Cut short
17. OK place
18. 666 – 15
19. Secret weapon
21. Epilogue